CONTENTS

A FIERY END

By Diana J Febry

Proofreading provided by the Hyper-Speller at https://www.wordrefiner.com
COVER IMAGE - BIGSTOCK
Cover design – Diana J Febry

CHAPTER ONE

Charlotte Searle stared dismally at her feet. What an idiot she had been. Maybe one day she would look back and laugh at her youthful gullibility, but right now she felt beyond stupid and wanted her day from hell to be over. Her escape from the embarrassing situation couldn't come quick enough.

Thank God she hadn't told her friends where she was going. Not because he told her not to, but because from the start she had a sneaking suspicion that he was a phoney. As false as the blond wig, orange tan and startling, white teeth. She shuddered at the thought of his clammy hands touching her when he pushed and prodded her into position. It was the eyes that really got to her. Green, piercing, and so very cold. If they were the mirrors to his soul, that was a place she never wanted to go.

It was all her parents' fault and their ridiculous double-standards. If they hadn't been so horrified when she said she wanted to be a model, she wouldn't be wasting her time in a damp cellar with a couple of chavs and a weirdo. Her father had sparked her ambition in the first place when he forced her into doing the photo shoot for the horse feed company. Of course, that was completely different in their eyes. He considered that to be a fun opportunity for her. Because the clothes were high quality, country clothes he believed the shoot would be dignified and classy, and he could show off the end result to his country-set friends. On the day of the shoot, her mother had been too busy flirting with the camera man to notice she had been squeezed into jodhpurs that would split if she sat on a horse and a T-shirt so tight, she could hardly breathe. Despite her coy claims it was her parents' idea, she had ended up enjoying the fussing and fawning, and the photographer's encouragement had stirred a desire to be the centre of attention.

Today's grim experience would teach her to be more discerning in the future. In the car, on the way to the hellhole, she had clamped her hand over her mouth to stop herself from laughing when he gave his cock and bull story about wearing blindfolds in the car. Did he really think she believed him when he said the studio, they were going to, belonged to his famous friend who wanted to preserve his privacy? She should have demanded he stop the car and got out, there and then. She had been tempted, but she stayed and complied, saying nothing because a small sliver of her wanted to believe it might just be true.

How could she have been so naïve? Now, she felt dirty and cheap. The first thing she would do when she got home, was jump into the shower. Secondly, she would delete the telephone numbers they had exchanged in the back of the car before their phones were confiscated. Thirdly, she would erase all memory of the dreadful day from her mind.

Charlotte looked up at the closed door. Lisa was in there now. She bet she would agree to the "special pictures." She was still making her mind up about Megan. She glanced across at the sulky, dark-haired teenager. Without the constant pout and badly applied makeup, she could be stunning.

Charlotte cleared her throat and asked the question that had been burning inside since they were introduced to one another in the car. "Hey, Megan. Is your dad a plumber? Connor Ambrose?"

Megan Ambrose continued to stare straight ahead, sitting upright with her knees pressed firmly. Her attention left the closed door for a second to look Charlotte over. On making eye contact, she blushed and mumbled, "Yeah. How did you know that?"

"He did some work at my home. He's a nice man," Charlotte replied, realising her initial impression of Megan was wrong. She wasn't hardened and arrogant. The girl whose gaze and returned to the door was shy and incredibly nervous.

"Thanks, I think," Megan quietly mumbled.

The soft reply reinforced Charlotte's sense of responsibility. Megan looked like her dad, and she knew Connor would be upset if he knew what his precious daughter was up to. She leaned forwards to gain her full attention and hopefully, her trust. "Look. A bit of a heads up." Nodding toward the closed door, she said in a low voice, "He's a creep. He'll ask ..." The warning dried in her throat when the door opened, and Lisa walked out looking red and flustered.

"You're next. Go right in," Lisa Navaro said, in the vague direction of Megan without looking at her.

Looking like a frightened rabbit, Megan jumped from her seat and scurried through the door. Charlotte turned her attention to Lisa as she took her seat, reassessing her earlier assumption about her. "Did he ...?"

"He asked," Lisa replied, scowling. "I told him where to shove it."

"So, you got just the crappy headshots for £50, then?"

"Yeah. You?"

"Same as you," Charlotte replied, with a grin of solidarity. "Told him not a chance in hell was I getting naked. He laughed and said I was too skinny and you two would make a better twosome on film."

Lisa gave a look of disgust. "Arse. He told me you had already agreed and were looking forward to our romp together. Let's hope Megan tells him to get lost, and we don't have to wait much longer. Did you warn her?"

"I tried...I should have tried harder."

"Oh well," Lisa said dismissively, flicking her hair. "We'll know soon enough. Do you think he'll give us our phones back like he promised?"

"He had better. Mines brand new," Charlotte replied, wondering how she would explain another lost phone to her father.

They looked up when the door swung open. The ageing surfer boy poked his head through the door. With a sickly smile, he announced, "Megan's shots are going to take a little longer. Would you like to join us?"

"No, thanks," Charlotte replied. Nonchalantly examining her fingernails while trying not to think about Megan or her father, she asked, "How long will you be? I'm starving."

Pointing to a side door, he said, "There's a small kitchen through there. Help yourself to whatever you find, but don't go anywhere else. The rest of the house is alarmed."

"Come on. What are you waiting for?" Charlotte said, heading for the door. When Lisa followed her into the small, functional kitchen, Charlotte grabbed her arm. "They will be ages. Let's have a snoop around the rest of the place. See who this house really belongs to. It could belong to someone at least vaguely famous. If we pick up some interesting souvenirs the day won't be entirely wasted."

Lisa hung back. "Didn't you hear him. It's alarmed."

"I bet it isn't. If an alarm goes off, I'll say it was me, and I was looking for the toilet."

Lisa followed Charlotte up the steep stone steps to the first floor and crept through into the grand hallway holding her breath.

"See, I told you. There's no alarm," Charlotte said, smirking.

"Ever hear of a silent one?"

Charlotte shrugged. "If someone turns up, we'll get to leave earlier. Either way, we win."

The rooms lining the spacious hallway were decorated as living rooms with comfortable chairs, lamps and low tables. Each room had a different colour scheme, but they all contained a drinks cabinet filled with spirits and red wine. Charlotte darted into the last room they checked and opened the double doors of a drink cabinet. "Great, it's unlocked." She grabbed a couple of glasses and clumsily sloshed brandy into them. She handed one to Lisa while she knocked hers back in one. With eyes smarting, she wiped her mouth with the back of her hand and said, "That was good." Pouring herself a second glass, she laughed at Lisa's grimace as she sipped her brandy. "It's quality gear, but we haven't all day. I want to see what's upstairs."

Lisa obediently took another sip, before nervously asking, "Do you think we should? What happens if he comes out and finds us gone?"

"Hurry up and drink up, then. I reckon we've got a good half hour," Charlotte replied, already heading for the central staircase.

The wooden staircase creaked and groaned over the hollow thud of their footsteps. Charlotte started a running commentary in her mind, pretending she was a famous actress in a horror movie. As the central character, she would survive, unlike the supporting actors who would die terrible deaths at the hands of the dark evil that lurked in the shadows. At the top of the stairs, she ordered, "You go that way. I'll check out the doors this side."

"No! We should stick together," Lisa said.

"Come on then scaredy-cat. This way." After a few steps, Charlotte turned and shouted, "Boo!"

Lisa screamed and scuttled backwards, nearly tripping. Regaining her composure, she narrowed her eyes and shook her head. "You idiot!"

Charlotte raised her hands in a conciliatory gesture. "Sorry. My bad." With a toss of her head, she moved on. "Let's start trying the doors."

Tiptoeing along the corridor, they tried each door in turn, finding them all locked. Disappointed, they retraced their steps back to the top of the staircase and tried the other way with the same result.

"Boring," Charlotte announced. "We'll go back down and have another brandy. Maybe we'll find something interesting in one of the cabinets."

"What was that?" Lisa said, grabbing Charlotte's arm.

"Shh!" Charlotte said, putting her finger on her lips. "It sounded like the front door."

Male voices and the sound of stamping feet reverberated through the empty corridors.

"What do we do?" Lisa whispered.

"Shut up. I can't hear," Charlotte snapped.

"Damn. Damn. Damn," Lisa repeated, starting to panic and walk in small circles. With wild eyes, she said, "They're going to come up here and find us."

Scanning the long, narrow corridor with uninterrupted views Charlotte bundled Lisa towards the large grandfather clock at the top of the stairs. With no rooms to hide in, the only place they could conceal themselves was on one side and hope the men went in the opposite direction. With her heart beating in time with the clock's mechanism, she counted the thud of footsteps coming closer and closer up the stairs. Concerned Lisa was going to do something stupid like scream she placed a hand over her mouth and gave her a warning look. On the surface, she played the courageous heroine with panache. Inside, she was shaking and praying the men would turn to go in the other direction.

Facing each other, almost nose to nose Charlotte saw the relief in Lisa's eyes as the footsteps stopped at the top of the stairs and clumped away from their inadequate hiding place. A key turned in a lock followed by the sound of a door clicking open. Charlotte extracted herself from Lisa's tight hold and peeked around the side of the clock. All she saw was the empty hallway.

Lisa dragged her back. "What are you doing? They'll see you."

Before Charlotte could complain, she was distracted by what sounded like the clanking of chains. Both girls pulled confused faces. This time Lisa was ready and pulled Charlotte back as soon as she made to step forward and peer around the side of the clock. They froze as they heard a door banging against a wall.

"Christ, she's heavy."

"What about the door?"

"Leave it. We'll come back and shut it later."

Charlotte stopped herself from crying out when Lisa pinched her skin as she clutched hold of her. She blocked out the pain and held her breath as the slow footsteps came closer. She felt Lisa sag in relief at the first creak of the staircase and the pinch hold relax. She was too quick for Lisa to catch and pull her back. She edged along the corridor, craning to catch a glimpse of what was going on while Lisa stayed behind, clinging to the clock in horror.

Crouching at the top of the landing, Charlotte looked down through the bannisters at the two men. She told herself to stop being so stupid. It was her imagination running wild after being spooked by Lisa. They weren't really carrying a dead body wrapped in a blanket, even if that was what it looked like. It was probably a curled-up rug being taken for cleaning. Her hand shot to her mouth, and she sat back on her bottom when a long, slender arm flopped out of the blanket. Fear and brandy collided and pushed bile to the back of her throat. She nearly jumped out of her skin when Lisa tapped her on the shoulder. "Christ. Don't creep up on people like that."

"I heard the front door shut. Are they gone?" Lisa whispered.

"Yes."

"What are you waiting for? We need to return to the room we're supposed to be in before they finish."

"Absolutely," Charlotte said, swallowing back her horror and trying to regain her earlier façade of confidence. Had she seen what she thought she saw? It could have been a mannequin. Yes, that would make sense. If they use the house for filming, there would be props everywhere. Heaving a sigh of relief, she pulled herself to her feet. She was being stupid and melodramatic. How ridiculous would she have looked if she reported the murder of a dummy? She hesitated at the top of the stairs. She wanted to be sure. "I'm going to take a peek inside the room," she said, pointing to the open door at the end of the corridor.

"Make it quick then," Lisa said impatiently, following Charlotte across the landing.

Air rushed out of Charlotte's lungs when she looked inside the elegantly furnished room. A large four-poster bed dominated the space. A used syringe balanced delicately on one of the satin pillows. Her eyes widened at the thick, metal bars covering the closed window. Taking a step forward, she became fixated by the handcuffs hanging down from their crude attachment to the headboard.

"Eww. The place is an upmarket knocking shop," Lisa said.

Charlotte nodded, fighting to remain calm and in control. If she told Lisa what she saw, she would panic. Turning away, she said, "Yeah. Pretty much sums up the day, doesn't it? Time to get back downstairs and wait patiently for Megan's shoot to be over."

Stepping as lightly as she could, descending the stairs, Lisa asked, "Why do you think the windows were barred?"

"The bars looked fake to me. They were probably theatre props. I think more filming than sex goes on here," Charlotte replied, hoping she sounded convincing.

"I can't believe I thought this would be fun."

"Me neither," Charlotte said, leading the way down the cellar steps. Taking her seat from earlier, she whispered, "Don't say a word about it until we're well away from here. Okay?"

"I'm not that stupid."

Five minutes later, Megan and Surfer man emerged from their photo shoot looking flushed and dishevelled. Surfer man leered at Charlotte, making her feel queasy as he tucked in his shirt. "Ready for home, girls?"

In the car, Charlotte obediently slipped the mask over her eyes. She waited until, surfer man had turned the car around and accelerated out through the entrance gates, before scratching her face to lift a corner of the cloth. She only had a sliver of vision, but she hoped it would be enough to see any prominent landmark they passed. At the very least, she would know the general direction they were taking even if it wasn't enough for her to work out the exact location of the house.

"Okay, you can take off the masks, now. Drop off where I picked you up?" Surfer Man asked as they neared town.

Charlotte poked Lisa in the leg and said, "Could you drop me in town? I fancy doing a bit of shopping before going home."

"Me too, please," Lisa said.

Charlotte felt culpable when Surfer Man squeezed Megan's

thigh and smiled. "I'll drop you off last, then."

Leaning forward between the seats, Charlotte said, "Do you want to come shopping with us?"

Megan looked around. With a haughty look, she replied, "No. I'm expected at home."

Outside the main entrance to the shopping mall, Surfer Man released the child locks so Charlotte and Lisa could open the rear car doors. "Have fun, girls! Don't forget, Mum's the word. I'll be in contact in a few days."

Charlotte linked arms with Lisa and marched her toward the entrance without looking back.

"Ow! You're hurting me," Lisa complained.

Charlotte ignored her complaints and continued frogmarching her away until they were safely inside the mall. She released her grip on Lisa and slammed herself back into the wall. She raised her head, keeping her eyes tightly closed.

"What is it?" Lisa asked in a high-pitched voice.

Charlotte rubbed her face. Maintaining the bravado she had shown during the car journey had left her weak and faint. "Nothing. It's nothing."

"It doesn't look like nothing. You've gone pale. Are you sure you're okay?"

Charlotte let herself slide down the wall. She sat with her head between her knees, willing herself to stop trembling.

"Are you having a panic attack? I'll find someone," Lisa said, frantically looking around for assistance.

"No," Charlotte said, her hand shooting out to grab hold of Lisa. "I'll be fine in a minute." While gulping for air, she decided she wouldn't tell Lisa anything about what she had seen. The men hadn't seen them. It would be safer to collect the prints from Surfer Man like nothing had happened and forget all about it. As her breathing returned to normal, she asked, "You won't go back there or have anything to do with him, again, will you?"

"No way. Bloody creep. I reckon that other girl, Megan, will. Do you think she actually believed he could make her star?"

Because of Connor, Charlotte felt she should have done more

to protect Megan. "Possibly." Holding up her phone, she said, "I've got her number. I'll see if I can get hold of her when I get home."

"Do you think Bob King is his real name?"

Charlotte gave a hollow laugh. "I don't even think it was his real hair. Surfer Man suits him far better, don't you think?" Looking up, she said, "What a sleaze." She forced herself upright and asked, "How are you planning on getting home? I was going to call a taxi."

Lisa shrugged. "Walk, I guess. It's not far."

"Okay. Well, look after yourself," Charlotte said, feeling in her back pocket. Panicking, she checked all her packets. "Crap. I've lost it."

"What?"

"My fake ID card. It was in my pocket." Fear constricted her throat, making her voice sound high pitched and scratchy. "I must have dropped it somewhere in the house."

"Ask Bob to return it with the prints."

"You don't understand. I saw something I shouldn't have seen back there. Those men I saw. They said they were returning to close the door. They'll find the card before Surfer Man. They'll know we were there when..."

"Do you think they'll come looking for you?"

Charlotte shook her head. "I didn't use my details."

"So, what's the panic?"

"I used Megan's details. Damn." Charlotte pulled at her hair in frustration. "I've put her in danger. I'm going to have to call her dad and tell him."

"I didn't think you knew, Megan, let alone her parents. What was it you saw and what are you going to tell him?"

CHAPTER TWO

DI Fiona Williams leaned her head against the car window and closed her eyes, willing the relentless swish of the windscreen wipers to lull her to sleep. She tried to breathe in time with the repetitive forward and back movement, hoping it would calm the overwhelming sense that she was losing the stability she had always taken for granted. The very stability she had rebelled against and resented at times. Like a child, she wanted to withdraw into herself. Return to a time when there was no doubt, and there was always someone to catch her if she fell.

Thank God, her brother, Richard, had been visiting their parents. Recognising the symptoms of a stroke he had taken control and rushed them immediately to the local hospital.

By the time she arrived, her dad was already undergoing surgery. Through the blur of confusion and worry, everyone repeated he was one of the lucky ones to get there so fast. They had hope to hang on to. Now, it was a waiting game.

Her brother's comments in the sterile corridor as they were leaving had stung, largely because they were true. She should get her head out of the clouds, take stock of where her priorities lay and appreciate the sacrifices her parents made. To put it bluntly, grow up, stop being selfish and care for her family for a change.

Easy for him to say from the safety of an office job and a happy marriage. She had neither luxury. The phrase, work/life balance, like so many other on-trend phrases had been overused to the point of becoming meaningless. Article after article advising how to reset the balance in an ever more demanding world. How to make small adjustments to tip the scales to live a more enriched, happy life. Great in theory when it was laid out in glossy magazines, making it all sound so easy. None of it had any practical application to her work as a police detective and the helpful tips morphed into yet more sticks to beat herself up with.

She loved her parents, but she also loved her career and her freedom to please herself. She glanced across at her driver, DCI Peter Hatherall and sighed. Despite all the apparent loving of life, she felt lonely a lot of the time. She wondered how Peter felt living alone in the cottage. Did he fill his evenings with meaningful activity or mourning the end of his marriage?

Peter considered every violent death or serious assault in the area not only as a department failure but a personal one as well. He had a short temper and two failed marriages to show for it. Was she on the same slippery slope? Without the failed marriages, as she hadn't managed a long-term relationship for years. She didn't even have a private life.

With her father so ill, maybe this was time to make some changes. The timing of a request for some personal time off could be a lot worse. Peter said earlier that the station had been quiet while she was away on her three-month posting with the Metropolitan Police. Would a delay to her returning to regular duties make that much of a difference?

The recurring image of her dad motionless on the hospital bed returned. His grey skin altered his appearance, almost past recognition. A faint reminder of the man she had once been so close to. Growing up, he had been her rock, her voice of reason and the first person she turned to for advice and comfort. That role had slowly diminished as the job took over her life. If she was honest with herself, in many ways, she had allowed Peter to take over the role her father had played. It could explain why, although they skirted around the idea of a romantic relationship, they had never taken that final step.

A few short hours ago, she had been outside Peter's new cottage without a care in the world, preparing to leave for the cinema to watch *Jojo Rabbit*. She had been hoping for a peek inside to see how the decorations were going in his new bachelor home. Her brother's call had abruptly swept those casual thoughts away, leaving behind a constricting fear for the future.

"What the hell?" Peter exclaimed, slamming on the car brakes.

Fiona opened her eyes to see a bright flash of light streak across the inky-black, night sky a short distance ahead. A loud explosion that vibrated through her accompanied it. She glanced across at Peter, hurriedly selecting first gear and accelerating forwards. She stated the obvious, "An explosion of some sort."

"Of what? There's nothing out here," Peter replied

"A car accident?" Fiona suggested. Her voice was drowned out by a series of smaller explosions lighting up the night sky. "Okay. Not a car accident."

As they rounded the bend, in the centre of the road, a camper van engulfed in orange flames came into sight. Peter pulled over, and they ran through the torrential rain towards the scene. Fierce heat assaulted them, forcing them to keep their distance as they skirted around the rear of the vehicle. Drawing alongside, they could see the blackened silhouette of a person, sat upright in the driver's seat, holding the steering wheel and looking through the windscreen as though nothing out of the ordinary had happened. A wave of intense heat pushed them back, stinging their eyes and clogging their throats. Edging closer, Peter pulled his jacket over his head, preparing to rush forward to reach the driver's door when there was a succession of explosions from the rear of the vehicle.

Fiona grabbed his arm, pulling him back. "Gas canisters! There's nothing we can do."

Turning away from the searing heat, they saw a woman in heels struggling out of the rear passenger seat of a car parked further along the lane, facing them. The front windscreen was shattered, and splinters of glass reflecting the flames lay scattered across the road. They ran towards the car. Fiona headed towards the rear of the vehicle and steered the woman away from the scene while Peter rushed to the front of the car.

Fiona led the attractive, twenty-something woman to safety. The woman stopped after a few steps and looked back towards the car with a dazed look on her face. "My handbag. I need my handbag. It's on the front seat."

Fiona tightened her hold on the trembling woman's waist, urging her to continue moving. "Don't worry about that now. We can get it later."

"I bet Barney won't think to pick it up," the woman said, stumbling forward. "Typical man." She tried to stop and look back over her shoulder. "What's taking him so long?"

Determined to keep the woman moving, Fiona pulled the woman along. Stopping by a stone wall, Fiona glanced back at Peter, who was reaching into the open driver's door. Keeping the woman turned away from the car, she said, "We should be safe to wait here. How are you feeling?"

Pale-faced, the woman raised a shaky hand to rub her forehead. Mascara ran down her cheeks as her mouth silently opened and closed.

"It's okay," Fiona tried to reassure her. "What's your name?"

"India. India Williamson. We were travelling back from a meal to celebrate."

Fiona wriggled out of her raincoat and draped it over India's shoulders as she started to shiver. "What happened?"

"Barney pulled over into the layby. I needed some papers from my briefcase, but I couldn't reach them from the front seat. I ... umm ... I saw ... It doesn't matter. My briefcase. It had toppled from the seat. I was reaching down behind the seats to gather up my things, when ... I don't know ... I didn't see anything ... There was a loud bang and a surge of light ... Heat. Sorry. I'm not much help, am I?"

Fiona rubbed India's arm. "You're doing fine. Take deep breaths and try to stay calm."

The woman pulled back and turned toward the car. "Barney? Where's Barney?"

Peter wrenched open the car door, the metal of the handle hot to the touch. He reached forwards to check the man's pulse to confirm what his eyes already told him. He pulled his hand back, his fingers slick with blood. A large fragment of the windscreen jutted from the man's neck. His face had numerous cuts from the shattered windscreen. From the neck down, his once white shirt was red. Peter closed the car door and looked back towards the fireball engulfing the camper van. He took a deep breath and immediately regretted it as the acrid smoke irritated his throat. Coughing, he pulled his phone from his jacket pocket and called the emergency services, before running through a fresh downpour of rain towards Fiona.

The female passenger, who he assumed was the driver's partner, grabbed his jacket sleeve, her eyes wide in distress. "Barney? How is he?"

He conveyed the bad news to Fiona with a split-second look and said, "The emergency services are on their way. Let's get you to my car to wait in the dry."

India fell silent and meekly allowed herself to be led towards the burning vehicle. Peter positioned himself to shield her vision as they passed the vehicle she'd been travelling in. Fiona and India clambered into the back of his car. Peter climbed into the driver's seat to start the engine and turn the heater to full blast, before turning to face the two women.

"He's dead, isn't he?" India asked, in a flat voice.

"I'm very sorry," Peter said, before his voice was drowned out by the sound of approaching sirens. Rubbing the condensation from the side window to get a clearer view, he said, "Looks like a fire engine." His eyes darted around the empty countryside. "I wonder who called them ahead of me." Not waiting for a reply, he pushed open the car door. "Wait here, while I have a word."

Once the door slammed shut behind Peter, India said, "Dead? How could he be dead? We were talking one minute … and then …" She stopped, her eyes searching Fiona for answers.

"I don't know anything more than you do," Fiona said, looking down at India's tightly clenched hands.

"Suzie! I need to call Suzie. My phone is in my handbag."

Fiona grabbed India's hand to prevent her from opening the car door. "I'll ask Peter to bring it over." When India slumped back in her seat, she asked, "Who's Suzie?"

"Barney's wife. She's pregnant. How can I tell her? She'll be devastated. I'm not sure I can."

Pushing questions about what the two of them were really doing parked up in a layby at night on a country lane to the back of her mind, Fiona said, "Don't worry about that, now. Trained police will contact her. Do you know their address?" Fiona strained to hear the reply over the sound of approaching sirens. Once India had repeated the address, she wiped an area of the passenger window to peer out at an ambulance and two marked police cars screeching to a halt. The rain blurred the flashing lights making it difficult to see. Squinting, she picked out Peter, taking control of the situation with his usual confidence. Knowing his shape and the way he moved, she could find him in a crowd, anywhere. She watched him move along, speaking to the driver of each vehicle as it arrived, gesticulating with his arms.

An uneasy feeling crept under Fiona's skin. The dark silhouette of the camper van driver, along with the vehicle's position was too staged. Too perfectly aligned. Surely, the driver would have reacted when the fire started? Swerved to the side, even if he had no time to get the hell out of the burning vehicle.

If they had left the hospital a few moments sooner, they could have done something. The realisation created a surge of resentment towards her brother. What gave Richard the right to grill her about how she ran her life? To tell her she had to up her game and do more to help her parents? To complain that she couldn't continue to leave it all to Emma, her perfect sister-in-law?

Despite her exhaustion, physical and emotional, Fiona's instinct as a police officer clicked in. She reached for the car door handle, putting her brother's concerns about what she should and shouldn't be doing to the back of her mind. Her place was outside, where she was trained to make a difference. She turned to tell India to stay put while she joined her colleagues.

India's lips were moving. Fiona strained to hear what she was mumbling to herself. She caught something about seeing him before. On the television. Fiona let go of the car handle, and asked, "What was that about the man on television? Did you see something?"

"What?" India replied. She flinched at the question, looking startled, as though she hadn't realised, she'd been voicing her thoughts out loud. Turning away, she said, "Nothing. I told you. I didn't see anything. I was thinking about how unreal this all is. Like a television scene."

Unconvinced by the explanation, Fiona's senses were on alert. "Are you sure you didn't hear or see anything before the explosion?"

"No. I was rummaging about under the car seat, trying to recover my things when all hell broke loose without warning."

"And before? When you first parked up? Did you see or hear anything, then?"

India vigorously shook her head. "Nothing. Everything was in total blackness."

Fiona glanced out at the unfolding scene, before asking, "You didn't see the van's headlights or hear the engine?"

India frowned and dropped her head into her hands. "I didn't see anything, but then I wasn't looking. I was twisting around in the front seat trying to reach my briefcase. That was when I accidentally knocked it from the rear seat."

"You didn't hear the other vehicle approaching?" Fiona persisted.

"I'm not sure … The stereo was playing. Barney always has it turned up too loud. He didn't turn it down when he stopped."

Fiona looked around. They were in a desolate spot with no distractions other than the ball of flames and flashing lights of the attending vehicles. She hadn't heard music playing when she helped India from the car. "Why did Barney pull over here?"

"We were discussing a work matter. I couldn't remember some

of the figures. My briefcase with all the details inside was on the back seat. When I twisted around to grab it, I accidentally knocked it from the seat. Barney pulled over. Just for a second, so I could go around to the back and gather my things. I wasn't taking any notice of anything else. I mean, why would I? There's nothing to see here, even in the daylight."

Fiona tried to catch India's eye, but she had dropped her head into her hands and was quietly sobbing. Whatever the real reason for their stop, why hadn't India heard or seen the camper van's approach? The sudden explosion of a vehicle while moving was suspicious enough. What were the chances of a stationary vehicle turning into a ball of flames without warning? Watching the firemen battling to bring the vehicle fire under control, she continued to probe. "You said you didn't hear or see the campervan approaching. Could it have been stationary when you pulled over?"

India rubbed her eyes with the heel of her palms and looked away. "It was dark, and my attention was elsewhere. Sorry, I can't remember." Her tone had changed to one of a sulky teenager.

Fiona's attention was drawn towards the fire. From behind the flashing lights, Peter appeared and walked towards them. He nodded at Fiona before walking around to India's side of the car. Opening the passenger door wide, he said, "Everything okay in here?" Without waiting for a reply, he held out his hand to India. "The ambulance crew want to check you over, and the traffic officers are keen to talk to you afterwards."

India shrank back in her seat, ignoring Peter's outstretched hand. "I'm not hurt, and I didn't see anything. Could you give me a lift home?"

"I'm afraid not," Peter said. "Come on, out you come."

Fiona remained silent. It wasn't like Peter to be less than charming with a woman in distress. Even one who had probably been making out with her pregnant friend's husband. Guessing he was equally suspicious of the accident circumstances, she tried to catch his eye, but his attention was set firmly on India.

Reluctantly, India huffed and puffed as she slid herself along the seat towards the door. Ignoring Peter's hand, she snapped, "I can manage."

Fiona watched Peter escort India to the back of the ambulance while she moved to the front passenger seat. When Peter returned and took up position in the driver's seat, she noticed his hand on the gear stick trembled. "Are you okay?"

Peter started the car engine, but instead of selecting first gear, he remained motionless looking out the front windscreen. He took a deep breath before turning towards Fiona. "I'm fine. I had a bit of a flashback earlier. When the gas canisters went off. Of that night. When Nick Tattner was ..." He pushed the car into gear and accelerated away without completing the sentence.

Fiona covered his hand with hers. "I get it." She removed her hand to allow Peter to travel up through the gears. She should have realised. The explosion had reminded Peter of the night a young constable from the station had been killed.

Events of that night came flooding back to her. Peter and Nick were checking the property for a suspected murderer. Nick had gone to the front of the house while Peter had gone around the back. The front door had been wired with explosives, and Nick had to be formally identified from his dental records. The blast had rendered Peter briefly unconscious, but he had witnessed much of the aftermath. News of the incident had reached Fiona at the theatre, where she was helping out with a youth production of The Wizard of Oz. She had walked out in a confused daze and had never returned to the theatre group again.

That incident changed everything for Fiona. It had darkened her opinion of humanity and brought it home how much risk she and her colleagues put themselves in every day. From then on, she felt much closer to her colleagues and more distant from everyone else. It was far worse for Peter and the other officers who had experienced the blast first-hand.

Peter focussed his attention on the road ahead, and said, "Sorry. I shouldn't have said anything."

"You should say something more often," Fiona replied, noticing his knuckles had turned white from his tight grip on the steering wheel. His jaw was firmly clenched, and his full concentration remained stubbornly fixed on the road. She wanted to say something more, to somehow make everything better, but didn't know where to start. It was easier to shut out the personal and slip into work mode. As the light from the fire and emergency vehicles disappeared from their rear view, Fiona asked, "When you checked the driver of the car, was the stereo playing?"

"I don't think so." Peter frowned in concentration. "No. The radio was off. The keys were in the ignition, but the engine wasn't running. Why?"

"India said she was searching for something under the car seat so didn't see or hear the camper van approaching. The car door would have been open. When I queried her about not hearing anything, she said the stereo was playing at full blast. Strange, don't you think?"

"The whole scene was unusual," Peter said, slowly.

"What do you think really happened?"

Peter ran a hand over his face before glancing across at Fiona. "We'll be back at mine in fifteen minutes. It's gone two in the morning. Do you want to stay over? The spare bedroom is made up."

Fiona's first thought was, what did he see that made him avoid answering her question, before realising he was probably still thinking about Nick. What she really wanted to do was take something to get rid of her pounding headache and crawl into her own bed, so she could process the jumbled events of the past five hours.

"Well?" Peter asked. "I can find you a clean shirt to sleep in."

Fiona felt a lump forming in her throat. She swallowed, asking herself why her throat was constricting. Smoke inhalation from earlier, possibly. Or was it the vulnerability she heard in Peter's voice? Glancing across as a muscle twitched across Peter's clenched jaw. Fiona caught his eye and smiled. "Thanks. I'm tired, and it will save me the drive home."

A short while later, Peter said, "Whatever happened back there, it was no accident."

Deciding that gave her the green light to start discussing the fire, Fiona, replied, "Agreed. Did the fire officials say anything?"

"Too soon to draw any conclusions." Giving Fiona a worried look, Peter added, "You look done in. Don't speculate about it now. Let's wait and see what tomorrow brings. There's a good chance it will be assigned to us."

Fiona turned to say something more. Peter's eyes flitted between the rear-view mirror and the country lane ahead. The silence was exploded by the wail of police sirens.

Peter slowed the car and pulled over to the side of the lane. "What now?" he muttered, as two, marked police cars sped past.

A short distance later, the lane was blocked by the two cars that had passed them. A young traffic officer, Fiona didn't recognise, waved for Peter to stop and lower his window. "Sorry, Sir. This road is shut. You'll have to find an alternative route."

Peter flashed his warrant card, and said, "Busy night for you guys. We've just left an accident scene a few miles back. What's happened here?"

The officer moved closer to the car to let an ambulance through. "A fatal hit-and-run. A young lad on a moped. This lane is going to be shut for quite a while."

Peter nodded his understanding and raised the window to shut out the heavy rain. Turning the car around, he said, "Looks like we're taking the scenic route through Hinnegar Woods."

Fiona rested her head on the window and closed her eyes. She desperately wanted sleep, but her brain had other ideas. With a sinking feeling, she realised the new drama they witnessed probably put paid to her requesting a few days off work, as she had intended.

Peter reduced his speed as he turned into the twisty, single-track lane through the woods. Quiet in the day, but at night it was a common crossing point for wild deer and a popular route for locals driving home from the pub. A dangerous combination after dark. Tractors and quad bikes were a common sight in the early hours of the morning, dragging abandoned cars from the deep drainage ditches without involving the police.

"Strange, don't you think?" Fiona said. "The hit-and-run happening so close to the vehicle fire. Do you think they could be connected?"

"The thought had crossed my mind. Traffic will contact us soon enough if they have suspicions."

"A couple of things India said when we were talking in the car didn't make total sense. She was holding something back. Something she saw. I'm convinced she was lying to me and it was more than being embarrassed about being caught in a layby with a married man."

Peter turned off towards his cottage. "We'll be formally interviewing her. You can raise any doubts then."

"True," Fiona replied, before raising her hand to cover a yawn. "You haven't forgotten I'm driving mum back to the hospital tomorrow morning, so I won't be in until lunchtime?"

"Yes, you did say," Peter said.

Fiona stifled another yawn, before asking, "What do you think caused the vehicle fire? Could it have been a freak accident?"

Parking in his driveway, Peter leaned forwards with his forearms on the steering wheel and turned towards her. "I'm too shattered to think anything. I'm going to concentrate on a good night's sleep, so I'm rested for whatever tomorrow might bring."

In the dim light, Peter's face looked tired and drawn. Fiona conceded, "You're probably right."

Peter gave a satisfied nod of his head and opened his car door, ready to dash through the rain to his front door.

CHAPTER THREE

Megan maintained her calm exterior while she counted slowly to ten in her head after the door closed. An excited grin spread across her face, and she whooped for joy. "Yes! Yes! Yes!" She marvelled at the hi-tech kitchen and the elegant living space before taking a deep breath and pushing open the bedroom door. It was perfect. She resisted the urge to leap onto the bed and jump up and down. It was all so grown up and romantic. There would be plenty of time to check the bed springs later. She spun around in circles. "Wow! Wow! Wow!"

Spotting the hot tub through the sliding glass doors, she rushed over to look. She pulled back the cover and slipped her hand into the warm water. The veranda was covered, so while it would be chilly, there was no reason why they shouldn't use all the amenities. Hearing the front door open and close, she returned to the bedroom and slid the glass doors closed.

She smiled at the thud of the suitcases being dropped onto the floor. He was the perfect gentleman. She had said she could carry her own small suitcase, but he wouldn't hear of it. Her pink case had looked shabby and childish next to his leather holdall in the boot of his car. Next time she would be better prepared. It was her birthday soon. Sophisticated travel gear would be going to the top of her birthday list. She would need it once she was famous.

"Well? Do you like it?"

"It's wonderful. I'm going to freshen up," Megan called back, opening the side door to the bathroom. "I'll be out in a minute."

"Take all the time you need. I'll put the champagne on ice."

Megan locked the door to the small bathroom and sat on the

toilet, pinching herself. She tingled from head to toe, feeling she was the luckiest girl in the world. Dad always called her his princess, now she truly felt like one. She honestly thought nothing this wonderful could ever happen to her. She was too plain and boring. Nowhere near witty and charming enough. Yet here she was. Feeling loved and cherished by the man who was going to make all her dreams come true.

Shaking herself, she stood and examined her face in the mirror. She looked flushed, but not too bad. She leaned forward, peering closer, searching for imperfections. Stepping back, it dawned on her what the change in her appearance was. She was deliriously happy, and it showed.

If Charlotte and Lisa could see her now, they would be sick with envy. They were so immature. She smiled to herself at the sound of the champagne cork popping. Tonight was going to be a stepping stone to a bright, new future.

CHAPTER FOUR

Fiona woke before her alarm clock on her phone went off. She was surprised she'd managed to sleep considering the questions that had been clamouring for answers in her head. She lay on her back, listening to the unfamiliar sounds of the room in the dark. Bird song was accompanied by horses neighing nearby. She never thought Peter was the type to move out into the countryside, especially to such a tight-knit community.

With the ring road diverting all the through traffic, Topworth was cocooned from the rest of the world. Its peace was more likely to be disturbed by the sound of horse's hooves than car engines. The fact Peter could walk along an unlit, hardcore pathway to the Horseshoe Inn in the neighbouring village had something to do with his decision. She smiled when she recalled Peter's horrified reaction when he discovered his neighbour left the keys in her car's ignition overnight and her house keys in her front door lock permanently. His security lecture had been met with polite amusement. Only after giving up trying to persuade her to take her security seriously, was he slowly being accepted into the community.

The smile on Fiona's face quickly faded. She needed to move if she wanted enough time to pop home for a shower and a change of clothes before collecting her mother to take her to the hospital. She could smell the smoke from the previous evening in her hair and coating her skin. Dealing with her parents and the fall-out from the fire was going to make the days ahead frantically busy.

Her mother could drive, but chose not to. Not long journeys anyway. She would occasionally borrow her husband's car and manage a quick drive to the nearby post office or to visit friends who lived locally. Her decision to curtail driving was based on her perceived idea that other drivers were becoming progressively more impatient and aggressive. Those drivers had no concept of the fear experienced by her passengers and everyone, including Fiona, had been relieved by her decision to sell her car and hang up her car keys.

Her mother's loss of independence was minimal when her father was fit and well. Things would be a lot harder now. Her parents lived in a residential area of Streed. There was a small corner shop and pub in walking distance, but that was about it. Fiona made a mental note to ask the doctor if her father would be able to resume driving. With the vision of her becoming a taxi service in the coming months, Fiona swung herself out of bed and quickly dressed. She left a thank you note for Peter on the kitchen table and stepped out into a windy, wet day. With no security or streetlights outside, Fiona fumbled to switch on her phone's torch before making a dash for her car.

Her mother put on a cheerful voice, but her face was lined with worry. Judging from the black lines beneath her mother's eyes, Fiona concluded she probably hadn't slept at all last night. Possibly one of only a handful of nights she'd slept alone since her marriage over thirty years ago.

The news about her father was positive. He was staying in hospital while they ran another brain scan and set up appointments with a speech therapist and physiotherapist, but everything pointed to him making a good recovery. With a few adjustments, life could continue as before.

Fiona had no idea what their normal was anymore. Her eyes watered, seeing her father's confused looks as the conversation carried on around him. Her mother continued gossiping about the neighbours and their favourite television programmes blissfully unaware of these moments. Was she choosing to ignore them, or was it nothing new?

When was the last time she visited? Nearly five months ago, despite them living only an hour away. They used to meet up at pubs along the halfway point between their respective homes. The practice stopped because she had stood them up so many times due to unexpected work commitments.

Fiona acknowledged the other reason she found excuses not to visit was to avoid her mother's favourite conversation. The joy of being a grandmother. How she loved looking after Richard's children, and she couldn't wait to hold Fiona's first child. As Fiona approached thirty, the excited anticipation of these imaginary children had turned to a worried look and a reassuring, 'There's still time.' Whatever the reason, it was still five months! She vowed to do better in future, no matter how busy work became.

Her parents' marriage had always been as solid as a rock. She considered them an independent, self-contained unit that didn't need her involvement. How they would cope if something happened to one of them hadn't previously crossed her mind.

Racked with guilt for abandoning her parents in the impersonal hospital room, Fiona asked, "Are you sure I can't get you a coffee before I go? Or a magazine from the shop in the foyer?"

"We're fine, dear." Her mother said, looking anything but. "You go on. I know how busy you are at work. Don't worry about us. Emma will be along soon to give me a lift home."

With mixed feelings about her perfect sister-in-law, Fiona kissed her father on the cheek and gave her mother a hug. "Call me if you need anything." With a quick squeeze of her mother's arm, she picked up her coat and bag and gave her final farewells. While she hated leaving them, she was eager to escape the claustrophobic heat and smells of the hospital and breathe cool, fresh outside air.

Fiona stopped at the hospital main entrance to put on her padded jacket. It was warm, but not rainproof like her raincoat. That was still damp from the night before and was abandoned over a kitchen chair at Peter's. Outside looked grey and dreary. Black rain clouds had rolled in at the start of October and had failed to move on. Stepping outside, she was hit by a blast of ice-cold wind, which heralded another downpour of rain. Pulling up her collar, she ran across the car park, dodging puddles and potholes the best she could. The cold rain numbed the side of her face, and the wind tugged at her clothes. When she reached her car, a gust of wind flung the driver's door from her hand. In surprise, she stepped back into a deep puddle. Cursing, she threw herself and her bag into the car and wrestled with the door. Finally, she defeated the wind and pulled it closed behind her.

Her wet clothes instantly steamed up the windows. Waiting for the heater to clear the condensation, she switched her mobile back on. There was one message from Peter. Suspicions had been raised about the camper van fire, and preliminary reports were on their way. While waiting for her to return, he was revisiting the parents of two teenagers who had been reported missing a couple of days ago.

"Oh, you're back," Superintendent Ian Dewhurst said, when Fiona walked into an unusually empty department. "How did it go at the hospital?"

Fiona peeled off her damp coat and hung it on the back of the chair. Feeling instantly cold, she rubbed her upper arms. "Not too bad. The doctors are optimistic. A few minor adjustments and everything should be fine."

"Good, good. Will you need some compassionate leave?"

Fiona felt a prickle of regret and guilt. How could she go swanning off when the silhouette of the campervan driver was imprinted on the inside of her eyelids, and her conversation with India left her uneasy and full of unanswered questions? Why had Barney picked that spot to pull over? And why was he left in the firing line of the explosion while India found an excuse to take shelter behind the front seats? How had she not heard or seen anything? "They are going to need some help, but with my brother and sister-in-law I should be able to work around it."

"Are you sure?" Dewhurst asked.

"Positive. It's going to be a long-term thing. Maybe, when we're quieter, I could take some time then." Inwardly, Fiona convinced herself she could honour her silent promises to prioritise her family by pushing herself harder. There was no reason why she couldn't work her cases and help her parents. She would find the time from somewhere.

She lowered herself to her seat and fired up her computer screen as if to prove she was going nowhere. Dewhurst hovered over her desk, before saying, "Well, I'll leave you to it, then," and wandering off in the direction of his office.

Peter came in carrying two coffees and put one on Fiona's desk.

After taking a grateful sip, Fiona asked, "How did you know I was back?"

Pulling up a chair, Peter replied, "Dewhurst mentioned it."

"Did anything come in on a vehicle fire, overnight?"

"It did. The preliminary report confirms foul play is likely. There were an excessive number of gas canisters in the back of the camper van and more importantly, the vehicle wasn't in gear, and the driver's feet were nowhere near the pedals."

Flicking through the pile of reports on her desk, Fiona asked, "Is there anything here on the fatal hit-and-run?"

"Not yet."

"Where is everyone?"

"Litton and Jordan are chasing on the hit-and-run report so they can circulate details to the local garages. I've sent Humphries and Ward to speak to friends of the two missing teenagers, and Smith and Mann are door knocking on Connor Ambrose's neighbours."

"Who?"

"The owner of the burnt-out camper van. For now, I'm assuming he was also the driver." He pulled a slip of paper from the pile of paperwork on the adjacent desk and read from it. "Mr. Connor

Ambrose. A fit and healthy, 6-foot-tall, 52-year-old. He worked as a self-employed plumber and lived alone. He was divorced with a teenage daughter who lives with her mother. Once you have finished your coffee, we'll swing by his home and then visit his sister who is registered as his next of kin. David's team has gone through his home already. I asked him to call if they found anything particularly interesting, but I've heard nothing so far."

"Sounds good to me," Fiona said, wrapping her hands around the coffee cup. "What do you make of Dewhurst?"

"Not a great fan, so far. Why do you ask?"

Dewhurst had only taken up his role a few months before Fiona had joined the Met for a few months. Her initial impression was of a fair boss, happy to give his officers credit and support when it was due. The previous superintendent, Rogers, had let them all get on with things with minimal intervention and Dewhurst's hovering around her desk earlier had made her nervous. "Just wondering. When I came in, I was surprised to see him in here. I've no idea what he was doing."

"Checking up on us, I expect," Peter replied. "Are you ready to go?"

They parked at the rear of Connor Ambrose's home in Sapperton, a sprawling housing estate responsible for numerous callouts for minor disturbances. Typical of the area, access was from the rear of the house. They parked in front of the garage and made their way to the garden gate.

"How about you take the lead, and I'll be a quiet observer," Peter announced.

"Yes, sure," Fiona replied, feeling surprised as he usually liked to take the lead, especially at the start of an investigation.

They showed their warrant card to the uniformed officer standing outside. Fiona looked back at the assorted cars parked haphazardly in the road. "Has anyone checked inside his garage?"

The officer nodded. "Empty other than the usual collection of old, paint tins and other discarded rubbish."

Fiona turned to Peter. "I'm assuming he had some sort of work vehicle if he's a plumber. There's insufficient space here for him to have parked a camper van. I'm guessing he stored it somewhere else and that's where we'll find his work vehicle."

Peter nodded, his agreement. "I'll find the registration number and get it circulated."

The rear garden of overgrown grass was devoid of any plants to soften the uniformity of a small rectangle of patchy grass enclosed by weather-beaten wood panels. The back door led to a narrow kitchen with popular, mass-produced units. It was neat and tidy, almost sterile in appearance. The remaining ground floor space was made up of an open plan living room with an area designated for dining. The table for four pushed into the corner and the three-piece suite huddled around a large screen television did nothing to add any personality to the square room. A couple of popular prints hung forlornly from the magnolia walls. Peter searched the downstairs drawers while Fiona headed upstairs.

The bathroom and the first bedroom she checked offered up the same neat conformity. In the bathroom cabinet was a packet of repeat prescription anti-depressants hidden behind shampoo and shaving foam.

The second bedroom had been decorated with a teenage girl in mind. The surface of the dressing room table was bare other than a large, unusual vanity mirror, which drew Fiona's attention. Turning it around, she read the words carved into the back, 'Made for a beautiful princess. Dad.' Fiona sat on the dressing table stool and pulled out the side drawers. Their pristine condition and the waft of new wood suggested they had never been used. Fiona crossed the room and pulled open the wardrobe. It was empty and also had the strong smell of new wood. The creases on the duvet cover on the bed suggested they had never been slept under.

Returning down the stairs, Fiona said, "Any idea how recently he was divorced? It feels like he hadn't been here long enough to leave any personal traces."

"He's been divorced for several years, but I haven't checked how long he lived at this address. I agree he's made no effort to make the house, a home. There's nothing here to give us any clue about his personality, unless he was an incredibly bland, boring person," Peter said.

Fiona stepped out of the back door into the garden and said, "Ordinary people don't generally end up being killed the way he was. They tend to fade into the background. He must have done something of some note."

"True," Peter said, following her back to his car. "We'll see if his sister can shed any light on the situation. I looked but didn't find a work diary anywhere. Was there a laptop upstairs?"

"No."

"I expect he recorded his jobs, electronically on his phone which was probably burnt to a crisp with him. If we can't find a personal reason for his death, it would be helpful to discover where he had been working recently."

"We might get lucky and find he kept a diary in his work van," Fiona said. Settling in the passenger seat, she added, "It could be his death was mundane, and it was only the disposal of his body that was exceptional. Covering up something, maybe. An argument that got out of hand or a suicide. There's a cabinet full of anti-depressants upstairs. We'll also need to check the terms of his will, assuming he had one."

"However, he met his death, I have the feeling it didn't happen at home," Peter replied, entering Connor's sister's address into his sat-nav.

"Unless there's been a thorough clean up. To be so tidy with absolutely nothing out of place is unusual for a single man."

After an awkward silence, Peter said, "True."

Fiona bit her bottom lip and stared out the window. She had forgotten Peter was still adjusting to living alone after his recent divorce. To change the subject, she asked, "Does anyone know anything about Dewhurst's personal life?"

"Very little. To have risen through the ranks so quickly he either has good contacts or is married to the job." Handing Fiona a blank business card with a handwritten number scrawled across it, Peter said, "I found this in a kitchen drawer. Give the number a ring to see if he was working for them. If he had work lined up for this morning, there's less reason for him to have been driving around last night in his camper van."

Entering the number into her phone, Fiona said, "He could have been checking it was running okay? Filling it up with petrol in anticipation of a later trip or taking it in for its MOT?"

"After midnight? If he wasn't travelling, for say, an early, morning ferry crossing, was he transporting something? Something too large to fit in his work van that he didn't want people to see."

Ending the call, Fiona said, "He was contracted to work on the new homes Highfield Homes are building a few miles north of Tilbury, and he had been expected on site, this morning." She settled back in the seat to look out the window, kicking herself for making the stupid suggestion about a midnight MOT.

CHAPTER FIVE

Connor's sister lived in a three-bedroom, terraced cottage in Back Street, a narrow lane in the village of Tilbury. The cottages had been built before the universal ownership of cars, and despite it being midday, there were no available car spaces. Peter parked in the car park of the village pub, The Beaufort Arms. Locking the car, he said, "It would be rude to park here and not pop in after we've seen the sister."

As they walked towards Back Street, Fiona decided not to mention the constant reminders Peter threw in the bin that the force was cracking down on liquid lunches.

"I'm hungry and local pubs remain the best place for picking up gossip. Some of my finest moments have originated from the amber liquid."

Fiona shook her head in mock exasperation, wondering, not for the first time, if Peter had some extraordinary mind-reading skill or whether, despite her best intentions, her facial expressions were that obvious.

Checking the house numbers as they moved along the street, Fiona asked, "What's the sister's name?"

"Lucy Gibson. She is married to a teacher, and they have three, young children. She works part-time from home running her own business, making and fitting curtains and cushions."

After some thought, Fiona said, "Siblings with an independent streak." They came to a stop outside a small gate set in a waist-high, stone wall in front of number ten. "This looks like it."

The front door was opened, as they walked along the short garden path, by a slight woman, barefoot wearing a simple, smock dress. Her honey-coloured hair was tied back in a loose pony-tail. When Peter and Fiona held out their warrant cards, she re-trieved a hanky from her dress pocket to stem the flood of tears from her already red-rimmed eyes. Dabbing her eyes, she said, "Sorry, come in. I'm still trying to get my head around the fact he's gone."

They followed her into a newly fitted, oakwood kitchen with exposed beams. A flight of steps leading down to a cellar could be seen through an open door on their right. In front of them, a double window looked out over a large garden separated from the open countryside by a low stone wall. They took seats on bar stools surrounding a kitchen island while Lucy busied her-self, making them coffee.

Placing colourful ceramic mugs of strong-smelling coffee in front of Fiona and Peter, Lucy asked, "Did you find somewhere to park? Parking is a nightmare around here."

"We parked in the Beaufort Inn car park," Peter replied. "I've never been in there, before. It looks a pleasant place."

Lucy drew their attention to the open door. "Rumour has it, there once was a tunnel leading from here to the pub. Dan, that's my husband, often joked with Connor about the possibility of re-opening it."

"Did you and your husband see a lot of Connor?" Fiona asked.

Lucy dabbed away at a new set of tears. "We were always very close. After the divorce, Connor came over every Sunday for lunch. Occasionally, I cooked, but more often than not, we went to the Beaufort. The landlord, Tim, reserves the same table for us each week. In the snug at the back."

"Was Connor a drinker?" Fiona asked.

"He liked a pint, but no more than anyone else," Lucy said de-fensively. "*She* claimed he drank too much, but he only drank to excess to deal with her and her unreasonable demands. He had been so much happier recently. He was like a different man. Ready to move on with his life. And now this."

"By she, do you mean his ex-wife, Amanda Wagstaff?" Peter asked.

"Who else?" Lucy replied, before submitting to another round of tears. "Worst day of his life, the day he met her."

"Their divorce was a difficult one?" Fiona asked.

"No. A very easy one. Connor gave the money-grabbing witch whatever she demanded."

"We'll be paying Amanda a visit later. Has she ever made threats towards Connor or indicated she wished him harm?" Peter asked.

"Are you suggesting ..." Lucy swallowed, before continuing ... "That it wasn't an accident?"

"We're not ruling out anything at this stage," Peter said.

"She all but destroyed him when she went off with her fancy man taking their daughter with her. She made access as difficult as possible and tried to poison Meg against her father. Who knows what else she is capable of?" Glaring at Peter, Lucy said, "I suggest you ask her that question."

Watching the exchange, Fiona cleared her throat and said, "Connor was found in his camper van. Were you aware he was planning on taking a trip?"

"He didn't say anything when he was here on Sunday."

"Did he seem his usual self on Sunday?" Fiona asked.

"Yes. We had a lovely meal in the Beaufort. Got soaked to the skin running home when the heavens opened. Could have done with a useable tunnel," Lucy half-heartedly tried to joke. Realising it had fallen flat, she continued, "He came in to dry off for a bit before leaving. Now you mention it, he did say something about the weather getting him down and wanting to get away for a bit. But then, I think everyone is feeling that way, with the weather and all. He didn't give the impression it was a definite plan."

"Where did he keep his camper van?" Fiona asked.

"And that's another strange thing. He parks it up in a farmyard near here, and he always pops his head in when he's heading that way." Lucy pushed herself away from the central island and moved to a side cabinet. Rummaging through a drawer, she said over her shoulder, "I've Keith's number somewhere in here. I'll write it down along with his address once I find it."

"How often does he take trips in the van?" Fiona asked.

"In the winter, infrequently. Come the summer, whenever the weather is looking good for the weekend, he'll take off for a few days."

Fiona looked around the kitchen, taking in the quality finish of the matching units and the open countryside through the window over the double sink. A step up from her brother's soulless, modern estate house. She estimated it would be beyond the pocket of most teachers. She couldn't imagine curtain making was that profitable.

Lucy wrote a number on the back of a used envelope and handed it to Fiona. "We grew up with Keith. He doesn't do too much anymore, not since his heart attack. He mostly rents his fields out to other farmers. Cows and sheep mostly. He lets a woman keep her horses in the fields closest to his house, and he charges people to store things on the farmyard. Containers, caravans and the like."

Lucy stopped and burst into tears. She gave her eyes a final dab and slipped her hanky back into her pocket. "Sorry, I can't stop babbling. Anything to stop myself thinking about Connor. I can't believe I'll never see him again." She took a deep breath, and said, "Ignore me. Please carry on with your questions."

"Do you know of anyone else who might have had a grudge against Connor? A recent falling out, maybe? Or any ongoing issues with a job he'd completed?" Fiona asked.

"No. Nothing like that. Connor was quiet and reserved. Not the sort to pick fights. He would do anything for anyone."

"Could you give us a list of his friends?"

Lucy dabbed at her eyes. "I can't think of anyone in particular. He was a bit of a loner. Kept himself to himself, mostly. I know he popped into his local pub occasionally." Lucy was overcome with a fresh wave of tears. "Everyone loved him, though. He was too kind to make any enemies."

Fiona looked to Peter to check whether he had more questions.

Peter replied with a slight shake of his head before standing. "I think that's everything for now."

Fiona stood and pushed her stool under the island. "We're sorry for your loss. Is there anyone I can call for you before we leave?"

Lucy shook her head and waved Fiona's concerns away. "I'll be fine ... just ... If it wasn't an accident, promise me you'll find the person responsible."

"We'll do our best," Fiona replied.

"No, promise me."

Under the woman's intense stare, Fiona told her what she wanted to hear. "I promise." She looked away when Peter caught her eye, giving her a stern look. She knew she shouldn't make promises she couldn't keep. Well, maybe she would do her darndest to keep this one. "We'll see ourselves out. Thank you for your assistance."

Outside, they quickly agreed to have a late lunch in the Beaufort Inn, before visiting the farm where Connor stored his camper van to have a word with the landowner, Keith.

CHAPTER SIX

Peter and Fiona pulled up on a mud-covered lane outside an untidy sprawl of concrete farm buildings. A cardboard sign propped against a rusty gate advertised potatoes and eggs for sale. The gate's hinges were rusted away, and it took some persuasion and brute force to open it wide enough for them to pass through. Behind the farm buildings was an ugly, pebble-dashed house. They exchanged looks before Peter banged the heavy, metal door knocker and stood back to look up at the upper-floor windows.

Peter was about to knock again when they heard signs of movement. The front door creaked opened, and a middle-aged man with unbrushed, black hair poked his head out. "What do you want?"

Fiona stepped forward, holding out her warrant card, trying not to breathe in the pungent smells of cow manure and stale, human sweat. "Keith Higgins, isn't it? We would like to ask you some questions about Connor Ambrose. We believe he stored his camper van here."

"Hang on a minute," Keith replied gruffly, before closing the door on them.

Fiona gave Peter an exasperated look. "Charming."

"We'll give him ten minutes. Maybe he wanted to make himself look more presentable for you," Peter said, with a dismissive shrug. "If he hasn't reappeared by then, we'll take a look around by ourselves. That'll probably bring him running."

"So long as he's not running at us with a shotgun," Fiona replied, looking back up at the house. She stepped across to look through a downstairs window, but it was covered in a thick film of mud. She turned to look back at the motley collection of farm buildings and the scattering of mud-covered farm machinery littered around the area. The layers of mud and rust covering peeling paintwork made everything a uniform browny-red colour.

Fiona walked through the rotting corpses of the abandoned farm machinery. Weeds poked through the cracked concrete walkway that opened out to form a small yard surrounded by wooden stables. She turned in disgust at the sight of a dead cow pushed up against the side of one stable. Marks on the ground suggested it had been dragged across the ground and dumped there. Feeling nauseous, she walked back towards the house.

"Find anything?" Peter, who had waited by the front door, asked.

Fiona pulled a look of disgust. "A load of junk and a dead cow. Remind me not to buy my eggs from here."

"There must be another entrance somewhere," Peter said. "One wide enough for vehicles. Wait here, while I take a wander in the other direction."

Before Peter had taken more than a few steps, the farmhouse door creaked open, and Keith stepped out. His brown trousers were gathered at the waist and held up by what looked like rope. His button-down shirt with a frayed collar had probably been white once upon a time, before turning a dingy grey. He stomped towards them in his wellington boots. He came to a halt and stood with his hands on his generous hips. "This is private property." He glared at Fiona, before saying, "You've no right to go poking about without my say so."

Ignoring the man's threatening pose, Fiona said, "We'd like to see where Connor Ambrose parked his camper van."

"If the vehicle is lacking a MOT or insurance that's got nothing to do with me. The same if it has been in an accident. I just let the fella park it here when he's not using it."

"I'm guessing he pays you a handsome rent for the privilege and security," Fiona replied. She added sweetly, "I'm sure you keep records of the income you receive for providing storage and would be able to provide us with copies."

Keith jutted out his chin and moved forward as if to say something. He changed his mind and stepped back. "Well, yes … you see."

"Just show us where the damn thing was parked," Peter said. "We haven't got all day."

"This way," Keith replied, before walking on ahead of them, muttering beneath his breath.

At the rear of the house was a second yard area, with a track covered in hardcore that led via a five-bar gate to a side lane. Roughly twenty vehicles, a combination of caravans, camper vans and horse trailers were parked haphazardly in the area. A few didn't look anywhere near roadworthy, but most looked clean and well maintained if past their prime.

"Connor's spot is over here," Keith said gruffly, leading them behind a double horse trailer. He stopped and pointed. "That's where he normally parks it."

Unsurprisingly the allotted spot was empty, identified only by a dark oil stain and yellow, flattened weeds. To the side was a small, blue transit van, with the wording, Ambrose Plumbing marked on the side.

While Fiona walked around the parked van, peering in through the windows, Peter asked, "When was the vehicle moved?"

Keith scratched his head. "Not so sure, as I know. It was here last week."

Peter squinted at the gate at the end of the track. Nodding in its direction, he asked, "Is that kept locked?"

"Yes, but I give everyone a key. I don't want them bothering me every five minutes to let them in and out."

"When was the last time, you know for sure Connor's camper van was here?"

"Sunday. It was here Sunday, lunchtime."

"And the last time you saw Connor?"

"Months back. Way before Christmas. October time, maybe."

"How did he pay you?" Peter asked.

"Bank transfer. I insist on a month in advance before I let any of them have a gate key. I've learnt the hard way not to trust anyone."

"So, you'd have records of the owners of all the vehicles, back at the house."

"Aye. Back at the house."

"I'd like a list of them all before we leave," Peter said, walking over to join Fiona, who was studying the van. "Find anything?"

Fiona straightened up from peering through the driver's window. "I can't see a diary. How tall was Connor?"

Peter frowned. "Over 6 feet according to the initial report."

"That coincides with the family photograph, Lucy had on the side dresser in the kitchen. She was about 5 feet 8, and the man she was with, I assumed to be Connor, was several inches taller." Fiona nodded towards the van. "Whoever drove this van last was shorter. Much shorter judging from the seat's position."

Peter turned to Keith, who was hovering over his shoulder. "Did Connor ever bring company when he came to pick up his camper van?"

"Not so as I remember. No."

Peter pulled out his phone. Waiting for his call to be answered, he said to Keith, "A team will be coming today to remove the van. Can you make sure they have access via the gate?"

Keith scowled and opened his mouth to protest, then appeared to think better of it. He meekly replied, "I'll go and unlock it, now," before sloping away.

Peter called after him, "Come straight back here afterwards so we can go through those records of yours."

Fiona waited patiently for Peter to complete the call. "All arranged?"

"Yes," Peter replied.

Indicating the general area, Fiona said, "It's probably worth having a full search of this area, as well." Looking up at Peter, she asked, "What are you looking so thoughtful about?"

"Me?" Peter said, with a wry smile. "That I should leave you to carry out this investigation. I appear to be surplus to requirements."

Fiona laughed and quickly turned away, unsure how to react to the compliment.

"Our jolly farmer is on his way back," Peter said. "We might as well have a look through his records before the teams arrive. At least we'll know where he is and that he isn't damaging any important evidence, knowingly or unknowingly."

CHAPTER SEVEN

Their next stop was Connor's ex-wife, Mrs. Amanda Wagstaff. The sisters-in-law were chalk and cheese, and Fiona thought they probably would have clashed even if the marriage had survived. Where Lucy was emotional, artistic and earthy, Amanda was immaculately groomed, business-like and aloof. The death of her ex-husband a minor inconvenience to her hectic schedule. Something to be quickly dealt with and filed away.

Amanda lived in a detached house in Brierly with her new husband, Owen Wagstaff, their five-year-old son and her daughter from her marriage to Connor. Dry-eyed and uninterested, she invited Peter and Fiona into an open-plan living room. The décor was modern and minimalists, all straight lines in slightly differing shades of white. She drank a health drink while Peter and Fiona put their decaffeinated, fair-trade coffee to one side.

Peter left his drink untouched in protest. Fiona was more concerned about spilling the nearly black drink on the deep pile, white rug. After a cautious sip, she concluded the hint of milk in the drink probably came from a Yak. When asked about Connor, Amanda waved around the impersonal room as though it proved she had moved on and made a new life for herself. She rarely heard from Connor, much less cared what he did with his time or his pathetic, little motor home. "We go to Barbados every winter. Wouldn't catch me dead in his pokey, little van on a wet weekend in Bournemouth."

"Is that where he went in his camper van?" Fiona asked, discarding her coffee cup on a nearby table.

"No idea. It was a figment of speech," Amanda replied airily, batting her eyelids at Peter, who promptly ignored her. Narrowing her eyes in displeasure, she turned to Fiona and asked, "Is there anything else? Only I've a busy day."

Annoyed by her calculated and uncaring manner and guessing her busy day probably amounted to a trip to a beauty salon followed by retail therapy, Fiona asked, "What do you do? For work?"

"I don't," Amanda replied haughtily.

Keeping her voice neutral, Fiona asked, "How is your daughter taking the news?"

"I haven't told her, yet. She's staying away with a couple of friends. She claimed it was study leave, but I have my doubts. I expect they're having a great time. Not wasting it on studying."

"It might be best you contacted her before she hears about the death of her father from a news report," Fiona suggested, struggling to keep her astonishment from her tone.

"I very much doubt they're spending their time on news reports any more than their school studies. She may as well enjoy the rest of her break before I break the news."

Fiona chewed her bottom lip to prevent her from commenting on something that wasn't really her business. She couldn't help thinking the woman's cold detachment from the situation was obscene. There was no inkling that she anticipated her daughter would be devastated and need her comfort. The woman probably was callous enough to arrange for someone's death if it suited her plans. Even a small financial benefit would probably suffice. Whether the cold fish was passionate enough about anything to take drastic action, was a different matter. Even disposing of an irritating ex. "What does your current husband do?"

"Owen? Why should you want to know about him?"

"Answer the question, please," Fiona said, abandoning the struggle to hide her impatience.

"An architect, if you must know."

Fiona's head shot up. "Does he do any work for Highfield Homes, one of the local property developers?"

"No idea. I don't take much notice. You'll have to ask him."

Fiona guessed her interest in her husband's work rarely strayed from the amount that appeared in her bank account every month. "Have you a contact number for Owen?"

Amanda waved her hand in the direction of a side cabinet. "I think there's a couple of cards in there."

While Peter walked over to inspect the cabinet drawers, Fiona asked, "Where were you last night?"

"Is this really necessary?"

"To eliminate you from our enquiries, yes."

"I was at my regular, aqua, aerobics class at The Grange with a couple of friends." Amanda looked up and asked, "Will you have to trouble them with this nonsense?"

"Afraid so," Fiona replied. "We'll need their contact details. What did you do after your class finished?"

While scrolling through her phone, Amanda said, "We shared a bottle of bubbly in the bar. I left at about ten o'clock, came home and went to bed." She read out the numbers for her friends, Sharon and Liz, before saying, "You can't seriously think I had anything to do with that idiot managing to set himself alight in his own vehicle, do you? He never was the brightest button in the box. Heaven only knows what I saw in him." Shrugging one shoulder, she continued, "The folly of youth, I suppose. Why on earth you should think I would risk all this and my good reputation for a mistake I put behind me years ago is beyond me."

Not making any effort to reassure Amanda she wasn't under suspicion, Fiona asked, "Can anyone verify the time you returned home?"

"Owen was in his study. I knocked on the door before I went up to bed. Anything else you want to waste my time on?"

Gathering her things together, Fiona said, "That will be all for now. We'll be in touch."

Peter walked over, holding one of Owen Wagstaff's business cards he had found in a drawer. He placed it in front of Amanda and said, "Could you write your daughter's mobile number on the back?" Before she could make any comment, he pulled a pen from his jacket pocket and handed it to her. "The sooner we've spoken to everyone, the sooner we'll leave you in peace to get along with whatever it is you usually do," he said, with a forced smile.

Outside, the rain was hammering down, making up for the brief respite it had given earlier. Shaking the rain from her hair in the car, Fiona asked, "Are you going to call the daughter as you have the number?"

"I wanted to see how she reacted to the request. Technically, as a minor, we need permission before contacting her. She wasn't exactly the over-protective Mother, was she?"

"She didn't seem to care at all," Fiona replied. "I feel sorry for both of her husbands. If she has any redeeming qualities, she keeps them well hidden. I had thought her sister-in-law's dislike was down to family loyalty. Now, I know better."

"Unpleasant as she was, I don't think she was behind her ex's death, but we'll still have to check out her alibi with her friends. We may as well do that now unless you have any other suggestions?"

Fiona said, "I would like to get hold of India Williamson, to go over what happened in detail. The brief statement she gave to traffic at the scene tells us nothing."

"Sounds a solid plan."

Reaching into her bag, Fiona said, "I'll try her, now." She returned her phone to her bag. "Her phone is switched off."

"Do you have her work number?"

Checking the file, Fiona shook her head. "She ran the online publicity company with Barney Jones from home, and there's no alternative number. I appreciate she was in shock at the scene when I spoke to her, but I would like to clarify some of her comments as soon as possible. Not being able to get hold of her is adding to my suspicions."

"Any chance she's in hospital?" Peter asked.

"She wasn't injured in any way, so I doubt it."

"What's her address? We can swing by her home. It could be she just wanted to switch off for a while."

They parked at the rear of India's home, which although several streets away was in Sapperton, the same housing estate as Connor. That was where the similarity ended. Built on the edge of the estate, one side faced open countryside. Fairy lights twinkled in the drizzle, lighting their way through the garden as they followed the garden path across a rectangular pond via a stone walkway. The fencing panels were shielded by trees and bushes. The upper garden was dominated by a wooden sun house with decking and a four-person hot tub.

When they knocked, the door was swung open by a woman in sports gear holding a white terrier. Her animated face fell when she saw them, and a look of suspicion crossed her face. "Who the hell are you?" she asked over the dog's yapping.

Fiona held up her warrant card. "We're investigating the accident India Williamson was involved in last night. Is she here?"

"I'm afraid not. When you knocked on the door, I thought it might have been her, and she had forgotten to pick up her keys, again."

"Any idea where she was going or when she'll be back?" Fiona asked.

"Sorry. She didn't say."

Fiona pulled out a card and handed it to the woman. "Can you ask her to call me. I'm one of the detectives who were first on the scene last night."

"Sure. I'll let her know as soon as she comes back."

"Can I take your name?" Fiona asked.

"Barbara Bloom. Everyone calls me BB." With an apologetic shrug, she said, "It started in primary school and has kinda stuck."

They called on Amanda's two friends who were equally condescending, but they did confirm they spent the early evening together. Fiona tried India's number one last time before they headed back to the station. Peter disappeared home, leaving Fiona to write up a report of the day and add it to the case file before heading home.

CHAPTER EIGHT

Megan woke with a pounding headache, feeling nauseous and confused. Where the hell, was she?

"Morning sleepyhead."

Megan rubbed her aching forehead. "Oh, hi," she mumbled, forcing an unsure smile. Slowly, it came back to her. The few nights away in a friend's weekend cottage. She checked under the covers. Yup, she was naked. Did that mean they'd done it? She had no recollection of the evening at all. Should she say something? No, he would think she was a complete idiot. She didn't remember getting undressed, so they must have.

She cringed when he ran his hand over her face, pushing a strand of hair behind her ear. His hands felt so soft and gentle. Why had her mind blanked out what had happened between them? Wasn't that only supposed to happen with traumatic events, not enjoyable ones? Had she enjoyed it? Now she thought about it, she did feel a bit sore down there. Maybe he became carried away and was too rough? She knew all about date rape drugs. Where you woke up with no recollection of having sex.

"How does your head feel?"

Confused, Megan rubbed her temple. Could this be some crazy situation where she had been in an accident and lost the last six months of her life? "Umm. Sore, I guess."

"Sorry, Princess. I should have realised you weren't used to drinking quality champagne. I'll make you a coffee and some dry toast to settle your stomach."

Once the bedroom door shut, Megan sat up, covering herself with the duvet. She had a quick glance at herself to check for any bruising. There was none. Could she have passed out from drinking too much? It was possible. She usually only drank cheap cider with her friends, sharing the one-litre bottle around between them in the park. When her head felt less fuzzy, she could think up questions to discover what happened without admitting her memory of last night was blank.

She looked around the room for her clothes, wondering if she looked as awful as she felt. If she was quick, she would have sufficient time to splash a little water on her face to wake herself up before the coffee arrived. She groaned when she spotted her new lacy bra hanging from the lampshade and the remaining items of her clothing strewn across the floor. It looked like she had put on a display at some point in the evening, even if she couldn't remember it. She grabbed her T-shirt from the floor and fled to the bathroom.

When she came out of the bathroom wearing her T-shirt, a mug of coffee and a plate of toast was waiting for her on the bedside table. She slipped under the covers and feeling surprisingly hungry she tucked in.

"You should start to feel better soon."

Swallowing a mouthful of toast, Megan heard the Pycho theme tune of her mobile. She looked around for it and noticed Bob's hand go to his pocket, silencing it. "That's my phone."

"I want to spend the morning together. Just the two of us."

Disconcerted about why he had her phone in his pocket, Megan asked, "What did you have in mind?"

His response was interrupted by her phone ringing and being cut off again. "We could go for a romantic walk. What do you think?"

"Umm, I'm not sure." Small alarm bells were ringing in the back of her mind. Why did he have her phone? She finished her toast and took a sip of the coffee to play for time.

CHAPTER NINE

Despite not leaving her parents' home until gone midnight, Fiona was wide awake by five o'clock in the morning. She sat down for breakfast for the first time she could remember in years. There was no need to pull the curtains to check the weather. She could hear the wind howling as it threw wave after wave of rain at the windows in the inky blackness of a winter morning. In defiance of the gloomy grey that was pulling everyone down, she wore a sky-blue jumper. It was at the top end of what was deemed appropriate for work, but a sea of grey suits was adding to the general dreariness.

She felt surprisingly alert and keen to make a start on her day. Progress on discovering what led to the death of Connor Ambrose had been disappointing. Today, she was determined to make some headway.

They still had no idea why anyone would have wanted to kill him. Interviews of friends and neighbours hadn't told them much more than they had gleaned from visiting his home. Everyone described him as a quiet man who kept himself to himself and was an adequate plumber. He lived within his means and had no record of criminal activities. He even completed his tax returns early. His interests outside of work were trips in his camper van and watching classic movies. Hardly the activities likely to lead to hatred and violence. There had to be something more to his life to explain his untimely death in such unusual circumstances.

During the week before his death, other than Sunday lunch with his sister's family, his only social visit had been one trip to his local pub. As was his usual practice, he had sat at the bar while he drank two pints having only brief words with other customers. He had had no recent contact with his ex-wife and had last seen his daughter in a café two weeks earlier. There were no reports of recent changed behaviour or sightings of him the evening he was killed.

Contacting India Williamson and pinning her down on what she had seen was Fiona's number one priority. She was convinced India held the key to unravelling what had happened the night of the fire and equally sure the woman was intent on avoiding them.

Barney's death niggled away at her thoughts. She found it hard to accept that it was purely by chance that he pulled over where he did. He had been the proverbial sitting duck in the front seat of his car, facing a campervan crammed full of gas cylinders primed to go up like a million fireworks, while India shielded herself in the back seat. She hadn't met his young wife as Peter had taken Phil Humphries to visit the family. They reported she was devastated and there was nothing to arouse suspicions.

With thoughts whirling around her brain, Fiona poured the remains of her coffee down the sink, grabbed the last piece of toast and headed out of the door. There were some benefits of operating from a small station. Officially it didn't open until nine o'clock, and all overnight calls were directed to Birstall. At the station, she would have full access to files and reports that came in overnight and still have peace and quiet for a few hours.

In the eerie quiet of the office, Fiona re-read the statement India had given to the traffic police. Like a brass monkey, India claimed to have seen and heard nothing before the explosion. She and Barney had spent the evening in The Grange Hotel to celebrate landing a contract they had been pursuing for months to provide the publicity for Highfield Homes Property Developers. The same company that employed Connor. The possible connection was obvious, yet for reasons, he had yet to explain, Dewhurst had insisted they delayed contacting the company.

The contract was a substantial one, and the publicity company India set up with Barney was about to double in value.

With his death, she now had total control. It was a possible motivation for murdering Barney, but there was nothing to link her to Connor.

Fiona scan read the remaining reports. They confirmed further tests were needed to confirm the cause of death and the vehicle fire, but an accidental ignition had been ruled out. The autopsy date on Connor was yet to be confirmed.

In normal circumstances, before seven o'clock was too early to call a witness. But these weren't normal circumstances, and Fiona wasn't convinced India Williamson was an innocent witness. Pacing the room with her unanswered mobile, she was about to hang up and drive to India's house to drag her from her bed, when a croaky voice answered her call. Taking a seat, Fiona said, "Hello, India?"

"No. It's BB Who is this? Do you know what time it is?"

"DI Fiona Williams and I'm fully aware what time it is. Could you call India to the phone."

"Hold your horses. I'll go and see if she's awake."

Fiona continued to pace when the line went quiet. "Come on," she muttered. "How long does it take to run upstairs and wake up your friend?" While waiting, she wandered to the window and looked out over Tibberton high street. The shops were still in darkness. A lone car passed by, its headlights highlighting a light drizzle of rain. Another day in paradise in good old England. She decided as soon as the current workload settled down, she was booking a holiday. Somewhere warm and sunny. She needed something to get her through the dismal winter nights.

A breathless voice appeared on the line interrupting Fiona's daydream about long days on a deserted beach. "She's not there. Her bed hasn't been slept in."

"Didn't you realise she didn't come home last night?"

"I went out for the night. I didn't get back until late and went straight to bed. I didn't check whether she was home. Why would I?"

"Any idea where she might be? A boyfriend's maybe?"

"No, and she hasn't got one. Not since Carl."

"How long ago was Carl?"

"That was over months ago. Said he had put her off relationships for good. She was enjoying being single and concentrating on building up her business with Barney."

"No other close friends she might have stayed with overnight? Or family nearby?"

"I genuinely haven't a clue where she might be," BB said, with annoyance creeping into her tone. "I'm not her keeper. I'm going to have to get ready for work. I'll leave a note telling her to contact you urgently."

"Hang on. I need to talk to you about how she has been the last few days. Has she said or done anything unusual?"

"I was about to get in the shower when you rang. I'm going to be late for work if I don't get a move on. But there is something, maybe. I don't know if it was anything, but if she has disappeared, maybe I should tell someone."

"Tell someone, what?"

"Can we do this after work? Only, if I don't get there, the salon won't open, and I'll have a lot of disappointed customers. Not to mention cross staff, still expecting to be paid for a full day."

"How about I meet you at work. Where is it?"

"Reflections Hair and Beauty in the shopping precinct in Sapperton."

"I'll be there in half an hour."

"Could you make it for an hour. I need a coffee and to make myself presentable, and there's a delivery I need to sort through. We'll still have a good half hour before my first appointment."

"An hour, then," Fiona agreed. "But one more thing before I go. Could you run upstairs and check whether any of her clothes are missing? Anything to suggest India has disappeared of her own accord."

Fiona impatiently paced, waiting for BB to return to the line. She heard what sounded like running down the stairs and a clunky noise as BB picked up the phone.

"As far as I can see, nothing is missing."

Ending the call, Fiona looked up at the time. There was a good chance Peter would arrive in plenty of time for them to drive to the salon, together.

She returned to the search she had started on Highfield Homes and the people running it before she was told to back off. Their signs had become commonplace recently, but she didn't think they had been around all that long. The new kid on the block often had to struggle to get their foot in the door. Maybe Highfield Homes had used more devious measures. Done things to cut corners and undercut competitors. Things they would like to keep secret at any cost. Only, Connor Ambrose had stumbled upon something and threatened to oust them. That would work as a motive.

She found a report that convinced her they should be looking at the company, regardless of what Dewhurst said. The Managing Director was currently serving a prison sentence for a string of offences, including the employment of illegal immigrants on various building sites. In his absence, a nephew had travelled over from Romania to take command. She was attaching a copy to the main file when Peter walked in. "Morning," she said brightly. Handing the file to him, she said, "You're going to want to read this report."

After a quick read through, Peter said, "Interesting. What does Dewhurst say?"

"I was just on my way to his office. Do you know if he's in yet?"

"We walked in together from the car park."

Indicating the report in her hand, Fiona said, "We'll catch up, later. I want to get this to him as soon as possible."

Once Dewhurst told her to enter, Fiona placed the report on his desk. "Sir, I know you've been reluctant to involve Highfield Homes in our investigation, but I've found some interesting background information about their Managing Director, Darius Albu."

Ignoring the file, Dewhurst said, "Tell me, but make it quick."

"He has a history of drug and assault charges and he is currently serving a sentence for his involvement in employing illegal immigrants. He claimed in his defence that he found God and turned his life around and made an honest mistake employing the young men thinking he was helping them. He put his financial success down to his altruism and loyalty of his staff. Others think differently, and his working practices and financial arrangements have been under scrutiny several times. The company is currently being managed by a nephew called Stefan Albu. Could Connor and possibly Barney have stumbled upon something he wanted to remain hidden?"

Dewhurst opened the file and flicked through Fiona's notes. Without looking up, he said, "Leave this with me. Anything else?"

When Fiona told him about her meeting with BB, Dewhurst checked his watch, and said, "Let me know how it goes," before returning his attention to his computer screen.

Annoyed by her abrupt dismissal, Fiona returned to the incident room. Finding Peter, she told him about the appointment to interview India's housemate.

Instead of showing any interest, he replied, "The bank account details for the missing teenagers have at last been released. It seems they both withdrew an identical sum of money the day before they disappeared."

"So? They're runaways."

"There's something about these two girls that is bothering me. They have absolutely nothing in common except their looks and now the same amount of cash withdrawn. I want to speak to their circles of friends again." Nodding towards the back of the room, he said, "Take Abbie with you. She's not assigned to anything."

Fiona was unhappy at the thought of spending a morning with DS Abbie Ward. The last time they had worked closely together was during the aftermath of Nick Tattner's death. They became friends for a while, meeting up outside work. Until Abbie had gone behind her back, telling tales about her. They had barely spoken since other than when it was necessary. "India's housemate indicated she had something important to tell me. As seeing the girls' friends isn't urgent, how about putting it off until later today and coming with me instead."

Peter pulled a sorry-no-can-do face in response.

"Please."

"Sorry. I've just got off the phone persuading them to see me. What did Dewhurst say about Highfield Homes?"

"Not a lot. Just to leave it with him."

"Well, I need to go. Let me know how you get on."

Dewhurst poked his head in through the door and said to Peter, "When you get back, I want a full update on where you are with the checks I asked you to carry out yesterday."

The door shut and Dewhurst disappeared as quickly as he arrived. Fiona gave Peter a questioning look. He shook his head and walked to the door. Watching him go, a new thought occurred to Fiona. She dismissed it out of hand. Even if Dewhurst was up to something dubious, Peter would never have anything to do with it.

She wandered to Abbie's desk and cleared her throat to distract her from the reports she was poring over. "Are you up to date on the Ambrose vehicle fire?"

Abbie smiled and replied, "I'm reading through it now."

"We still haven't been able to get hold of India, but I've an appointment with her housemate. Peter suggested I take you along."

"I'll grab my coat," Abbie replied eagerly.

"Don't rush. I'm popping to the loo, first. Be ready to leave in about ten minutes."

Once outside the room in the corridor, Fiona pulled out her phone and searched for the contact number for PC Rachel Mann. Thinking about Abbie's betrayal of her trust had reminded her of the details surrounding Nick's death. She was halfway along the corridor to the toilets when her call was answered. "Hi, Rachel. Fiona, here. Could you check whether Emma Comley is still in prison for me?"

"Sure," came the bubbly reply. "Wasn't that the girl whose explosion killed Nick?"

"Yes," Fiona replied, wondering how she could be so blasé

about the subject. Especially as she remembered Rachel being in floods of tears, soaking up as much sympathy as she could for weeks afterwards. "It's quite urgent. Call me back on this number with the confirmation as soon as you can." As there was nobody else in the corridor there was no need to continue with the façade of visiting the bathroom, Fiona made an abrupt turn.

CHAPTER TEN

From the outside, BB's hairdressing salon looked upmarket. The tinted glass in keeping with the simple, classic black surround made it impossible to see inside. The lack of a price list outside supported the initial impression that it would cost an arm and a leg to get a sophisticated haircut.

Fiona's phone rang while they were waiting for BB to unlock the door. Fiona slipped the phone back into her bag after taking the call from PC Rachel Mann, relieved that Emma Comley was still safely behind bars. It was one less distraction to worry about. She could now focus on finding India and discovering what or who she saw moments before the explosion. She was pleased she hadn't voiced her suspicions about Comley being involved, out loud.

BB seemed far more agitated than when they had briefly met before. She led them through the shop where the theme of shiny black surfaces and straight lines continued until they reached the small staff room at the rear. The cosy feel of the room which included a scattering of colourful, comfortable sofas and sofas was blurred by the haze of cigarette smoke. BB stood at the far end by a complicated-looking coffee machine. "What would you like, ladies? Lattes, cappuccinos, mocha …"

Fiona interrupted her. "Two, plain, everyday coffees with milk will be fine." Before BB could say anything more, she added, "And hold the sprinkles."

Losing her smile, BB flicked on a kettle and pulled three mugs and a jar of instant coffee from an overhead cupboard. "Personally, I enjoy a latte."

Coughing into her hand, while her eyes watered, Abbie said, "Could we talk somewhere else? The smoke is irritating my allergies."

BB shrugged, as she placed her mug under the coffee machine and reached for a packet of cigarettes on the counter.

"It is illegal to smoke in the workplace and has been for some time," Abbie pointed out.

BB put down the cigarettes, grumbling, "Whatever." She sprayed an air freshener around which caused Abbie to descend into a coughing fit.

Fiona gave an exaggerated sigh. Abbie had a point, but contravening the smoking policy was not high on her list of concerns, and it was wasting time. She wanted to discover as much as she could about India, not give BB a fine for a breach of health and safety laws. To diffuse the situation, she stood up from the sofa she had just got comfortable on and said, "We'll wait back in the salon for you to finish making the coffees."

In the salon, Fiona dragged three padded chairs from their positions in front of mirrors and arranged them in a small circle. Taking her seat in one of them, she avoided any conversation with Abbie by flicking through a fashion magazine, she found on a counter in front of one of the mirrors. She put it to one side when BB joined them and handed out the coffees.

Reluctantly settling on one of the customers' chairs, BB said, "I'm not sure I can tell you anything more than I did earlier on the phone. India hasn't returned, and I haven't a clue where she might be. In fact, I was hoping you could give me some advice on whether I should report her as a missing person."

"Did you check to see whether anything else was missing from downstairs before you left home?" Fiona asked.

"No," BB replied, looking crestfallen as though she had just failed a test. "I didn't think to."

"Never mind. You could check on that later for us. Could you talk us through what happened the night she witnessed the vehicle fire?"

"Not really. I was in bed."

"I appreciate it would have been in the early hours of the morning, but did you hear her come in that night?"

"I knew she had gone out for a meal with Barney. It was some sort of celebration. So, I wasn't concerned about her not being back before I went up to bed. I think I heard her arriving home, but I've no idea what time it was. The door opening and closing woke me up. I turned over and went back to sleep."

"Do you know if they met anyone else at the meal?"

"I thought it was just the two of them, but I'm not completely sure."

"Did you speak to her the following morning and did she say or do anything out of the ordinary?"

"Sort of. It was my day off, so I had a lie-in. I was irritated by the sound of the television on in the living room. I went downstairs to ask her to turn the volume down. I was surprised to see the intent concentration on her face considering the junk she was watching."

"Which was?"

"One of those dreadful shopping programmes. You know. The ones that run all day with wannabe actors getting over-excited by the amazing price of the stunning jewellery which looks like a pile of crap."

"Does she normally watch the shopping channels?"

"No. I asked her why she was watching such rubbish, and she said she was waiting for something to come up. A phone or something. A friend had mentioned it was worth looking out or something along those lines. We chatted for a while, and I made us both some breakfast. All the time, she kept an eye on the television screen. It started to annoy me to tell you the truth. I asked if she had something better to do with her time, like work, but she didn't reply. She remained with the remote in her hand and her eyes glued to the screen. I was about to leave her to it when she thumped the air and shouted, 'Yes,' still watching the screen."

"I'm guessing this fancy phone with an incredible offer came on?" Fiona prompted.

"No, that's the weird thing. They were featuring a computer animation app for kids. She wrote down something on a scrap of paper and slipped it into her bag. I'm guessing it was the purchase details that run along the bottom of the screen. She continued watching until the feature ended and then switched the television off."

"Then what?"

"I asked her if she was going to buy it. She looked at me like I was crazy, and replied, she was getting ready to go out. When she reappeared fully dressed, I asked her where she was going and what time she would be back. She tapped the side of her nose and said, 'I'm going to see a man about a dog.' I followed her to the door and asked how her evening had gone. And do you know what she said?"

"Enlighten me."

"She said, 'Not great. Not for Barney anyway.' I asked her what she meant, but she just shrugged. Before closing the door, she looked back at me and said, 'Wish me luck. I'm off to meet a potential business investor. I think it could be the start of a beautiful relationship.' With that, she was gone. She never even mentioned the accident or that poor Barney was dead. I only found out about it because it was on the local radio. Can you believe it?"

"Unfortunately, I can." Fiona's satisfaction that her instincts had been right about India was tinged with the realisation she should have pressed her for more details while she had the chance. The callous attitude towards Barney suggested she may have been more than a witness. Considering how shaken India had been at the scene, Fiona hadn't seriously thought she was involved in setting up the scene and ensuring Barney parked his car where he did. Now, she wasn't so sure. But what on earth could be the relevance of a children's computer app? "Do you remember the name of the computer app India was so interested in?"

"Ruddles, I think it was called. It turned book characters into 3D images."

Fiona held up her hand to stop BB when her phone rang. She pressed reject without looking at the screen. "Did India ever talk about Darius or Stefan Albu?"

BB rolled her eyes and said, "On a few occasions," suggesting it was far more frequent than that. "She thought Stefan was a sleaze bag. Barney rarely leaves his computer screens, but India always made sure he was with her when she had to meet Stefan in person. She didn't want to allow him to try it on again with her, but at the same time, she desperately wanted the business. Highfield Homes was going to be their first major customer."

"What was her relationship with Barney?"

"They were friends and business partners." BB stopped and thought for a moment. "They spent time together, but I don't think there was anything more to it. His wife is pregnant."

"We know. Has India said anything about the fire or this computer app, since that morning?"

"Not really. I've been swamped with work, and we've been like ships passing in the night. If I'm honest, I was too annoyed about her attitude towards poor Barney to want to speak to her. I'm thinking of asking her to move out."

Irritation flashed as Fiona's phone rang again. She pulled it out to switch it off when she saw the name on the screen. "Sorry, I'm going to have to take this." She stood and walked to the front area of the shop. Looking through the window, she watched delivery drivers carrying boxes to shop entrances and office workers exiting the coffee shop opposite with steaming coffee cartons. She pressed to accept Peter's call. "Hi. What is it? I'm in the middle of speaking to India's housemate."

"End the conversation and meet me at the entrance to the byway that runs through Lordswood."

"That's an invitation I don't receive every day. Should I wear anything in my buttonhole?" Fiona said sarcastically.

Ignoring her comment, Peter said, "I'm on my way over there with Humphries, now. The body of a young woman has been found."

CHAPTER ELEVEN

A marked police car was parked across the byway, blocking the entrance. Once they had shown their warrant cards, Fiona and Abbie were allowed through and directed along the overgrown track and through a metal, five-bar gate on their right. Peter stood shoulder to shoulder with Humphries just inside a three-sided hay barn. They parted as Fiona approached and she looked down at the crumpled body on the ground.

"Well?" Peter asked. "It's her, isn't it?"

Apart from the obvious, there was another reason Peter asked for confirmation. As well as being alive the last time they'd seen her, she had been dressed for an evening out. Much of her makeup may have been smeared, but she was smartly dressed, with her hair styled. The girl on the ground was dressed in jeans, sweatshirt and trainers with her hair tied back in a ponytail. Devoid of makeup, she looked much younger and vulnerable. Fiona fought the urge to pull down her sweatshirt which had been hitched up, revealing her toned stomach. A croak caught in her throat, as she said, "Yes. It's India."

Peter gave a final look and turned away. "It looks like she was strangled."

The bruising around India's neck, made the statement redundant. Ramming her hands inside her coat pocket, Fiona muttered, "Stupid girl. Why didn't she say something to me when she had the chance?" For one surreal moment, she thought she saw a tear roll down India's face. She looked up at the black clouds rolling across the sky as rain started to fall. She glanced around the half-filled hay barn and spotted a roll of tarpaulin abandoned in the corner. Pointing at it, she turned around to ask, "Is there any way we could use that to protect her from the rain?"

Peter stepped forward and reached for her elbow. "A team will be here any minute to set up a tent." On cue, white vans pulled up behind them, and doors swished open and slammed shut as the crew clambered out and started to pull on their protective equipment.

"We're going to get drenched in a minute," Peter said. "Let's leave them to do their job and get back to our cars before the rain really kicks in." Leading them back along the track, he asked Fiona to update him on the conversation with BB in the dry of his car. Humphries took the front passenger seat, leaving Fiona to climb in the back with Abbie. As they closed the car doors, the threatened storm arrived, battering the roof with hailstones mixed in with the rain.

When Fiona had completed telling BB's account, she said, "I suggest we head out to Highfield Homes to ask Stefan Albu where he was last night. That's two, possibly three deaths in a row with a clear link to the company."

Peter looked directly at Fiona and replied, "I'll take Humphries and see if we can track him down. I want you and Abbie to find out all you can about this computer app and check whether India had any other contact with the product or the shopping channel."

"You what!" Fiona said, failing to hide her annoyance.

"You heard me. From what you said, I think India was watching that channel for a reason and something she saw excited her and possibly led to her death. Check the television footage to see if you can spot what it was that sparked her reaction."

Although seething inside, Fiona couldn't ignore a direct order in front of two other officers. Although she thought of Peter as a friend, he was also her superior, and the look he was giving her was making that position abundantly clear. She sensed Humphries and Abbie were holding their breaths waiting for her to react. Probably wishing they had popcorn to munch on while they watched the drama unfold from their front row seats. She was going to disappoint them. When she expressed her griev-ance, it would be later and in private. Through gritted teeth, she said, "Of course, Sir."

Without acknowledging the bitterness in her tone, Peter asked, "We also need to find India's car and contact her next of kin. Did you find out from chatting to her housemate whether her family live in the area?"

"No. I was interrupted before I could finish the interview," Fiona replied, failing to keep her resentment from her tone.

"Never mind. Could I leave you to arrange the official search of the house and the collection of her laptop and work records?"

Fiona flung open the car door. "The rain is easing off. I'll make a start." Slamming the door behind her, she ran through the rain to her car, leaving Abbie to follow in her wake.

During the car journey, Fiona responded to Abbie's questions with a grunt until she finally fell silent. She was too busy keeping her anger in check and deciding precisely what she intended to say to Peter to hold any sort of conversation.

Thinking back to Dewhurst's reaction earlier, she wondered if there was a connection between her exclusion from the visit to Highfield Homes and what else Peter was doing for him in the background. Before Dewhurst arrived to take up his post, there had been rumours that he was a freemason. Conspiracy theories regularly went around about their infiltration into the force to protect other members from prosecutions, but she rarely took any notice. She had never experienced anything before to sug-gest it was more than idle gossip, but there was a first time for everything. Something was stinking to high heaven, and even Peter was a part of it.

At the station, it didn't take her long to arrange a search of the house India shared with BB. Next, she pulled up the details for the Ruddles app. It was a clever piece of technology, but she thought it likely to be no more than a short-lived fad. The books were designed to be read to young children. As the parent turned the page and read, the child held a phone over the page and clicked the corresponding app to make the characters appear as moving holograms acting out the scenes. Expensive too. Outside the pocket of many parents. Especially as you had to buy a different app for each book.

The app was advertised extensively in America, so Fiona assumed that was where it was invented. She rapidly lost interest in the subject as she thought it a complete waste of her time. She couldn't see how it could be connected to the deaths. Not unless she was living in a fantasy world and the campervan fire had been an illusion. A hologram created by a computer app. Only she dealt with reality, and she didn't live in a parallel universe. She had been there and felt the heat of the fire. The stench of smoke still lingered in her hair.

She closed the page on her computer screen and googled the company behind the app. Her mind wandered to how the interview at Highfield Homes with Stefan Albu was going and how by rights she should be there as she flicked through the screens, skim-reading as she went. The registered owners of Ruddles looked like geeky schoolboys, one dark-haired and the other blond. Were they destined to become millionaires before they were old enough to grow beards or bankrupt and disillusioned by their thirties? Her irritation with Peter was temporarily forgotten when she discovered the app designers were British and the one who shared his name with the app lived in Sapperton not far from Conner or India. A connection could be within the realms of possibility.

Abbie called across the office, disturbing Fiona's concentration. "I think I've got the footage from the shopping channel that India would have seen. Do you want to come over and watch?"

Before walking over to join her colleague, Fiona glanced at the photograph that filled her screen of the app designer called John Ruddle. A plump face with round glasses, grinning inanely under an untidy mop of dark hair. In a different setting, the look could be described as unnerving. Definitely creepy.

Abbie had paused the film and waited until Fiona sat next to her before pressing play. The cogs in Fiona's brain started to churn over as soon as the film started running. The cheesy presenter promoting the app was the designer whose face she had been examining moments earlier. He was a few years older than his website picture suggested, but it was him.

"So, what do you think?" Abbie asked. "Do you see something there that would have caused India's reaction?"

Fiona stared intently at the screen, watching the presenter's every movement. She waved her hand to Abbie to keep quiet. When the segment finished, Fiona asked Abbie to restart it so she could watch it again.

She leaned back in her chair after watching it through the second time. There was nothing unusual in the background, no subtle hand signal or odd phraseology. Nothing that would cause the average viewer to suddenly leave the house. Nothing except the possibility that they could have seen the presenter running from the scene of a fatal vehicle fire the day before.

"Fiona?"

Abbie's voice broke through the chatter going on inside Fiona's head. Still staring at the screen, Fiona said, "The man we just watched is also the inventor of the app. He also just happens to be a local lad from Sapperton."

CHAPTER TWELVE

Can you get hold of John Ruddle's company and home address? We're going to pay him a visit." Walking back to her own desk, Fiona added, "I'm going to see if I can find any obvious previous connections between him and Connor, India or Highfields Homes."

Peter hadn't called in by the time they were ready to leave for Ruddle's home address. The company used a mailbox as a registered address, so she assumed he worked from home. Fiona made a quick note for the case file and a second, brief note for Peter which she stuck to the back of his chair. Knowing them, she thought they were probably having a long, leisurely lunch in a pub somewhere.

With a new lead, her irritation reduced. Guiltily, she admitted to herself, she was relieved she had avoided being present when they broke the news of India's death to her family. A duty, nobody enjoyed. To his credit, Peter could have delegated the responsibility very easily, but rarely did.

The initial unguarded reaction to a sudden death often left an emotional mark on the officer breaking the news. The polite, nervous smile turning to confusion and denial before the full horror of their worst nightmare drained the colour from their face. As the news gradually sunk in, some turned deathly quiet, lost in their grief, forgetting they weren't alone. If they spoke, it was in a whisper. If they didn't say it out loud, it couldn't be true. Other erupted giving voice to their anguish. Fiona touched the faint scar above her right eyebrow where a bereaved fiancée had thrown a framed photograph from the wall at her for bringing death to her door and destroying her dreams.

As they were drawing near to the house, Abbie broke the silence in the car. "I know you're still cross with me, but I was worried about you. I'm really sorry, we're not still friends."

The full force of Fiona's irritation bubbled to the surface. She regularly moaned about Peter keeping things to himself and not saying how he felt, but she wasn't so keen on things swinging so far the other way. She wanted to concentrate on what she was going to say to John Ruddle not listen to Abbie trying to justify why she had betrayed her trust.

Before Abbie had gone and ruined things, she had enjoyed her friendship. In a mostly male-dominated station, it had been good to let her hair down with someone who understood the pressures of the job. The black humour and inside jokes. Which was why the betrayal had hurt so much. Releasing emotions that had been coiled up inside for months, Fiona blurted out, "If we were friends, why did you go behind my back and speak to Peter? Why didn't you talk to me?"

"I tried. If you remember, you either blanked me or told me to mind my own business."

"Maybe that's what you should have done."

"And let someone I cared about get hurt? I'll never be that person, and I won't apologise for it. That's what friends do."

Fiona had no intention of wading in on that one and pointing out it showed a complete lack of faith in her ability to sort her own private life out. "Can we forget about it for now and move on?"

"I would like that."

Fiona gave a small smile, and said half-jokingly, "I meant leave the personal stuff alone and concentrate on where we're heading."

"Oh. Okay," Abbie said, turning her head to look out of the window. Five minutes later, she broke the silence by saying, "You're thinking that seeing John Ruddle and this computer app on the television is what set India off. Which was the important bit? John or the app?"

"My money is on John. At the scene of the fire, India said something about television. When I questioned her, she mumbled that it was like watching a scene on television. I thought at the time she was lying about not seeing or hearing anything. I think she may have seen John Ruddle. What he was doing there? I have no idea. I didn't find anything to connect him to Connor, India or Highfield Homes. But I only had a quick look, and I'm convinced there must be a link, somewhere."

"I understand looking for a link with Connor and India, but why should there be a link to Highfield Homes?"

"Because Connor worked for them and India had been out with Barney to celebrate signing a contract with them."

They pulled up outside a small, terraced cottage fronted by a pretty garden that pre-dated the newer developments in Sapperton. The rain stopped, and the sun put in a surprise appearance, glistening on the wet grass. The burst of sun gave the cottage stonework a yellow tinge. Reaching for her bag, Fiona said, "Let's hope that's a sign of something good coming our way."

Climbing out the other side, Abbie, asked, "Have you worked through what you're going to say?"

Fiona pushed the car door closed with the hip. She chose not to sour things further by pointing out her thought process had been hijacked by Abbie's need to clear the air. "I'm going to play it by ear."

Approaching the front door, they could hear sounds inside the house of running on wooden floorboards and children's high-pitched shouts. The door was opened by a painfully thin, dark-haired woman. Fiona deducted from the heavy rimmed glasses she wore that it was John Ruddle's wife. A couple wearing matching glasses was a new revelation to her. It struck her as oddly disturbing. Glasses on some people add a hint of seriousness and intelligence. On these two, they added an element of goofiness to their blank expressions.

She was about to raise her warrant card and introduce herself when two screaming children shot along the hallway colliding with the woman, who had to steady herself from the impact by holding onto the wall.

"How many times do I have to tell you. Go upstairs and play something quiet." As the children retreated, laughing, the woman turned back to them. "Sorry. What was it you wanted?"

Fiona caught a strong whiff of wine which explained the woman's slurred words and glazed look. Holding up her card, she said, "We're police officers. Is your husband at home?"

The woman slumped against the wall with a resigned look on her face. "What's he done?"

"Is he here?" Fiona repeated.

Pushing herself off the wall, the woman stumbled a few steps forwards. "He's on the other side of the world!"

A woman shouted from inside the house. "Who is it, Karen?"

Ignoring the question, Karen asked, "Anything else?"

"It's important we speak to your husband to confirm his recent movements."

Struggling to focus, Karen stood back from the door and said, "Come on in!" She turned to lead them along the short hallway. Swaying side to side, she asked, "Would you like a glass of wine?"

The hallway led to a small, modern kitchen where a young woman sat at the central island behind two bottles of wine. Her heavy makeup made her resemble a child's doll. She looked up and belched before disintegrating into a fit of giggles. Karen retook her stool beside her friend and joined in the laughter. Two toddlers were asleep in a double child's buggy parked in the corner of the room.

Fiona cleared her throat and said, "Mrs. Ruddle. Could you tell me the current whereabouts of your husband?"

Karen's friend stopped giggling and looked at them suspiciously. She poured herself a fresh glass of wine, and slurred, "What's it to you?"

"Shh, Becky!" Karen said, nudging her friend, causing her to spill her drink. "They're police officers."

Becky narrowed her eyes and slurred, "Why do you want to know about John?"

Ignoring the friend, Fiona addressed Karen, "You said at the door, he was on the other side of the world? Did you mean figuratively?"

Karen's face crumpled in confusion. "What does figer ... fig ... that word you said mean?"

Running out of patience, Fiona asked, "Where is your husband?"

"In the United States of America. The land of the brave or something or other," Karen replied, standing up and pretending to wave a flag.

"How long has he been there?"

Karen slumped back onto her stool and said, "His flight left early yesterday."

"Do you know what flight he was on?"

Karen shrugged. "Not a clue. He was flying from Gatwick, I think."

"Any idea where in the States he is?"

"New York. Promoting his little app, so we can all live a life of luxury."

"Where has he been all this week?"

"He's been in London doing promotion and stuff," Karen replied.

"So, he claims," Becky said darkly. "He's never around when you need him." Rubbing her thumb and fingertips together, she added, "If his app is doing as well as he says, where's the money? I don't see him bringing it home, girl."

"They had to invest a lot to get it up and running. And there's the cost of all this publicity," Karen said defensively.

"Yeah, right. Who knows where he and his geeky friend spend their money? If he was my husband, I would have slung him out on his ear, years ago."

"He's not your husband," Karen snapped.

"Good job, too," Becky replied, before throwing back her head and laughing. "Sold his soul and forgot to collect his forty pieces of silver!"

"Shut up, Becky!" Karen said, slamming her wine glass on the countertop.

"What do you mean by sold his soul?" Fiona asked.

"Nothing!" Karen said. "She doesn't mean anything. She's drunk!"

"Becky?" Fiona asked.

Becky looked from her wine glass to her friend and back to her wine. Shrugging one shoulder, she said, "Don't take any notice of me. I'm drunk."

"Yes, you are," Karen said. "You're talking gibberish."

Becky raised her wine glass and waved it in the air. "I know nothing, don't you know?"

Karen glared at her friend before standing to face Fiona. "Are you done?"

Not wanting to become involved in a drunken brawl between the two women, Fiona replied, "For now. Could you give me his mobile number before we leave?"

"Which one?" Karen asked. "He has them all colour coordinated."

Becky snorted with laughter, spewing a mouthful of wine across the counter. "He's such an idiot."

Fiona chose not to comment on Becky's observation. "Could you give us the numbers he most frequently uses? The ones we're likely to be able to contact him on."

Back in the car, Abbie said, "Where does that leave us? He couldn't have killed India if he was in London and New York."

"We'll re-watch the television clip to see if there's something else we missed but don't discount him just yet. I doubt his wife knows what time of the week it is most days. We need to find out when his piece was recorded for the shopping channel. It could have been days or even weeks ago. And check what flight he took to New York. He could be feeding his wife a pack of lies for all we know. Did she look like a happy, contented wife and mother to you?"

"Point taken." Checking her watch, Abbie said, "Although,

being out of her brains on wine by the middle of the afternoon could have been a one-off. Maybe she hadn't seen her friend for a while."

"My gut feeling is their meetings are a regular thing. Helps them get through the day. Which would be fine if they weren't responsible for young children. I'm no expert, but the two asleep looked to be less than three years old. The ones running about, three and five years old. Hardly responsible parenting at its best."

"Agreed."

"If what his wife said is true, then John Ruddle is a dead end. But not until it has been fully checked out," Fiona said.

After a brief silence, Abbie asked, "Are you seeing anyone?"

"No. You?"

Abbie broke into a smile. "Yes. Fingers crossed this one's a keeper."

Fiona knew this was where she should ask the obvious questions. How did you meet? How long ago? And then listen to details of the perfect relationship. Instead, she replied, "I'm pleased for you," and closed the conversation down. Clearing the air between them so they could maintain a good working relationship on the case was a good thing. But she wasn't ready to let bygones be bygones and rekindle the friendship they shared before. Especially when she felt the whole situation with them being thrown together had been manipulated by Peter for some unknown reason.

Fiona struggled to make close friends, and Abbie had hurt her badly. She frequently sensed an invisible barrier between her and other people. With Abbie, there had been a shared understanding. She could relax and be herself, laugh and even have fun. She missed those times, but the trust had been broken.

Difficulty making friends was nothing new for her. Some of it she put down to her being a police officer. She represented authority and was considered a killjoy. They never saw the horrific repercussions of just having a little fun, like she did every day. The last-minute cancellations of plans due to work didn't help.

Not that she could blame it all on her job. At school, she had thought she was being helpful, pouring cold water on her classmates' devilish plans, outlining the flaws and the likely punishments if they were caught. Often to hoots of laughter followed by a disgruntled, "Suit yourself Goody-Two-Shoes. We weren't asking you along, anyway." Left alone, she would console herself with her studies, pretending she didn't care and preferred her own company. Alone, she became the perfect target for schoolyard bullies, and the resulting scars ran deep.

Fiona's phone rang, bringing her back to the present time. Seeing the caller, she pulled over to take the call outside the car. Returning to her seat, she said, "That was my brother. I'm going to drop you back at the station and shoot over to my parents. Can you complete the checks on John Ruddle?"

"Sure. Is everything okay? Peter said your dad was in hospital."

Fiona's hackles raised. What else did they discuss behind her back? "It's nothing serious. Can you update me one way or another about Ruddle? I'll keep my phone on."

CHAPTER THIRTEEN

Fiona's resentment towards her brother grew as she drove towards her parents' house. It was so typically frustrating of him to change everything last minute and expect her to fit in with whatever had been arranged. It made perfect sense for her mother to skip the hospital visit if she was feeling unwell. It was her exclusion from the decision and the assumption she would be free to spend the evening with her mother than rankled. What if she already had plans for a big night out? The fact she didn't, added to her irritation.

When she arrived, her mother looked pale, wrapped in a blanket watching television. Fiona hoped it was exhaustion rather than anything more serious. Her annoyance turned to concern when her mother admitted she had not eaten all day as she felt nauseous. Fiona persuaded her to at least try some soup and toast and disappeared into the kitchen to make it.

She was buttering toast when her phone rang. Seeing it was Peter, her first instinct was to ignore it. When the phone stopped ringing, curiosity about how the interview with Stefan Albu had gone got the better of her. Wiping her hands on a dishcloth, she called Peter back. He refused to tell her anything over the phone and insisted she go around to his cottage, 'to talk things through.'

"Can't you tell me now? I'm going to be here for at least another couple of hours."

"That's okay. It's still early. Come around when you finish."

Although she felt exhausted, she knew she wouldn't be able to sleep without knowing how things had gone. "I'll call you when I'm leaving."

Deep in thought, she carried the soup through to the living room. Considering Stefan Albu's family history, he should have been interviewed days ago. She couldn't help questioning the delay as she urged her mother to eat. She encouraged her mother to eat most of the soup, but it worried her how lethargic and averse to conversation her usually chatty mother remained. Accepting her cajoling was making the situation worse, she found her mother's favourite film, *Casablanca*, on Netflix. They had both watched it a hundred times so could drift off in thought while cocooned in nostalgia.

When the film finished, her mother had fallen asleep in the chair. Fiona woke her and helped her up to bed. Downstairs, she tidied the room and washed up their bowls from earlier. She was about to call Peter to say she was on her way when Abbie rang. John Ruddle had missed his booked flight to New York and had taken an early morning one the next day. She was still trying to confirm his whereabouts for the previous week. Feeling guilty that Abbie was still working while she had been lounging in front of the television, Fiona thanked her and said, "You needn't do it all tonight. We'll go through his diary together in the morning." Ending the call, she set off for Peter's cottage.

Peter met her at the door, in jeans and a sweatshirt. His hair still wet from the shower. "Come in. Come in. Have you eaten?"

Fiona replied yes, although she wasn't sure the thin chicken soup she had found in her mother's cupboard and a piece of dry toast counted as a meal. She caught her reflection in the hallway mirror. She wasn't just looking older, but more hard-hearted as well. Every callous act she witnessed was etched on her face reflecting her increasing indifference to suffering.

"How was your mother? Is everything okay?"

"Everything is fine. She wanted some company this evening. I'll make the time up tomorrow."

"Don't be so hard on yourself. Let me get you a drink. Wine?"

Fiona followed him into the kitchen and watched while he poured two glasses of wine and pulled some snacks, he had prepared from the fridge. He handed her a glass of wine and led her through to the living room. The coffee table and couch were strewn with handwritten notes, leaving nowhere to sit down without moving them. Another surge of guilt hit her. She was the only one who had been slacking.

Gathering the sheets of paper together, Peter said, "I popped into the Horseshoe Inn earlier. Gladys and Dick asked after you and I said I would pass their good wishes on."

"Thank you." Fiona took a seat in an armchair and took a sip of wine before asking, "How did the interview of Stefan Albu go?"

"We kept it very brief and his alibi for the two nights stacks up."

Fiona put her glass to one side, hardly believing what she was hearing. Her voice rose, reflecting her surprise and confusion. "What do you mean, you kept it brief? He has a direct involvement with three murders, and you kept it brief! What's that all about? I should have been there. I would have said something and not kept it brief."

"Maybe."

"Is that why you took Humphries?"

"Humphries was in the station when the call came in about India. At the time, I thought it could have been one of the missing teenagers."

"I thought ..."

"A debit card belonging to one of them has been used. Until we find them safe and well, that doesn't mean much."

"You and Dewhurst virtually blanked me when I suggested Albu warranted a closer look." Fiona took a sip of wine to create enough time to organise her thoughts. After working with Peter for five years, it was out of character for him to be happy tracing a couple of teenagers rather than be at the helm of an investigation into a double murder. Putting her glass to one side, she asked, "What is it, you're not telling me? There's something off, here. Too many things aren't adding up."

Peter reached for the glass of wine he'd left on the table and took a sip. "If I tell you what I think, it is to go no further. Not yet, anyway."

"Go on."

"I think Dewhurst is watching his back. If I tell you what I know, you have to promise not to say anything and watch my back."

"I promise," Fiona said, crossing her fingers behind her back.

"Without crossing your fingers." After taking another sip of wine, Peter continued, "While you were in London, Stefan Albu's name came up in connection with an assault, but Dewhurst asked me not to follow up on it."

"Really? Fiona reached for her glass and took a sip.

"When his name came up again in connection with the vehicle fire, Dewhurst admitted he was contacted by Peter Strickland from Birstall Station."

"Strickland? He's vice, isn't he?"

Peter nodded, before draining his glass of wine and reaching for the bottle to refill it.

"What else is this guy into? Dodgy work and financial practices. Assault. And now, murder."

Peter shook his head. "He's not squeaky clean by any stretch of the imagination, but that isn't the whole story. His uncle is in jail for employing illegals on his building sites, not him. Stefan is bound by family loyalty, but he is anti-drugs and the trafficking of young girls."

"Oh, come on," Fiona said, looking sceptical.

"This is to stay between us. Do you remember the truck carrying Romanians hidden in the back that was stopped by Birstall police on a minor vehicle defect about five months ago? That was due to a tip-off from Stefan."

"So, as Strickland's informer, Stefan Albu is untouchable. Even if he's involved in murder?"

"The way I read it is, not if you find something that connects him to your case. But it has to be concrete evidence."

"So, if his name comes up again, I can have free rein investigating him?" When Peter gave a non-committal shrug, Fiona asked, "Is he working for Strickland, now?"

"It is more of a general request that he listens out for anything that might interest Strickland. Who by the way, thinks we may have sex traffickers, pushed out from Birstall, lying low in the area, so he wants us to tread carefully."

"Why wasn't I told?" A sudden thought that would explain Peter's attitude crossed Fiona's mind. "Do you think the missing teenagers are somehow connected to this Birstall gang?"

"Strickland says, not. The group they're investigating is only interested in bringing foreign girls into the country." Peter leaned back in his chair. "Dewhurst isn't convinced there's a connection, either. Although, I did raise the possibility that as Connor worked for Albu, his killing could have been by these people in retaliation for him helping the police."

"Oh," Fiona said, thinking over the possibility. "What did Dewhurst think of that?"

"My imagination has gone into overdrive. I should stop dreaming and stick to the facts."

"That sounds like one hell of a put-down. What did you say to him?"

"I don't like Dewhurst, but I think he is as unhappy as you about having his hands tied when it comes to Stefan Albu. I also suspect he knows I would end up telling you."

Still mulling the situation over in her head, Fiona said, "Thanks for trusting me." She felt a little foolish for entertaining the thought Peter would be involved in a cover-up and much of her anger dissipated.

"I always have. How did it go with Abbie, today?" Peter asked.

"Great," Fiona said, miming shooting herself in the head. "I feel like a school kid who has been split up from my playmate for chatting too much in class and is forced to sit next to someone else."

"You two used to be such good friends. Is there no chance of you burying the hatchet?"

"Only in the back of her head. You mentioned trust. I trust her about as far as I could throw her. She has too long a track record of failing to keep her mouth shut." Pushing her feelings about Abbie to one side, Fiona took a sip of wine. "If you're satisfied their disappearance has nothing to do with this gang, why are you so preoccupied with the two missing teenagers?"

"I can't quite put my finger on it, but something is bugging me about them. Not least, why they should have disappeared together."

"Such as?"

"The two girls have nothing in common. Charlotte is a straight-A student at a private school with loving parents and a couple of horses. Her social life revolved around the local Pony Club. The only other thing of note is she recently did a photo shoot for a company that sells expensive riding wear and equipment. The other girl, Lisa, is a tearaway known to the local police. When she bothers to attend, she goes to the local comprehensive. She spends her free time busking in Bristol and uploading songs she has written and performed to social media sites. She has a long history of disappearing, but only for short periods."

"An unlikely partnership, I agree. Any mutual friends or clubs?"

"None. The one thing they have in common is they could have been viewed nationally by numerous people outside of their social group. This is what is worrying me," Peter said, sorting through a pile of photographs on the table. Handing two to Fiona, he said unnecessarily, "They look so similar they could be twins despite all their other differences."

Looking between the two pictures, Fiona had to agree. "You think someone has selected them specifically for the way they look after seeing their images online?"

"In the absence of anything else to connect them. Pretty much, yes."

Checking the time, Fiona handed back the pictures and said, "I can see your point with the girls."

"How did it go with John Ruddle?"

"It didn't. According to his wife he's in New York."

"So, he's off the hook, then?"

"Not necessarily. He missed his booked flight and took a later

one, so he was in the country the night India was strangled."
Stifling a yawn, Fiona said, "It's getting late, I had best get going.
You've given me a lot to think about, tonight." She didn't add
that while he had explained his continued interest in the two
runaways, she still had doubts about Dewhirst's protection of
Stefan Albu.

Peter picked up the empty wine glasses and followed Fiona
along the corridor. At the doorway, he held out a torch. "Take
this. There's no street lighting," before leaning in and kissing her
good night.

CHAPTER FOURTEEN

Recent events slowly came back to Megan in snatches. She dared to hope he didn't intend killing her as he ordered her to get dressed before dragging her outside. The secluded cottage no longer a romantic rendezvous, but the perfect place for her murder. Her vision blurred as she struggled against him. Her mind frantically trying to work out where they were and to plan her escape route.

When she saw where they were heading, she automatically realised his intention. She screamed and fought to be free. Digging her feet into the muddy ground to stop the inevitable. When that didn't work, she collapsed to the ground. She was prepared to try anything to slow their progression to her final resting place, regardless of how futile. She nearly passed out from the pain when he wrenched her to her feet by her arm, tearing her shoulder muscles. She held onto consciousness by her fingertips as he dragged her along behind him. She had only a short distance to free herself from certain death. Ignoring the pain, she screamed and fought, clawing at him with her free hand.

When they arrived, she fell to her knees and begged for her life through her tears. With the back of her hand, she wiped away the snot running from her nose mingling with her tears. She looked up at his face one last time. Daring to hope, she tried a smile. He threw back his head and laughed. "You stupid, ugly, little bitch." Her nose crunched as it took the full brunt of his kick and she felt herself falling backwards, headfirst into the abyss. Frantically waving her arms and legs to slow her plummet through the darkness. Intense pain followed by nothing.

CHAPTER FIFTEEN

After a night of very little sleep, but plenty of tossing and turning, Fiona disentangled herself from her duvet and rolled out of bed. Her night of turmoil had some benefits. She was clear on the next steps in the case. While John Ruddle was in America, she would concentrate on discovering his whereabouts leading up to the deaths and any previous connection to Connor and India. She would be discrete as the last thing she wanted was for him to get wind of their suspicions and decide to stay in America.

She had resolved a few personal issues as well. She was going to take the olive branch Abbie held out. That didn't mean she was ready to trust her again. She was a once bitten, twice shy type of girl. In her line of work, what else could she be?

It was Peter's revelation about Stefan Albu and the possibility an organised, people-smuggling gang was operating in the area that had sparked her imagination and kept her awake. One of the reasons she had applied for the temporary position with the Met was to escape small-town policing for a while, and she had flirted with the idea of seeking a permanent transfer. With her father so ill, that was no longer an option, but it seemed the area wasn't as immune to organised crime as she thought. Logically, with plenty of space and isolated old farm cottages, here was as suitable a place as anywhere for their operations.

Opening her front door to leave, the landline rang. She was tempted to ignore it. It was probably cold callers. The only other people who used the number were her parents, and if they didn't receive a reply, they would switch to calling her mobile.

She dithered in the doorway before stomping back to take the call.

It was her mother calling to double-check she was still okay to collect her at the end of the hospital's evening visiting hours. She was feeling much better and keen to make up for the lost gossiping time. When Fiona finally ended the call, her mobile rang. She was irritated to discover it was her brother calling to check she was picking her mother up from the hospital that evening. Tempted though she was, she decided it wasn't the time to start an argument. She masked her annoyance through the brief chat and headed for her car. Although the phone calls had delayed her for less than half an hour, she would now hit the rush hour traffic at its peak, and she was going to be late arriving at the station.

Fiona watched the white clouds skitter across a rare glimpse of blue sky as she drummed her hands on the steering wheel in the stop-start traffic. The congestion was caused by the relentless building of barn conversions and small, executive-style housing developments, none of them big enough to warrant an overhaul of the road system. The area was still served by roads and lanes that were laid down when car ownership was a luxury owned by the few. Add in a trundling tractor and cars parked on the road due to a lack of garages and the lanes quickly became clogged.

Fiona rotated her neck to release her rising tension and resist the urge to take her frustration out on the other drivers. No one had a choice other than to join the slow-moving throng. Public transport was a joke in the area. The few buses that did run, wound their way through numerous villages at a leisurely pace before ending their destination hours after the average workday start. Local councillors argued for them to keep running as a vital link without considering why they ran almost empty. They also couldn't see the need for food banks or drug programmes. If they didn't acknowledge the need, it didn't exist. Those problems were the scourge of the cities, not an issue in England's green and pleasant lands.

Fiona accelerated as she passed the main bottleneck to join the one major road into Birkbury. A song came on the radio that reminded her of an old boyfriend. Thinking of easier times relieved some of her tension.

The dry weather was holding when she arrived at the station. She hurried across the car park and took the stairs two at a time in the vain hope it could shave minutes off her late arrival. In the corridor, she met Humphries carrying a cardboard tray of coffees. Giving his usual big grin, he said, "Late again."

Catching her breath, Fiona fell into step with him. She was pleased about his recent promotion to detective sergeant. She had worked alongside him for several years and trusted him as a colleague and friend. For some reason, no one called him Phil. Humphries seemed to suit his large frame and friendly disposition, perfectly. Unusually for him, his suit looked crumpled and his face unshaven. Half-jokingly, she asked, "What did you get up to last night? It looks like you never reached home."

"I didn't." Humphries' face broke into a wide grin.

Humphries had a long track record of being unlucky with women, and Fiona was nervous about asking for more details. He was the decent, understanding chap that women wanted to unburden their problems on, but not date. She knew he had been having an on-off relationship with an ex-reporter with a traumatic past for several years. She hoped it wasn't her, leading him on again. "Someone, I know?"

"Grab the door for me."

Following him into the incident room, Fiona caught an unguarded disapproving look from Abbie quickly covered with a smile. Abbie was flanked by DCs Andrew Litten and Eddie Jordan who turned and smiled. She acknowledged them and gave Peter a friendly nod before taking a seat in the corner of the room, next to Humphries. "Will you tell me who the lucky lady is, later?" She was distracted by Peter walking to the front of the room to address them.

"Grab your coffees, and we'll start," Peter said. "For the benefit of Fiona, who may not have heard, Connor Ambrose's daughter,

Megan, was reported missing this morning."

Fiona's eyes widened in surprise, and she put down the cup she was about to drink from.

Peter continued, "Megan told her mother she was taking a study leave break with a couple of friends. When she didn't arrive home, it was discovered there was no trip."

Abbie interrupted, "Could there be a connection to the two teenagers who disappeared last week?"

"There has been a development there, as well. One of the girls, Charlotte has withdrawn money from a cash point in Plymouth. Her parents failed to mention they own a holiday home down there. That needs to be followed up on today, but it looks unlikely there is any connection to Megan Ambrose's disappearance. Unless anything else comes to light, Megan's disappearance is more likely to be connected to the death of her father."

Peter gave a brief summary of the investigation to date into the suspicious vehicle fire before saying, "His autopsy is taking place this morning. We have no idea why he was killed or who by. We don't even know why he was travelling in his camper van at that time of night."

"Transporting something?" Humphries said.

Peter raised his hands in a who-knows gesture. "The vehicle fire also claimed the life of Barney Jones, whose vehicle was parked nearby. Initial thoughts were that it was incredibly bad luck on his part. He pulled over at the wrong time and place. As we are getting nowhere, it might be worth re-examining our assumptions about him. Especially as his business partner, who was his passenger at the time, has been killed." Peter caught Fiona's eye. "We have a new line of investigation on her death. Do you want to update us on where you are with the possible lead you have for John Ruddle?"

Fiona stood up, but didn't move to the front of the room. "India Williamson had been travelling as a passenger in Barney Jones's car and as far as we're aware was the only witness to the fire that killed Connor Ambrose and Barney Jones. Rather conveniently, she had moved to the rear of the vehicle moments before the explosion. Yesterday, she was found strangled and dumped on the byway that runs through Lordswood. According to her housemate, after the vehicle fire, India tuned their television to the shopping channel and watched it obsessively. When a segment hosted by a local man was shown, she disappeared into her room, dressed and left the house in a hurry. We are unsure of the significance, but we have discovered the local presenter she watched, John Ruddle, was not where he told his wife he would be the night India was strangled." Fiona ended with, "We're still following up on this. He is currently in America, but is due to return home soon.

I would like enquiries concerning his background to be discrete until I have the opportunity to speak to him."

Peter stood and said, "Have you made any progress with the hit-and-run the same night as the vehicle fire, Eddie?"

Eddie Litton half-rose and said, "We've spoken to local garages, but nothing so far."

Without looking over, Peter said, "Fiona, I want you and Abbie to continue working on the Ruddle angle. Before that, as you previously met Megan's mother, I want you to talk to her about her daughter's disappearance. When you have details of her friends and activities, pass them back to Andrew and Rachel for follow up interviews." Checking his watch, he said, "I'm due at Connor Ambrose's autopsy in half an hour. If anything major crops up, call me."

Fiona read through Abbie's case notes from the night before. Abbie had been thorough and efficient. After tracing the website and social media sites John Ruddle used to promote his product, she had contacted his wife, persuading her to read his business appointments from his diary and to give a couple of his closest friends' details. From this, she had compiled a list of computer and toy shops he claimed to be canvassing. Reading the report, she wondered if the handwritten diary was a fantasy created to pacify his wife, while his genuine list of engagements was electronically stored on his phone.

Abbie crossed the room to join her. "Sorry, I didn't get very far with it,"

"This is good. I'm surprised you managed to get this much from his wife. Interesting that he missed his flight and the shop owners he was supposed to be meeting last week had never heard of him. Keeping his activities secret from his wife is interesting. He could have been anywhere, including in the area meeting India. What time did you finish last night?"

Abbie shrugged. "Late. Do you think he could be involved? Other than the fact he lies to his wife about his whereabouts, I didn't find anything else. He has not been in trouble with the law before. He doesn't even have any driving violations. While he may not be the husband of the year, I didn't get the feeling there was any violence in the marriage."

"We might get a different picture once we've spoken to some of his friends. India rushed out to meet someone after watching him on the television. When India was in shock, at the scene of the fire, she made an unguarded comment about being on television. My gut feeling is that she saw him there. She watched the channel to be sure it was him."

"He wasn't there when you and Peter arrived at the scene of the fire. Where do you think he went? And how?"

"Good question. India denied seeing anyone in the area, let alone a car driving away. If he was there innocently, why did he leave without stopping to help? The set up with the camper van suggests a degree of planning and knowledge of Connor's habits. There must be something to link the two men. We just need to find it."

"Maybe Megan's mother, could point us in the right direction? She was married to Connor, after all." Abbie suggested.

"We'll ask the questions, but we'll need to be tactful. Officially we will be there to ask about her daughter's disappearance. Are you ready to go?"

"I need to grab my coat from the other room."

Fiona flicked through the website for the Ruddles app and the promotional social media posts, waiting for Abbie to return.

The publicity shots projected the image of a cheeky, boy-next-door geek who got lucky with his creation. The website included a couple of posed pictures with his family. After flicking through them a few times, Fiona looked up his date of birth. She wasn't great on ages, but she estimated he was ten to fifteen years older than his wife. She sensed Abbie looking over her shoulder.

"Did you see something, I missed?" Abbie asked.

"No, I don't think so," Fiona said, closing the screen, and grabbing her coat and bag. "Let's get the interview with Amanda over. She wasn't upset by the death of her ex-husband and told us very little. I'm hoping with the disappearance of her daughter, things will be different."

CHAPTER SIXTEEN

Megan knew she had been falling in and out of consciousness, but had no idea for how long. The first time she had stirred, she had thought she was in heaven for a few moments. The agonising pain in her leg and the penetrating cold shattered that illusion. This time, she forced herself to stay calm and still while she came around before trying to move. He had thought the fall would kill her, but she was alive. While she was alive, there was hope. She could escape, or someone would rescue her.

She slowly opened her eyes and looked around. The stone walls of the disused well closed in around her. She was laying on her side, surrounded by junk and rusty tin cans. There was a deep, long gash along her left forearm, which had bled while she slept, staining the ground around her. She laughed hysterically. Even to herself, she sounded crazy. Maybe she was. The reason she was alive was that along with their general rubbish, someone had thrown an old mattress down the well. She laughed until she cried, and exhaustion took over. She closed her eyes. She was so tired. If it wasn't so cold and damp, she would curl up on the soft mattress and go to sleep.

She shook thoughts of sleep from her mind. Considering the amount of junk on top of the mattress, people must walk this way. She remembered, when she had been dragged along the floor, she had seen discarded, empty beer cans hidden under a bush a short distance away. Teenagers must come here to party. She had to keep awake, listening for them to arrive, so she could call for help.

She twisted her head to look up. The circle of grey light seemed so far away. Would they hear her shouts for help? Looking around, her heart leapt for joy. A metal ladder was bolted to the side of the well. It looked rusty and old. As long as it held, freedom was a short climb away. Her attempt to roll over and sit up shot powerful surges of pain through her shoulder. She lay on her side, breathing through the pain as it came in waves. When the pain subsided to a manageable level, she looked down to find an alternative way to sit up. She caught sight of her foot, sticking out at the wrong angle to her leg. Startled, she quickly turned. The intense pain created pinpricks of light in her peripheral vision as the bile rose in her throat, and she slipped back into unconsciousness.

CHAPTER SEVENTEEN

Heading towards Amanda Wagstaff's home in Brierley, a small village that valiantly fought every planning application to prevent it from being swallowed by the nearby sprawling mass of Sapperton, Fiona's phone rang. Not recognising the number, she pulled over to the side of the road to take the call. She wondered if she was becoming paranoid. Progress was being made, but she didn't trust Abbie not to repeat details if it turned out to be a private conversation.

After the caller introduced herself and explained why she was calling, the colour drained from Fiona's face. "Hang on a minute. I've someone with me." Fiona ignored Abbie's questioning look and stepped out of the car. Once she was a safe distance away, she said, "Where did you get that information?" Listening to the reply, she glanced back at Abbie, who was watching her. She ended the call and raised her hand to Abbie to indicate she would be another five minutes. When her call was answered, she turned her back on Abbie and walked further away from the parked car.

Peter made it clear he was not happy about being interrupted in the middle of an autopsy. Fiona apologised, but stressed she needed to speak to him. She walked small circles while she waited for him to make his apologies and leave the room. The longer she waited, the more irritated she felt at the betrayal of the investigation. Her list of suspects was small, and she couldn't fathom what any of them could hope to gain from leaking details to the press.

Finally, Peter returned on the line. "What is? Make it quick so I can get back in there."

"I've just received a call from a Miss Emma Thorpe, claiming to be from Birstall Gazette. She knew everything about our investigation and intends to submit a report saying we're investigating John Ruddle in this evening's edition. We don't even know for sure if he is our man and I absolutely don't want him to get wind of anything before he boards his plane to return to England. He could decide to stay in America, which would ruin everything."

"Calm down and tell me what she said." Once Fiona had relayed the details of the conversation, Peter said, "I'll ring the editor now. He won't want to do anything to jeopardise the good relationship we have."

"Thank you. I considered calling him myself, but because of your friendship, I thought it would do better coming from you."

"Did the reporter say where she got her information from?"

"She wouldn't say, but it has got to be someone in this morning's briefing. One of them must have rung the paper within minutes of the meeting ending. The thought of it makes me feel sick."

"You haven't mentioned anything about what I told you about Stefan Albu to anyone, have you? If that got out, the repercussions could be serious."

"Of course, not. You asked me not to," Fiona snapped, annoyed he was more concerned about protecting Albu than someone leaking case details to the press.

"Sorry for questioning you. I had to be sure. Have you spoken to Abbie about the reporter, yet?"

"No." Fiona glanced back at Abbie, waiting in the car. "My priority was to contact you to get the story closed down."

"I'm on it."

"What if the journalist takes it to a different paper?"

"I don't recognise the name. Whoever she is, she's new. Jeff should be able to explain it will be the end of her career if she does. He already owes me a favour or three. Ask Abbie about it. If you discover anything, text, don't call. I don't want to interrupt the autopsy a second time."

Fiona ended the call feeling only slightly calmer. She knew every officer in the briefing. She hated to think of one of them being responsible when she had made it clear she wanted to catch Ruddle unaware of their interest in him when he landed. It didn't even make sense. If someone wanted to warn Ruddle, why didn't they call him direct?

Was it possible that someone outside the morning meeting knew about Ruddle's possible involvement? India might have contacted the reporter before her death as some sort of insurance policy. But if that was the case, why was the reporter so coy about protecting her source? The way she had spoken suggested she expected more information would be coming her way.

"Is everything okay?" Abbie called through the open car window.

Already in a foul mood, her shrill tone was like chalk on a blackboard to Fiona's ears. She turned, forced a smile and walked back to the car. Sliding into the driver's seat, she asked. "Do you know someone called Emma Thorpe?"

"Yes," Abbie said slowly. "Why do you ask?" A look of panic spread across her face. "Has something happened to her?"

Fiona dropped her forehead to the steering wheel, telling herself to take deep breaths and stay calm. Just because Abbie knew the name didn't mean she was the leak. If Abbie knew her then maybe other officers in the station did as well. She slowly raised her head, trying to create alternative reasons for the look of concern on Abbie's face, from the obvious one. "How do you know her?"

With a flushed face, Abbie said, "I started to tell you about her yesterday. We only met a few months ago, but she's the one. I'm sure of it."

Fiona forced herself to remain composed. Before she tore into Abbie, she needed to know just how stupid and naïve the woman was. Between gritted teeth, she asked, "What does she do for a living?"

Abbie reached forward and lifted her bag from the floor. "She's a writer of historical fiction. I've a copy of her book here. Would you like a look. She's good."

Fiona felt like she was about to explode. With an incredulous look, she said, "No. I don't want to read her stupid book."

"What?" Abbie said, her unguarded look one of anger rather than surprise. "What is your problem? I thought we were trying to get along like civilised human beings."

"I'll tell you the problem. Your girlfriend is a journalist. Or she was. Peter is speaking to her boss now. She rang me a few minutes ago demanding I make a comment on the story she intends to run in tonight's paper. All about our imminent arrest of a local television personality for strangling India Williamson." Fiona slowly clapped her hands together, three times. "Well done."

"But I ... I didn't ... Oh God, you've got to believe me."

Fiona stared out the front windscreen, trying to think straight through her anger. "I think you should get out of the car."

"I can explain."

Fiona couldn't bear to look at her. She'd had been in some crap relationships and made some terrible decisions, but never anything like this. "No, you can't. Which bit of get out of the car are you not understanding?"

Finally, Abbie gathered up her things and got out. Through the open door, she said, "I'm so sorry."

Looking straight ahead, Fiona said, "Shut the door." Her eyes remained fixed on a building in front of her as the car shook from the door slamming. She took deep breaths, looking in the opposite direction to avoid watching Abbie, the blabbermouth, walk away. After five minutes, the adrenaline rush that had fuelled her anger slipped away, leaving her feeling vulnerable and shaky. She glanced around to check Abbie was nowhere to be seen, sent a brief text to Peter and started the car engine.

When she pulled up outside Amanda Wagstaff's house, dark clouds rolled in, and rain started to fall. The sky looked as turmoiled as she felt. She flicked through her notepad, forcing herself to concentrate on the job in hand as the rain hammered down on the roof of the car. Despite the time of day, lights turned on inside the house. Deciding her anger had fallen to a manageable level, she checked herself in the car mirror and prepared to make a dash to the front door.

CHAPTER EIGHTEEN

Amanda opened the door, smartly dressed in black trousers and a grey sweater, her makeup looking freshly applied. "Oh, it's you." Opening the door wider, she added, "I suppose you had better come in."

Fiona followed her to the living room where nothing had changed since their previous visit. No refreshment was offered after Fiona took her seat.

Amanda hovered over the chair. "Don't you usually travel in pairs?"

"Not always. Can we talk about your daughter, Megan? You reported her missing this morning."

"I'm rather regretting it now. It seems I overreacted." Amanda picked up her mobile phone from a side cabinet. She scrolled through the screens, before handing it to Fiona. "She messaged me a few moments ago. See? She says she's safe, but needs some time away. She specifically asked I don't try to find her. I assume that she intends to return when she is good and ready, but not before. Like her father, she has always been stubborn and strong-willed, so I think I've rather wasted your time."

Fiona frowned as she blocked out Amanda's voice and read the text message. She looked up at Amanda, thinking of ways to express her uneasy doubts. In other circumstances, she would tread carefully, trying not to increase a parent's anxiety. She wasn't convinced that applied in Amanda's case. "Could I hold on to this?" she asked, referring to the phone.

"Not really, no," Amanda replied, holding out her hand for the phone's return. "Megan is clearly safe and well, so your involvement isn't necessary. I was about to call to explain."

Fiona reluctantly handed the phone over. "How can you be so sure the message is from your daughter? Anyone could have taken her phone and sent it."

Amanda took a seat on the couch and crossed her legs. "Why do you think it's not from Megan?"

"I can't say for sure, but there have been other cases where text messages have been sent from victims' phones. Occasionally, the recipient notices that the messages don't sound like the sender."

"How very clever of them to hear text messages." Before Fiona could say anything, Amanda twirled her hand in the air. "I'm being facetious. Have you heard of black humour? It's a well-known coping mechanism." Looking down at the screen, she added, "It sounds exactly like something Megan would send. The sub-text reads, 'You've done something to cause me to need to take some time away.'" Looking up, she asked, "Do you have a teenage daughter?"

"No, but I'm not sure that's relevant here."

"Trust me, it is. The mother-daughter relationship is complex and difficult. Get it right, and I believe it is rewarding and profound. Get it wrong, and it is fraught with resentment and tension, which ultimately leads to disappointment, on both sides. Our relationship fell into the latter category before she hit double figures. I have no doubt in my mind this is just another of her stunts to punish me for my obvious failings as a mother."

"Could you entertain the idea for one moment, that she has not left of her own accord and is being held against her will? For the length of this conversation, at least?"

"I'll play make-believe for a few moments, if that will make you happy. After which, I will have better things to do with my time."

"The last time I was here, you said Megan was vacationing with friends on study leave. When were you expecting her to return home?"

"Yesterday afternoon. I went out to dinner last night. I noticed she hadn't returned this morning."

"Did you check in on her when you returned from your dinner date?"

"The lights were out, and no sounds were coming from her room, so I naturally assumed she had switched off her television and gone to bed."

"That's a no, then," Fiona said, recalling how her mother would never fall asleep until she was sure she had arrived home safely from nights out. After school trips, her mother was always there to greet the coach, waving frantically. "Have you checked in her wardrobe to see if anything new is missing?"

"I haven't checked the cupboards, no. When I poked my head in her room it looked undisturbed. She doesn't like me to go in there." As if aware of Fiona's internal judgement, Amanda added, "I'm not the sort of parent who snoops around. I respect her privacy."

"Could you give me a list of her friends and their contact numbers. And anyone else she might have decided to stay with for a couple of nights."

Amanda slid open a drawer under the coffee table and placed a sheet of paper with a handwritten list of names and telephone numbers on the surface. "I anticipated you asking and wrote these down before I received her text."

Fiona pulled herself out of the armchair and reached for the paper. Slipping it into her bag, she thanked Amanda for her foresight. "How about your daughter's hobbies and interests? That might give us some clues as to where she is."

"Social media, clothes shopping and antagonising me, mostly."

"Boyfriends?"

"If she did, she didn't confide in me." Amanda's attention shifted. After staring into space, she gave a hollow laugh. "Not since I failed to take sufficient interest in the man, she had a crush on, back in the summer. He was twice her age, possibly even older."

Fiona automatically thought of John Ruddle, years older than his wife. "Oh? What happened?"

"Nothing as far as I'm aware. The school failed to find her a work experience placement last year, so she trailed after her father for a week. She couldn't stop talking about someone she met there. I telephoned Connor to ask who it was. He laughed and told me not to worry. She was talking about the boss man, and there was little chance of him being interested."

"Do you remember his name?"

"It was foreign-sounding. Stefan something or another."

"Stefan Albu?"

"Yes, that's it. I can't imagine he would be so stupid as to run off with her. She's under sixteen."

"It's something I'll be looking into," Fiona said, "How often did Megan see her father?"

"Rarely."

"Why was that?"

"She found him ... overwhelming. Too desperate to please. Always so eager, like an annoying puppy. I know I shouldn't talk ill of the dead and all that, but he made people uncomfortable."

"People or you?"

"I'm a person, and that's how he made me feel. Socially awkward, I believe, is the phrase for people like him."

Fiona gathered up her things. "Before I go, could I take a look around Megan's bedroom?"

CHAPTER NINETEEN

From her car, Fiona rang the station and gave a list of Megan's closest friends and of the clothes her mother believed were missing from her wardrobe. It hadn't taken her long to decide she wasn't going to update Peter of her intention to visit Albu. Far better to be criticised after the event than to be prevented going. A trick she had learnt as a teenager if she was determined to attend a party her parents would disapprove of.

Her reasons for visiting Albu were solid, and Peter hadn't said she couldn't go after him. Just that she needed rock-solid evidence before bringing him in. His name had come up in connection with Megan's disappearance, so it was only reasonable she followed up on it, before returning her attention to John Ruddle.

In her early teens, she had fantasied along with numerous other teenagers of somehow meeting her favourite pop stars. If her dreams had become a reality, she wondered how she would have reacted. Would she have run off with one of them if the opportunity arose, without a second thought? Today's youngsters generally seemed less naïve and more worldly-wise than she had been. But if encouraged by the person they idolised, anything was possible. Could that be the connection to her father's murder? Had he discovered the relationship and threatened to expose Albu's activities with young girls? Maybe Ruddle and Albu were members of an online group of men interested in underage girls. India had told BB, Albu was a sleaze and she avoided being alone with him.

She knew from Peter's report on the interview that Albu didn't have a permanent office. His practice was to set up one on his current development project and reside there until the last house was sold. She turned her car around and headed towards Highfield Homes. Whatever protection Albu thought he had through his contacts at Birstall Station, his name was linked to three deaths and the disappearance of a teenager. No amount of assistance to another station was worth that level of immunity.

From the start, the ignoring of Albu and the eagerness to channel enquiries elsewhere had felt wrong. She had never previously questioned an officer's integrity, especially one as high ranking at Dewhurst, and wasn't sure where to start or who she should speak to. Peter would never allow himself to be swayed from pursuing the truth by anyone, no matter what pressure was applied. He would normally be her first choice of confidant. But even he seemed happy to follow Dewhurst's instructions when he came to Albu. Rogers, their previous Superintendent was trustworthy. Although he was retired, maybe she could contact him.

Dewhurst was an unknown quantity. All she knew about him was his glittering progression through the ranks, apparently on the back of his excellent detective skills. There had been hushed suggestions that it took more than that for such a speedy rise, but she had dismissed it as idle gossip.

She reminded herself to take one step at a time. First, she had to speak to Albu. She wouldn't be questioning him about the recent deaths. She would be asking him about the disappearance of a teenager, a completely different matter. She would play ignorant and not draw attention to the services he provided for Birstall and see if he raised the subject himself.

Parking on a side street across from Highfield homes, she recalled BB's comment about how India referred to Albu as a sleaze. Checking her tired reflection in the interior mirror, she doubted she was worth anyone making a pass.

The reception area of Highfield Homes smelled of new carpets and furniture. The attractive salesgirl who greeted her reeked of perfume and hair spray. The combination of scents caused Fiona's eyes to water and tickled her throat as she raised her warrant card and asked to see Mr. Albu.

Fiona looked around the sales display while she waited. There was nothing about the company or the current manager, only the development itself. The glossy, professional photographs showed a range of tastefully decorated houses that claimed to meet everyone's budget. They were outside Fiona's price range, but if she had that amount of money to spend, she wouldn't touch them. Her dream home was a cosy cottage with a sprawling garden, preferably next to a stream. Peter's cottage, but with a much larger garden came close to that ideal.

"Mr. Albu will see you now. Follow me."

They left the sales area through the door behind the girl's desk and set off along a narrow corridor. It would be easy to forget the passage was temporary, made from cheap plasterboard in what would eventually be the last executive home sold on the plot. With paintings lining the wall and plush carpet underfoot it felt solid and durable, identical to countless, permanent, office buildings. Fiona wondered what other facades the fake charlatan, she was about to see, created.

When she entered the room, Albu was looking out over the development with his back to her. There was an open laptop on the desk, but it seemed out of place among rows of paper filing. The room would have warmed Peter's heart with his Luddite tendencies. The impression the room gave was contradicted by the man's fashion sense. A suit would have been in keeping with the traditional office of solid, wooden furniture and wall-papered walls. Instead, Albu wore jeans, heavy-duty work boots and the most hideous, navy-and-lime striped, hoody Fiona had ever seen. Physically, he looked like he could match any of his builders in strength and fitness. The office furniture probably belonged to the uncle, currently residing in prison.

Albu turned. For a fraction of a second, Fiona was mesmerised by bright, blue eyes in a vacuum of nothingness. The world rushed back, punctuated with the clanging of a pneumatic drill starting up. Albu shut the window and grinned. "Sorry if the noise startled you. Please, take a seat."

Shaking off her surprised reaction, Fiona settled on one of three chairs in front of the desk. Ignoring the pounding of her heart, she sat primly with the case file on her lap and pulled out her notepad. Looking up, prepared to start, she took in Albu's appearance. With his shaggy mane of black hair, smooth olive skin and chiselled features, he looked like a male model in a fashion magazine. On him, the gaudy sweatshirt looked a designer fashion statement rather than an unfortunate gift from an elderly relative. She could see why Megan might have fallen for his charms. His cheeky smile nearly had her fooled. Behind the sparkling, blue eyes that had hypnotised her earlier, she was sure lurked coldness and a healthy dose of danger. Flicking open her notepad, Fiona said, "Thank you for seeing me at short notice, Mr. Albu."

"Stefan, please. And the pleasure is all mine." Lifting the handset on his desk, he asked if she would like coffee or tea.

"Neither, Mr. Albu. I'm short on time, and I'm here to ask you about a young girl, Megan Ambrose."

Albu replaced the receiver. "You have me, how do you say, at rather a disadvantage. Meegan? Who is this Meegan?"

Fiona looked him over, telling herself she was immune to his nonsense and bad boy looks. The mispronunciation aimed to give the impression that English wasn't his first language didn't convince her. Especially as she heard a faint twang of an Irish accent. "Megan," she corrected. "The daughter of your recently deceased plumber, Connor Ambrose?"

Albu's face lit up with a wide smile. It showed a row of perfect, white teeth. "Maybe, you have a picture, yes? This would be good. I could look and see if I know this girl?"

Fiona slid the photograph of Megan from her file and pushed it across the desktop. Albu examined the picture without touching it. His long, curled eyelashes blinked several times as he looked down at the image.

Fiona prompted. "She spent a week doing work experience with her father in June of this year. I understand you met."

Albu pushed himself back from the desk. With a satisfied grin, he said, "I remember. A good girl helping her Papa. Very bright girl."

"Bright? How do you mean?"

"Happy. Full of the gay of spring."

Fiona glared at him. How stupid and naïve did he think she was? The act might work as a pick-up ploy in a bar, but it was hardly appropriate in the current situation. "Where did you go to form this impression?"

"Go? We no go anywhere. I see with Papa. Good girl. She respects her father." His look of confusion shifted to one of concern. "Why you ask these questions? She's not dead like her Papa?"

"She's missing." Fiona didn't say anything more, waiting to see if he would volunteer any more information.

Albu handed the photograph back to Fiona. "She was fond of Papa, no? Upset by his death. She maybe wanted to be alone. It is dangerous for a young girl, like her. You must find her."

Fiona slid the photograph back into the file. "Are you able to account for your movements over the last few days and nights?"

"In the days, why, I am always here." Albu opened a side drawer of the desk and brought out a leather diary. He placed it open on the desk facing Fiona. Jabbing at entries with his finger, he said, "See? I have been every night at council meetings in the town hall. Always busy." He grinned at Fiona, confident that it being written down in his office diary was all the proof needed of his innocence.

"Can I have some names of who else attended these meetings?" Once she jotted them down, Fiona asked, "Where do you go after these meetings end?"

"I go home."

"Can anyone verify that?"

Pulling a sad face, Albu replied, "Alas, I live alone."

After a loud knock, the salesgirl poked her head around the door. "Sorry to disturb you. Your next appointment, Mr. Dervishi, is here to see you."

Albu glanced at his gold watch and stood. "Hours fly, but I

think he is early. Please see to his comfort and tell him I am sorry to keep him waiting. I will be a few more minutes." As soon as the receptionist withdrew from the room, he asked, "Is that finished?"

On impulse, Fiona slid out the photograph she had of John Ruddle. "One more thing. Do you recognise this man?"

Albu walked out from behind the desk and took the picture. Frowning, he carefully studied it before looking up, "Who is this man? Do you have a name?"

"John Ruddle. Is the name familiar to you?"

Albu's jaw twitched, but he shook his head. "Sorry. No. How is he connected to the missing girl?"

"I'm afraid I can't tell you."

Returning the photograph, Albu said, "Please, I do not wish to be late for meeting."

Fiona felt his hand hold on to hers a fraction longer than necessary as she took the picture from him. "I might want to talk to you again."

"I would like that very much." Looking troubled, he said, "Take care of safety. I would hate to see you hurt."

Fiona hardly had a chance to register the sinister undertones before the heat of his hand on the hollow of her back ushered her from the room and along the corridor. She nodded at the man in the reception area who stood to greet Albu as they entered. He was how she had expected Albu to look. A balding, middle-aged man squeezed into a cheap suit. Leaving the room, she heard the man greet Albu in broken English.

CHAPTER TWENTY

Megan had no idea how long she had been slipping in and out of consciousness. Everything seemed to come in waves. Waves of physical agony, crippling self-hatred and grief for her father. How could she have been so stupid and self-centred? She should have realised she was being taken for a fool. Who could ever love someone as ugly and stupid as her? Only her father had ever loved her and called her a princess. Now, he was dead because of her and her idiotic fantasies.

She painfully pulled herself into a tighter ball as the rain started up again. She was desperate to go back to sleep. Her teeth were chattering, and she was shivering so much even oblivion was beyond her. Sleeping was forgetting, if only she could. Giving up, she gingerly tried to sit up. Every movement sent shock waves of pain through her. Gritting her teeth, she finally manoeuvred herself into a half-sitting position, with her back against the cold, damp wall of the well.

She spotted a crumpled, black, bin liner, half under the mattress. Pushing with her uninjured leg, she shuffled her bottom along, so her weight wasn't pressing down on the mattress, and she could free it. She had no idea what damage had been done to her shoulder when he yanked it from its socket, but her whole arm felt weak, and she had difficulty moving it. She doubted it would have the strength to pull the liner free. Her other arm felt hot and swollen from the deep gouges on her forearm from catching it on the rough walls during her descent, but it was less painful to move and felt stronger. She reached out with it and started to pull at the liner. Bit by bit, she wriggled it. She gave an extra-strong tug, and it finally came free. Dragging it towards her, she could see the bulge of rubbish inside of it.

The stench of the contents was overpowering as she peered inside. Amongst the decomposing rubbish that turned her stomach was the red flash of a coke can. Turning her head away, she groped through, feeling for the metal. Her heart sank at the weight. It was empty. A quick shake suggested there might be a dribble left inside. Fighting the urge to gag, she lifted the can to her lips and drank the flat, gritty liquid. It didn't taste anything like cola as it trickled down her dry, parched throat. She emptied the rest of the bag's rotting contents out and with her good arm wrapped the bag around her shoulders. Already soaked to the skin, it provided little comfort.

She looked at the foul mush of rotting food around her and started to cry at the realisation she was going to die in a rubbish tip. No one was going to find her, and her death was going to be slow and painful. Local kids might come to the area to drink and smoke in secret during the summer, but they sure as hell weren't going to bother in the pouring rain. She would be a rotting corpse by the time they returned in the spring.

She glanced up at the rusty ladder. She wasn't good at distances, but she judged the distance to the top of the well to be about the height of the school gym. Not that it made any difference. It might as well be a mile high for the good it would do her. She would be nervous climbing it with four fully functioning limbs. With a broken ankle and dislocated shoulder, it would be impossible.

In frustration, she threw the empty can at the ladder and shouted, "Why?!" The can clanged against the ladder disturbing particles of dust and rust before landing back on the mattress with a quiet thud. Pulling the ends of the stinking, bin liner around her, she leaned against the wall and gave in to her tears. They finally stopped leaving her drained and sleepy.

Her tired, sore eyes were starting to close as she looked up at the ladder. If she didn't at least try to climb out, her only other alternative was slowly dying in her own filth. If she fell when she was partway up at least, her death would be swift. She shuffled her bottom along so she could lie down again. If she was going to attempt it, she stood more chance of being successful if she was fully rested. She closed her eyes and drifted back to sleep.

CHAPTER
TWENTY-ONE

Back at the station, Fiona hurried along the corridor, past the closed door to Dewhurst' office, crossing her fingers he was occupied inside. She was surprised to find the incident room empty. She hoped a quick review of the case files would provide something to support her argument that Albu should be viewed as a potential suspect, and she wasn't questioning Dewhurst's motives for no good reason. She was still undecided about who she would turn to for advice if she found his exclusion from the investigation was more than a simple error.

The brief report of Albu's previous interview didn't add anything. Catching sight of the inconclusive report on Connor's work van she recalled how the driver's seat had been pulled forwards. It could have been an attempt to deflect attention from a taller man such as Albu or to aid pulling a lifeless body from the rear seat. As the lab had been unable to obtain any clear fingerprints, it didn't help.

She fired up her laptop, determined to find a connection between Albu and Ruddle. She didn't imagine the twitch in Albu's jaw when she showed him the photograph of Ruddle. Nothing came up when she compared the history of the two companies, but something else caught her eye. They hadn't looked at John Ruddle's business partner, Robert Murray. If there was anything in John's closet, with the right encouragement, Robert might be happy to fill in the details.

"There you are. Why didn't you call to say you were back?"

Fiona spun around and greeted Peter with a quick smile. "I wanted to check something," she said, closing her laptop. If he asked where she had been, she would say she had been continuing to investigate Ruddle, with a reasonable, and very minor detour to follow up on Megan's schoolgirl crush.

"Did you find what you were looking for?"

"Possibly. John Ruddle had a business partner. He's my next point of call."

"Sounds promising." Peter crossed the room and perched on the end of her desk. "They haven't been able to trace who reported the vehicle fire or the hit-and-run accident, which is annoying. How did you get on with Amanda Wagstaff? Was she any more upset by the disappearance of her daughter than the death of her ex-husband?"

"Not by a great margin, but in her defence, she has received a message from Megan, and she is convinced that she is safe somewhere."

"Did you find anything to link her disappearance to her father's death?"

"I did. Megan did work experience with her father during the summer term and developed a crush on Stefan Albu, so I popped out to Highfield Homes to have a word with him. He claimed he had never spoken to her, but I wasn't wholly convinced. It could be there was a relationship, and her father was unhappy about it. Maybe he confronted Albu, and the situation became heated. I think he should be up on the board as a potential suspect."

"You should have told me you were visiting Albu and why."

"Oh?" Fiona replied with an innocent expression.

"You know why. I'm surprised I didn't receive a complaint the second you walked in there."

"I wasn't aware he was totally off-limits. I was only asking if he remembered Megan," Fiona said, preparing her argument for why Albu should be under investigation.

Peter quickly changed the subject. "There's something else I wanted to talk to you about. Abbie came to see me after you threw her out on the street."

"That's an exaggeration of the truth! She compromised the investigation by relaying everything to the press, and I asked her to leave the car."

They turned as Abbie and Rachel walked into the room.

"How are the interviews going?" Peter asked.

"Other than Megan didn't get along with her mother we've made little progress," Rachel said, while Abbie stared at the floor. "No one has seen or spoken to her for a few days. Several have said they weren't surprised she took off after the death of her father, but they have no idea where she might have gone. We've something else to follow up on. She recently joined an amateur dramatics group and was in their last production."

When Peter looked expectantly at Fiona, she said, "Her mother didn't mention anything."

"We got the impression they hardly spoke, and the mother doesn't take much notice what Megan did with her spare time," Abbie said.

"While we're waiting to hear back from the drama group's committee, we've come back to grab something to eat in the canteen," Rachel added.

"Keep me updated," Peter said. He crossed the room and held the door open for Fiona.

In his office, Fiona gave her account of the morning. She paused regularly, expecting Peter to comment, but he waved her to continue to the end. She was on edge and flustered by the time she finished. She held her breath in the silence, wishing he would say something. Anything.

"I'm surprised at the way you handled the situation with Abbie. It's not like you to be so impulsive ... and callous. Is everything okay at home?"

Fiona cringed at the criticism and the underlying suggestion she might not be coping with her father's stroke. She could have handled things more compassionately, but the fact remained that Abbie was out order. Her mistake could have destroyed their investigation of Ruddle. "Everything is fine at home. I'm concerned that if Ruddle discovers we're investigating him, that he could avoid us for months by staying in America."

"I understand your viewpoint, but I'm unimpressed by the way you managed the unfortunate episode."

"With hindsight, I admit I could have done things differently, but in the heat of the moment, I was too angry."

"At least you recognise you made a mistake."

Fiona bit down hard on her tongue. She made a mistake! "What about Abbie?"

"We're too short-staffed to let a good officer go. I shouldn't have partnered the two of you."

Fiona heard the silent accusation of her and started to object.

Peter spoke over her. "She has explained what happened and I believe her. She considered the young woman to be a friend and was unaware she was a reporter."

Furiously shaking her head, Fiona asked, "How did she explain her conduct?"

"Had you been less hasty, you would know the answer to that question. To please you, she wanted to get the background information you requested so took her notes home with her. She was late getting ready for her prearranged night out. She left Emma Thorpe downstairs while she was in the shower. Emma must have read through the notes while unattended."

Running through that version of events in her head, Fiona felt a pang of guilt. It took the wind out of her righteous indignation. "If it happened that way, then I'm truly sorry. I probably was too harsh with her today."

"Probably?"

"Okay. I should have checked the details, first," Fiona snapped.

"Yes, you should. And that's what worries me. Normally, you would."

Fiona cringed under Peter's penetrating stare. Maybe she had been a little hot-headed recently. It was probably due to tiredness, and things would settle down soon. It was terrible timing, her father having a stroke the night of the vehicle fire. "I'll speak to Abbie when I see her."

"To apologise?"

"Yes." Fiona felt herself blush and experienced a sinking feeling inside, as she considered the events from Abbie's point of view. Abbie had discovered she had been used by someone she thought she had future with and treated with contempt by a colleague within the space of a few minutes. "I'll look for her in the canteen as soon as we've finished here."

"Good," Peter said, sounding relieved he could move on from personal issues. "You shouldn't have approached Albu alone without even checking in and telling anyone where you were headed."

"The daughter's crush sounded promising. I wanted to check it out straight away," Fiona replied defensively.

"It is interesting," Peter replied. "Although it sounds like a one-way thing, I agree it's worth following up on. Keep the enquiries discrete, and if you find anything, any other approaches to Albu should be run by me. Understand?"

"Yes."

"What is the situation with John Ruddle?"

"His flight lands in Heathrow at 7 o'clock tomorrow tonight. He left his car in the airport car park, so will be driving himself home. His wife is expecting him to arrive at about 9 o'clock. I will be waiting outside for him."

"You're not meeting him at the airport?"

"So long as the newspaper doesn't print anything, I don't think he's a flight risk."

"What do you intend doing between now and then?"

"I'm hoping to speak to his business partner and see where I go from there."

"Fancy a coffee? I'm on my way to the canteen. You can get your apology over and done with."

Peter suggesting the canteen when he usually avoided it was strange. Although she felt she was being manipulated, it probably was best she spoke to Abbie straight away rather than brooding over it. "Sure." While she knew it was the right thing to do, she wasn't looking forward to approaching Abbie, and she certainly didn't want to talk to Peter anymore about it. "What's happening with the two missing girls?"

"Haven't you heard? They have turned up at Charlotte's parents' place in Plymouth. Local police found them, and they're on their way home."

"That's good, isn't it?"

"I've spoken to Charlotte on the telephone, and I'm not happy about a few things."

Fiona took a deep breath as they entered the unusually quiet canteen. She checked the tables, but couldn't see Abbie and Rachel. By the time they had bought their coffees and settled at a corner table by a window, she had accepted she had missed them. After taking a sip of her coffee, she asked, "What is it about the teenagers you're still not happy about?"

"Everything. I'm convinced there's something more to their adventure. Things just don't add up."

"Like?"

"I've told you the girls have nothing in common. They told Plymouth police that they met by chance in the train station. Only, we went through all the footage from the station cameras. It was one of the first things we did. Neither of them were there."

"I'm guessing there are blind spots. Maybe they met in the toilets?" Fiona replied, wondering if that might be where Abbie and Rachel were.

"They still would have been picked up by at least one of the cameras. They're really vague about what they've been doing the last few days."

"But they're safe and well? Not hurt in any way?"

"So, they say."

Putting her coffee cup to one side, Fiona asked, "Why would they lie?"

"Fear. Charlotte sounded as nervous as hell."

"It could be that they met up with boyfriends, who drove them down there, went to a rave and took drugs and they don't want their parents finding out," Fiona suggested.

"There is something more to it than that. Throughout the call, I had the impression there was something she wanted to say, but was too scared."

"I've not been involved in their disappearance. Maybe, I could give a fresh perspective? We could find time to see the girls. After they finish school, maybe? Did Charlotte say why they stayed together?"

"She claims they instantly got along. Which doesn't make sense as they're like chalk and cheese. Charlotte's father is a top London barrister while Lisa doesn't know who her father is, and her mother barely makes ends meet. They're not the sort to normally cross paths, let alone decide to go off on a jolly jaunt together."

"They do say opposites attract," Fiona replied. "I'll let you know what I think when I meet them. Are you coming with me to see Ruddle's business partner?"

"I wish I could. I'm late already for a meeting with Dewhurst." With a shrug, he added, "He has some concerns about the way I file my paperwork."

CHAPTER TWENTY-TWO

Megan woke with her tongue stuck to the roof of her mouth, it was so dry. Feeling weak and light-headed, she slowly and painfully pulled herself to a sitting position. With tears of despair running down her face, she licked droplets of rainwater from the plastic bin bag she had wrapped herself in. Thoughts of dying amongst filthy litter tore at her heart. She looked up at the rusty ladder, glistening with raindrops. It would be better to die trying than to lie down amongst rotting garbage to await her painful death.

She was stiff from the cold and rain, but it had a small, numbing effect on the pain from her injuries. Cradling her injured arm and pushing off with her good leg, she shuffled along on her bottom until she reached the other side of the well. Stretching up with her good arm, she could just reach the bottom rung of the ladder. She could barely move either arm, and she had no idea whether her foot, stuck out at a strange angle would bear any weight.

She was tempted to rest. Getting onto that first rung would be the greatest challenge. If she could get that far, she stood a chance of making it all the way to the top. There was no time limit. She could carefully take her time to minimise the risk of falling as she moved upwards. Shaking off her drowsiness, she decided she could rest when she got herself upright.

Using the wall to support her back, she bent her good leg ready to propel her to her feet. She placed the palm of her left hand flat on the wall to help push herself up. Partway up she screamed in agony as she accidentally transferred some weight onto her twisted foot. She saved herself from slipping back down by ramming all her weight into the wall. She vowed to herself she would not countenance any backwards movement. Once she was on the ladder, she would focus her mind on one thing. Moving upwards towards the light. The pain subsided, and she reached around for an indentation in the brick wall she could use as a handhold. Finding one, she closed her eyes and called on every, last ounce of energy to drive herself to a standing position.

Panting, she turned to face the wall. She locked her arm around a ladder rung to stop herself from falling, as waves of dizziness threatened to overwhelm her. She clung to the cold, rusty metal, as her legs shook and threatened to crumple under her, knowing her life depended on her remaining upright. Slowly, her giddiness subsided. She rewarded herself with the promised, brief rest.

She opened her eyes and looked up, along the ladder rungs to the circle of light above her. She wanted to fix the image in her head before she started her climb to freedom. She had to get up there. If not for her, for her father. She angrily wiped her tears away. There would be time for them later, along with her tears of self-incrimination. Once she had obtained justice for her dad and the rotten bastard was locked away for good.

Stretching up, she could reach the third rung. Although her left arm appeared to be working normally and could hold her weight, she had lost her sense of touch. She would keep her eyes on each rung as she couldn't feel whether she was holding on tight or not. She took a deep breath, took all her weight onto her arm and swung her good leg onto the bottom rung. Sweat poured off her as she pulled and pushed until she was standing upright on the bottom rung.

She feared losing her grip on the rung, already slick from the earlier rain. Pressing herself against the ladder, her forehead touching the wall, she watched in horror as her hand started to slide off the rung. Keeping her weight as far forward as possible, she dipped and pushed with her good leg, catching herself in time with her elbow looped over the rung. She rubbed her palm dry on her sweatshirt. Looking down, she noticed her hand had left a light brown smear. Checking her palm, she saw it was stained an orangey-brown colour that reminded her of the fake tan girls at school were so fond of. She closed her eyes with her weight still held by her elbow. Thinking about those bullies wasn't important right now. She needed to focus on her climb. To make it to the top, she would need to repeat the dipping manoeuvre to return her hand to the rung and move on to the next one. Over and over again.

Doubt filled her mind as she froze. Could she do this on every rung until she reached the top? Every time she did it, she would risk falling. The risk increasing the more tired she became. If she fell, she knew she would never find the strength to start again. The alternative was to lie down on a foul-smelling mattress and accept her fate. If she did that, no one would know who killed her dad or why. She took a deep breath and prepared to dip and push to grab the next rung.

CHAPTER TWENTY-THREE

Walking from the canteen, Fiona couldn't shake her uneasy feeling about Peter's meeting with Dewhurst. His attention to admin was chaotic, but she wondered if that was the real reason for his summons. She couldn't share her concerns about Dewhurst with him, until she was sure where his loyalties lay.

Deep in thought, she bumped into Abbie and Rachel in the corridor. "Abbie. Could I have a quick word?" When Abbie hesitated and it became clear Rachel had no intention of leaving her side, Fiona said, "I'm really sorry about what happened earlier. I should have listened to your explanation."

Abbie shrugged and mumbled, "Forget it," before Rachel dragged her away along the corridor.

Certain that Rachel would encourage Abbie not to forget about it, Fiona felt relieved she had at least said something. It was one less thing she had to worry about. In the empty incident room, she pushed what they both might be saying about her from her head. She also closed her mind to her growing doubts about Dewhurst so she could focus on the case.

Details of John Ruddle's business partner, Robert Murray were easy to find and he agreed to see Fiona. Reaching his house proved to be a little harder. He had told her she couldn't miss the house as it was the only building for miles around. He failed to warn her that she would intermittently lose the internet connection for her sat nav as the narrow lanes wound through dense woodland and up a steep incline. She was convinced she had missed a turning and was about to turn around when a modern white house, clinging to the side of the hill, appeared from nowhere. Her car clattered over a cattle grid and climbed the steep, gravelled drive to the side of the house. She double checked the handbrake was on and left the car in gear before getting out. She didn't want to exit the house to find her car several miles away at the bottom of the hill.

When she knocked on the door it was opened as far as the chain would allow. A quiet voice asked her to open her warrant card and place it on the ground facing him. He had said on the telephone he was a recluse and visitors made him anxious, so Fiona complied without questioning the request. After a short while a gloved hand placed two, sealed packages on the ground. "Please, put these on."

Inside the plastic Fiona found a face mask and a pair of surgical gloves. Looking at them doubtfully, Fiona asked, "Is this really necessary?"

"If you want to come in, they are. One can never be too careful."

Reluctantly, Fiona attached the mask and pulled on the gloves. "Okay. I'm wearing them."

As the door opened, Fiona took a step back as she considered Robert Murray clad in protective overalls, mask and gloves, nervously fidgeting in the doorway. His pale skin suggested he rarely saw any fresh air and his tousled, blond hair looked like it hadn't seen a comb in days.

"Come in. But please try to not touch anything." Robert nervously bounced around the wide, tiled entrance, explaining the downstairs was bedrooms and the living area was upstairs. By the time they reached an expansive, open-plan kitchen, his joke about inviting strange women upstairs on a first meeting were wearing thin.

From the kitchen area, they entered a living room with sliding glass doors onto a large, terraced area which led down to the split-level garden. Fiona sank down onto a lemon, leather sofa covered with a plastic sheet, hoping the constant, running commentary would come to an end naturally without her having to ask him to stop. She took in the impressive view while he rambled on about the house design and the history of the area. From the matching, black floor tiles throughout the house, to the smell of new leather and the Porsche parked outside, it was clear Robert had few financial worries. It was equally obvious he had some major issues with the outside world.

"It's here, already, you know."

"What is?" Fiona asked, turning her attention back to Robert.

"The virus. It was made in Russia and released all over the world. China is suffering now, but Europe will be next. Then it will spread throughout America and Africa. Russia will hold the world to ransom. You wait and see."

Not wanting to disappear down a rabbit hole, Fiona nodded and smiled politely before saying, "You've a beautiful home. I'm here to talk about your business partner, John Ruddle." She waited, wondering how he would react. A deadly silence followed. Robert's eyes that had previously darted around the room in time with his jerky movements, stared resolutely at the floor. Fiona prompted him, "Is your partnership an amicable one?"

The waiting game finally provoked a response. "We don't mix socially. I rarely mix with people at all. Sorry am I talking too much? I sometimes don't talk to anyone for days."

"That's okay. You're doing fine. How did you meet John?"

"Over the internet. I advertised the position and he was my chosen candidate to be the face of my creations."

"How does your partnership work?"

"I have the ideas and the design skills. John is the face of the product. He couldn't do what I do, and I certainly couldn't do what he does. We complement each other, you could say."

"Do you get along when you are together?"

"I only met him once." With an erratic waving of his hand, Robert added, "It created a professional difference."

"Professional? Not personal?" Fiona asked, quietly.

Robert gave a dramatic shudder. "I don't like his attitude. But I should warn you, I feel that way about most people. I'm not a sociable person. I prefer my own company."

Feeling like she was pulling teeth, Fiona asked, "Attitude to what? Life? People? The business? You?"

"All of the above."

Aware time was ticking by, during the long silences, Fiona bluntly asked, "Which causes the greatest issue between you?" Sighing, looking at the fading light outside, she added, "Are there any particular problems?"

Robert pulled a small device from his pocket. He pressed a button to turn on the lights. He pressed another and the curtains closed in spasmodic, juddering movements, similar to his own. "I must get that seen to," he muttered as they fully closed.

"You were telling me about the problems you had with John Ruddle, the one time you met?" Fiona reminded him.

Blushing, Robert said, "He brought a girl to my house, uninvited."

"A girl? Are we talking a very, young girl?"

"She claimed to be over sixteen."

"You didn't believe her?"

Robert nervously wrung his hands. "You're missing the point. He brought her here. To see me. We argued. I asked him to leave."

"Did you catch the name of this girl?"

"Sorry, no. I think the silly, giggling thing realised I disapproved, and remained silent."

"Would you recognise the girl if you saw her again?"

"I'm not sure. Possibly."

Pulling her tablet from her bag, Fiona said, "I would like you to look at a couple of pictures for me." She turned the screen around to show a series of girls, including Megan.

Robert took his time studying the pictures from a safe distance, but shook his head at each image. "Sorry, I've never seen any of them before." Looking up, he shrugged and added, "To be fair, the girl we argued about looked slightly older than these."

Not looking forward to the journey back through the unlit unfamiliar lanes, and not seeing what more Robert could tell her about Ruddle if they only met the once, Fiona prepared to leave. She tried to hand Robert a card, but he recoiled in horror, refusing to take it. "I don't need that. The number you called from earlier has already been stored."

Fiona returned the card to her pocket. "Thank you, for your help. Please call me if you do remember anything more about the girl."

"Yes, of course," Robert replied, nodding enthusiastically. "I hope I haven't given you the wrong impression about John. I don't think he would physically harm anyone." Blushing, he quickly added, "Well ... I'm not sure how relevant my thoughts are. I rarely leave this building. I'm probably very out of step with lots of things people accept as normal. Today has been a good day."

"What's a bad day like?"

"I would have had to cancel our meeting. The anxiety would have been too much for me. ... I should have asked earlier. Has something happened to some young girls?"

"It's nothing for you to worry about," Fiona said, standing. "Thank you, again. I'll see myself out."

Rushing to the door, Robert said, "No. Please don't touch the door handles. I'll see you out."

Driving back through the winding lanes, Fiona processed the strange meeting with Robert. If he was as reclusive as his performance suggested there was no point investigating him further. There were no grounds to request his medical records, so she did the next best thing and followed the signs to the nearest village. The two ladies in the cramped, corner shop and the landlord of the pub confirmed Robert was regularly talked about because no one in the area had ever seen him. The only person they had seen arriving and leaving the house was a young gardener he employed.

Leaving the village behind, she decided against calling Peter. She would update him in the morning. Robert Murray could be discounted as a suspect, but John Ruddle's interest in young girls was interesting. It might be worth asking Charlotte and Lisa if they recognised him. It was tight, but Fiona pulled up outside her mother's home just in time to drive her to the hospital.

CHAPTER TWENTY-FOUR

After the morning's briefing, Fiona moved to her desk and opened the sandwich she had picked up on her way in. She hadn't had time to eat anything the day before and was ravenous. She played with a paper clip while she ate. Sleep had been elusive the night before. Something that lay just out of reach was bugging her. Although she couldn't put her finger on what it was, she felt sure it was important. Lost in thought, she was startled to find Peter had pulled up a chair next to her without her realising.

"Penny for them," Peter said.

"Sorry, I was miles away. I'm convinced I've missed something important."

"Those things often come to you out of the blue when you're thinking about something completely different. Are you still okay to pick me up this evening to wait for John Ruddle?"

"Of course."

"Robert Murray sounded a strange one."

"He was. Obviously incredibly rich and a computer expert. Sad to think he rarely leaves his house, beautiful though it was. I'm surprised his family has allowed him to lock himself away like he has."

"Maybe they tried in the past and have given up. You didn't explain how he came to be in a partnership with Ruddle."

"I did. They connected online. Murray advertised for someone to be the face of his inventions, and Ruddle applied."

"How did he select him? Surely they must have met at some point if even only to go through contract terms?"

"No. He chose Ruddle from his online profile, and everything was set up online." Fiona straightened her now-empty sandwich wrapper out on the desk, and said, "I still think Stefan Albu is worth a closer look. If Connor discovered he was having a relationship with his daughter, he could have decided to have words, and things became heated. Connor's death could have been accidental, and the campervan fire was staged in a half-baked attempt to cover it up."

"It's one possibility, but where's your evidence?"

Fiona shrugged. "I'm still looking for it.

"We're investigating Ruddle because we think India saw him running away from the scene. How does Albu fit in with that? How do they even know each other?"

Fiona shrugged. "We'll never know what she saw. If Ruddle met his business partner online, maybe that is how he met Albu. Via a site specialising in young girls."

"You've really got an issue with Stefan Albu, haven't you?"

"You're convinced there's more to the two runaways, without any real evidence. What's the difference?"

"Shrugging, Peter said, "The lack of any progress on this case is worrying. We're still scrambling around in the dark with no idea why Connor was killed or why his daughter has disappeared."

Fiona rubbed her forehead in frustration. "Whoever drove Connor's work van out to where he stored his camper van was short."

"As is Ruddle. Albu is tall," Peter pointed out.

"That's it!" Fiona said, screwing the sandwich packaging into a ball and throwing it towards the wastepaper basket. "That's what has been staring me in the face. If someone drove Connor's van out to the farm and then bundled him into the campervan to stage the fire, how did he leave the scene? It's the middle of nowhere. Two people must be involved."

"Unless," Peter said, turning her laptop towards him and tapping on the keyboard. Frowning at the map he brought up, he said, "There is one cottage out there. I don't remember seeing any lights, but I was surprised at the time how quickly the emergency vehicles turned up."

"We need to find out who lives there and pay them a visit."

Peter stood up. "Let me know what you discover."

"You're not coming?"

"I've a few loose ends to tie up. Once I have, you'll have my undivided attention."

Fiona watched Peter walk towards his office, wondering whether his loose ends had something to do with his private meetings with Dewhurst. She was disappointed he wasn't coming with her out to the cottage as they worked better as a team. She guessed she had hit a raw nerve referring to his obsession with the two runaways. Without him to bounce ideas off, her mind ran around in undisciplined circles.

Fiona parked her car outside the padlocked gates to Lilac Cottage. They were too high to climb, and a quick rattle confirmed the padlock was secure. Through the bars, she could see a gravelled drive through the grounds leading to the house. Because of the way the road twisted back on itself, the distance to where Connor's van was set alight was a couple of miles. The direct route across open farmland was far shorter.

The letting agent who handled the holiday property had promised someone would meet her with the keys. She had half an hour before he was due to arrive. She pulled her wellingtons from the boot of her car to walk the perimeter in the hope she could get a preview. The high stone wall continued around the property, and she ended up back at the front of the property.

Looking at the ground, she could see muddy footprints leading from the gates to a wooded area off to the side. She thought it strange as the agent said the property was only let during the summer months. She decided to follow the tracks to see where they led.

After a short distance, the footprints joined up with a muddy, waterlogged path leading into the woods. Fiona glanced back at the house to check the agent hadn't arrived early before carrying on.

The clay soil clung to her boots, and her calves complained about the heavy going. The view to the cottage was blocked by trees. She decided she would continue to the fork ahead in the track and then turn back. Reaching that point, she looked along the two alternative paths. What looked like a bundle of rags lay in the middle of the left track a short distance away. Checking the time, she resolved to inspect what it was before turning back. As she neared, she broke into a run. A young girl lay face down in the mud. One arm was outstretched as if reaching for help, while one foot stuck out at a strange angle. She crouched down, expecting the worse and felt for a pulse. It was weak, but it was there.

She threw off her coat and covered the girl while calling for an ambulance. It was hard to tell from the mud-splattered, ghostly pale face turned to the side, but the girl fitted the description of Megan Ambrose. She rang the station and spoke to Peter. From her crouched position she could see drag marks in the mud stretching out behind the girl. She was torn between waiting for the ambulance to arrive and investigating where they led. There was nothing she could do for the girl, and she couldn't discount the possibility there might be other girls, they didn't know about in need of help. She ran as best she could along the slippery path.

Her heart fell when she came to a clearing. The drag marks led directly to an old well. Taking a deep breath to prepare herself for the worst, Fiona peered over the side and down into the darkness. Without a torch, she couldn't see the bottom. Realising the injured girl had climbed the ladder and dragged herself through the mud made her feel sick. She wasn't a fan of heights, but she swung her legs over the side of the well and descended the ladder.

In the enclosed space, the smell of rotting food and damp became more overwhelming the deeper she climbed. Jumping away from the ladder onto a mattress, she nearly gagged at the stench of congealed food waste. Feeling nauseous, she pulled up a rotting mattress to check what was under it. She wasted no time checking there were no more bodies to be found before quickly climbing back up the ladder to return to wait for the ambulance.

Crouched by the young girl, the stink of putrefied food lingered. The damp slime of the well's walls seemed to have seeped through her skin, chilling her insides.

Once the paramedics had arrived and taken charge, Fiona walked back to the cottage where she found a shaken letting agent talking to two police constables who had been sent out to secure the property. Taking them to one side, she explained about the disused well that also needed to be protected and then examined. She didn't envy whoever received the task of sifting through the garbage, but at least they would be wearing protective gear. After only being down there for a few minutes she had an overpowering desire to peel off her damp clothing and have a long, hot shower.

While they discussed setting up tape around both sites, the letting agent, a grey-haired man near retirement, had returned to his car. When Fiona introduced herself, he looked up from the driver's seat and muttered, "In all my born days, I've never known anything like it. Terrible. Quite terrible."

"Did the officers ask you for the keys to the cottage?"

The agent shook his head and glanced at the set of keys on the passenger seat. "I'm not sure I should ... I mean, I've never been in this position before. Should I ask the owners for permission, first?"

Fiona held out her hand. "A young girl has been seriously assaulted. As the agent, you have the authority to hand over the keys to customers, don't you? I promise I'll take good care of them and return them as soon as possible."

They turned to watch the paramedics carry the stretcher to the rear of the ambulance. Still holding out her hand, Fiona said, "The keys, please."

Diverting his attention from the ambulance, the agent snatched up the keys and handed them over. "Am I free to leave, now?"

"After a few questions, you can be on your way."

Mopping his brow with a handkerchief, the agent replied, "I'll do my best, but I don't know anything."

"You said when I rang earlier, that you thought there had been no bookings for months for the cottage, but you would double-check that for me."

"Yes, yes. I did that, before I left. According to our records, the last booking via us was in October."

"Were you the sole agent for the cottage?"

"We always encourage our customers to only use us to avoid the risk of double-booking."

"That doesn't answer my question. Were all the bookings made via you?"

"I believe in the past, there have been occasions when the owners made their own arrangements."

"Who owned the property?"

"An elderly gentleman, I think," the agent replied, picking up a file from the passenger seat and flicking through it. "I don't seem to have his details with the file. They'll be back at the office."

Handing over her card, Fiona said, "When you find them, call me on this number. Could you also put a list together of all the bookings for Lilac Cottage last year?"

"That should be easy enough to do."

"Thanks. How does the system work? Do people collect the keys from you or do you meet them here?"

"From the office whenever possible."

"And in between bookings. Do you employ a cleaner or some-one to air the cottage for new arrivals?"

"We employ a lady in the village. She's very reliable," the agent replied. He pulled a pen from his shirt pocket. "I'll write her name and address on the back of one of my cards." Handing it over, he asked, "Is there anything else?"

"That's all for now, but we may have to speak again. And, of course, I'll need to return the key."

The agent pulled the car door shut and accelerated away, narrowly missing a vehicle travelling towards the cottage. Fiona smiled as Peter stepped out of the car. "I thought you were tied up elsewhere, today?"

"So, did I. What has been happening here?" After Fiona updated him, he said, "Probably best we don't trample on any more evidence before the experts arrive. Leave the keys with the constable, and we'll see if we can locate this local housekeeper."

The housekeeper for the cottage was a retired publican, who looked after several holiday properties in the area for the letting agents to keep herself active. She was unaware of any recent bookings and had not been to check on the property for several months. She confirmed there had been past occasions where the owners had organised private lettings, but that had been months ago.

CHAPTER TWENTY-FIVE

Fiona's phone rang while they were parked across the street from Ruddle's house, awaiting his return from the airport. Ending the call, she said, "That was the hospital returning my earlier call. They're doing what they can, but Megan is in a bad way, and they can't guarantee she'll make it."

"From what you've said, the kid has shown an amazing will to survive. Let's hope she's still fighting." Wiping condensation from the window with his sleeve, to get a clear view of the house, Peter asked, "How easy would it have been for India to contact Ruddle? Have you checked whether she rang the television studios to ask to speak to him?"

"No, but it was pre-recorded, so he wouldn't have been there, anyway. I doubt they would have handed out his number, but I will check, later." Pulling out her mobile, she entered John Ruddle's name into the telephone directory. Showing the screen to Peter, she said, "If she knew he was local, she could have used the telephone directory like I just did."

"Fair point." Glancing up at the house again, Peter said, "He's running late."

"He could have been held up in the airport or in traffic. We know he was on the flight and it landed on time. He should be here soon."

"I hope he hurries up. It's starting to get cold."

"There's a blanket in the back. I'll grab it if you like."

"Maybe later. Hopefully, he will turn up soon, and we'll be inside in the warm."

Peter wiped the side window clear again. "Come on. Hurry up."

Fiona checked the time. She was starting to get worried that Ruddle knew they were waiting for him and had decided to disappear. She hoped she hadn't made a massive mistake by not driving to Heathrow to meet his flight. She rechecked the sightlines. Their car wouldn't be visible from the house, but a friendly neighbour could have spotted them. Looking up and down the empty street, there were no obvious signs of twitching curtains, but that didn't mean they hadn't been scrutinized earlier. She glanced across at Peter pondering whether to voice the possibility. The thought had probably entered his mind already.

"We'll give it another twenty minutes," Peter said. "Then I'll ask the wife, whether he's been in contact to warn her that he's been delayed. Anything might have come up. I don't want to spend the night here if he's decided to spend the night in London."

"Okay," Fiona agreed. She scanned the street again for any sign they were under observation. Settling back into her seat, she said, "Have you seen anything about the new disease in China? It's all over Twitter. I looked it up after meeting Murray. People are dropping down dead in the street, and the government is so worried about it spreading they're locking people inside apartment blocks."

Peter gave her a dismissive look. "You're not stupid enough to believe all that social media rubbish, are you?"

"I looked it up after speaking to Ruddle's partner. The World Health Organisation is looking into it. If they're getting involved, it suggests there is something going on."

"What sort of illness is it?"

"A type of flu, but it gets really bad. Patients' lungs fill up with liquid, and they basically drown."

"Nasty."

"Do you think it will spread to here?"

"You worry too much," Peter replied, shaking his head. "If it does, I doubt we'll be instructed to lock people in their homes."

They were interrupted by Fiona's phone ringing. She glanced over at Peter several times as she listened to the caller. Peter always said there was no such thing as an innocent coincidence, and she was starting to believe him. She ended the call and said, "That was the guy from Heathrow security I spoke to earlier. Ruddle was mugged while walking across the car park to collect his car. He's been taken to Hillingdon Hospital where he'll be staying at least overnight." She started up the car engine.

Peter nodded towards the house. "Shouldn't we inform the wife?"

"Already done."

Bagging up the empty sandwich containers and coke cans, Peter said, "Fancy popping into The Horseshoe for something more substantial to eat?"

"Sounds good. I'll ring the hospital to see if we can interview Ruddle tomorrow morning."

CHAPTER
TWENTY-SIX

When they arrived on the ward in Hillingdon Hospital, Fiona spotted a group of nurses huddled around the central desk, enjoying a coffee. They looked up as one on their approach, irritation at being disturbed flitted across their faces to be replaced by tired smiles. Peter and Fiona held up their warrant cards and introduced themselves.

Looking down at the paperwork strewn across the desk, Fiona guessed they had interrupted a shift change rather than a relaxing break. "Sorry to disturb you. I rang earlier. We're here to see Mr. Ruddle."

"So, you did," a male nurse said. "You spoke to me. He's in one of our side wards. Hang on here, and I'll check he's awake."

Fiona nodded her thanks and moved away from the central desk to wait. She knew from the police report, Ruddle had been set upon by two, hooded figures. One had held his arm behind his back so tightly it had dislocated his shoulder while the other person had kicked and thumped him. Luckily for Ruddle, the altercation had been seen by a fellow traveller who had raised the alarm and the two attackers had fled empty-handed when he approached. While a chance mugging couldn't be ruled out, it sounded more like a pre-meditated beating.

Her suspicions about the attack were reinforced when they entered the side room, and she spotted an open laptop and a Pro Max iPhone on the side of Ruddle's bed. His face was heavily bruised, but he managed a brief smile in greeting.

"I don't suppose there's any chance of finding the little sods,"

Ruddle said in a resigned voice.

Peter leaned against the wall while Fiona drew up a chair. She nodded to the electrical appliances. "That's a quality phone. I'm surprised they didn't grab it before they ran."

Fortunately, the attack was disturbed by a passer-by. I guess my guardian angel was looking out for me, last night."

"I heard. It was brave of him to come to your rescue." Even though she knew the answer, she asked, "Did they get away with anything else?"

"No. They got nothing for their trouble."

"I understand you regularly guest on one of the shopping channels. You won't be able to do that for a while."

Ruddle looked smug at the thought of being recognised as a television presenter. "True, but I still feel I am a very, lucky man. I'm afraid I'm not going to be able to help you very much with catching them. I didn't get a look at their faces."

"Not to worry. Local officers will be talking to you about the attack. I'm here on another matter. How do you know Connor Ambrose?"

"I'm not sure I know anyone by that name. Who is he?"

"A local plumber."

"We use a firm called Just Heating to check the boiler every year. Does he work for them? I don't think I've ever been at home when they've called. You'll have to check with my wife."

"Maybe, you knew him through his daughter. Megan Ambrose?"

Ruddle shook his head. "Nope. Neither name means anything to me. Should they?"

Fiona considered Ruddle, searching for signs he was lying. There was nothing obvious to suggest he was, but it was helpful he had given flat denials of knowing Connor or his daughter. If she later found evidence to contradict his denials, she would have something to work with. She debated telling him Megan was in hospital, but discounted the idea. She didn't want to put the girl in any more danger. Keeping a close eye on his reaction, she said, "I've another name for you. India Williamson?"

"Sorry, none of these names mean anything to me."

Fiona pulled out her notepad and jotted down a few things before raising her head and asking, "Where were you last Sunday night?"

For the first time, she spotted a change in Ruddle's open demeanour. His eyes narrowed in a guarded expression, and his tone went up a notch, when he asked, "Sorry, when was that again?"

Despite the slight change of attitude, Fiona could still detect an air of smugness. She anticipated a watertight alibi was on its way. "Last Sunday."

Ruddle scrolled through screens on his phone, before breaking into a smile. "Ah. It was that evening," he said, handing it to Fiona. "I bumped into an old school friend, Dale Wood and I'm afraid we got very carried away reminiscing. We chatted into the early hours in his front room. Unplanned evenings like that are the best. Don't you think?"

Suspecting he was going to give another alibi for his whereabouts the evening India disappeared, she half-heartedly asked the question and returned the phone.

After a quick look at his phone, Ruddle replied, "Would you believe, I was with Dale again. Having got carried away the first evening, I left my coat behind. I popped back to collect it and ended up staying for supper."

Fiona asked for Wood's number and jotted it down despite being quite sure he would collaborate Ruddle's story.

Peter pushed himself off the wall, took the slip of paper from Fiona and asked, "Would you mind if I ring your long-lost friend now? We will need a full statement from him at some point."

Ruddle rested his head against the pillows and closed his eyes. "Go ahead." After watching Peter leave, he wearily added, "The pain killers I took before you arrived are kicking in. Do you mind if I rest my eyes while he makes his call?"

"Just a few more questions before you do," Fiona said. "Do you know Stefan Albu?"

Ruddle opened his eyes a crack and dreamily said, "Sorry?

Who?"

Peter re-entered the room, shaking his head. Fiona stood and slung her bag over her shoulder. Glancing at the watch on the bedside table and the tech gear on the bed, she was far from convinced Ruddle was the victim of a random mugging. Until she had something more, there was nothing to gain talking to him in his drugged state. "We can talk again once you're home and feeling better. Have they said when they'll be discharging you?"

Ruddle fully opened one eye. "Tomorrow morning at the earliest, I believe. They want to run some tests."

In the hospital corridor, Fiona asked, "What did the friend say?"

"Dale Wood reeled off the same story as Ruddle without hesitation. It was nearly a word-perfect repetition."

"An immediate red flag."

Nodding his agreement, Peter said, "I've arranged for us to take a written statement from him at his place of work."

"Let's hope when he realises, he is giving an official statement in a murder enquiry, his resolve to cover for Ruddle weakens." Fiona groaned at the sound of her phone ringing. "Who's this ringing now?" She glanced at the unknown number and accepted the call.

"Ah. Is this the police lady with fiery, red hair?"

Fiona rolled her eyes, recognising the false accent of Stefan Albu. She put the quickening of her heartbeat down to an adrenaline rush due to hoping Wood would reveal a chink in Ruddle's alibi. Abruptly she said, "DI Fiona Williams. Who am I talking to?"

"Stefan Albu. I ask some questions about the man you showed me in the photograph. I would like to meet with you to say what I have discovered."

Exiting the hospital and hurrying across the car park, Fiona said, "Can you tell me over the phone?"

"I think it is better we meet. For lunch, maybe. Do you know The Vine Tree at Moreton?"

Fiona juggled the phone and her bag as she opened her car door.

The Vine Tree was a beautiful restaurant, off the beaten path. The food made the journey through a maze of tiny lanes worthwhile, although it came with a hefty price tag. "I do, but I'm currently in London and short of time. I have another appointment to make. I'll drop into your office afterwards."

"Not so pleasant surroundings, but I look forward to seeing you. And Fiona, be careful. There are bad people in the world."

"I'll bear that in mind," Fiona replied, with a roll of her eyes before disconnecting the call. Slipping her phone away, she updated Peter. Inwardly she debated calling Humphries to ask him to pop out to Albu. She dismissed the idea. He had asked for her and sending someone else may lead to him withholding whatever information he thought he had. It might turn out to be a complete waste of time and a ruse to obtain a dinner date, but it could also be the vital link that connected up all the dots. "Whatever information he has, it had better be worthwhile. My gut feeling is it will be nothing of any use, and it will be a complete waste of our time."

Starting the car engine, Peter said, "I think the woman doth protest too much."

"What on earth do you mean by that?"

"Nothing. Nothing at all."

Shaking her head, Fiona admitted she couldn't remember the last time she was invited to a lunch date by a strange man. Smiling to herself, she conceded even though it related to a murder investigation, it was still a satisfying ego boost.

CHAPTER TWENTY-SEVEN

Peter parked in the car park of Teobald, Gibson, and Wood Solicitors with half an hour to spare before their appointment with Dale Wood. Fiona used the time to rest her tired eyes after the journey from London while Peter flicked through her notes on the interviews, she had completed without him.

Fiona nearly drifted off to sleep when she was jolted by the sound of car doors slamming. She looked up to see two men calling to one another, as they locked their vehicles. One had exited a gleaming, red, Vogue Range Rover and the other a dusty work van. Peter packed Fiona's notes away, and they followed the men towards the company entrance.

Waiting behind the men at the reception desk, their ears pricked up when the name, Dale Wood was mentioned. Trying not to make it look too obvious they were eavesdropping, they learned his car was being returned after bodywork repairs to the front following a recent prang. After a brief telephone call, the receptionist confirmed they could leave the keys with her.

When they left, Fiona and Peter stepped up to the desk and were invited to take a seat by the window to wait for Dale Wood to collect them. Fiona flicked through the company brochure while they waited. They discretely watched Wood collect his car keys from the receptionist. He was unremarkable looking, with middle-age spread and balding hair. His dark suit was crumpled and tired. Not noticing them, he started towards the exit with the car keys in his hands.

Peter stood to call after him, but was beaten to it by the receptionist. "Mr. Wood. There are two detectives waiting to see you," she said, waving her hand in their general direction.

Wood spun on his heels, looking startled and confused. Catching sight of them, he quickly slipped the car keys in his jacket pocket and returned to greet them. Visibly unsettled and nervous he led them to the lift doors and along the corridor to his office. By the time they reached his office door with a brass plaque with his name in large, bold letters, he had needed to mop sweat from his brow with a handkerchief several times.

An awkward silence between them continued while he seated himself on a leather computer chair behind a sturdy desk, and Peter and Fiona pulled up two hardback chairs. Wood clasped his hands in front of him on the desk, looked down his bulbous nose from his higher position, and said, "I've another appointment in half an hour, and I'm not sure I can add anything to what I said over the telephone."

Peter smiled brightly, and replied, "If you're short of time we could go over a few points now, and then you could come into the station to make a formal statement, later at a time that would suit you better."

Wood dabbed his forehead again. "Let's get on with it, shall we?"

"Of course." Fiona watched his expression as he retold the two alibis for Ruddle. As Peter nodded in all the appropriate places, Wood settled into his story and his overall demeanour changed from nervousness, through tentative confidence to one of superiority. Once he finished, Fiona smiled and closed her notepad. When Wood leaned back in his chair, Peter turned to her and said, and asked, "Did you have any questions?"

Fiona fixed Wood with a long stare before taking him backwards and forwards over the salient points. As he deflected question after question without interruption, a look of smugness crept in.

"I think that will do for now," Fiona said, starting to rise.

Peter remained seated and casually asked, "What happened to your car?"

Panic briefly flit across Wood's face. "What do you mean?"

"Your Range Rover? Wasn't it just returned from a garage?"

"Oh, yes. Someone hit it in a supermarket car park. Of course, they didn't have the decency to leave their contact details."

"Annoying," Peter sympathised.

Wood escorted them to the lift, where he left them after they shook hands. On the ground floor, Peter quickly crossed to the reception desk. "Hi, I've some damage to the side of my car. Mr. Wood recommended the company that did some work for him, but he couldn't remember their name. Did you happen to catch it when they dropped off the keys?"

The receptionist efficiently whipped out a notepad and pen from under the desk and wrote down the company name. After a few taps on her computer screen, she added their telephone number.

Crossing the car park, Peter said, "That's interesting. The garage looks like a small, family-run affair and is miles away." Nodding towards the gleaming Range Rover, he added, "The obvious place to take it would have been the main dealers in Birstall."

Fiona agreed. "The only time Woods appeared even vaguely rattled was when you mentioned the damage to his car."

"Can you ring the garage and ask for a copy of the repair report? If we could prove his car was involved in that hit-and-run accident, it would be our first substantial breakthrough. It throws suspicion on to him and drives a hole through the centre of the alibi he's providing for Ruddle. If they are working together, Wood will be the weakest link and the one most likely to crack under pressure."

Fiona's thoughts were interrupted by a loud rumble of her stomach, reminding her she hadn't eaten for hours. It also reminded her of the lunch date with Albu she had declined. She was about to call the garage when her phone rang, the screen showing her it was Humphries. Before she could say anything, he said, "We've had an interesting development, at last. One of Megan's classmates knew Charlotte Searle."

Fiona frowned, trying to place the girl in the order of events.

"That's one of the girls who went missing. Hang on. Peter will want to hear this. I'll put you on speakerphone."

"Charlotte's parents recently had a problem with their heating system that needed several visits from a plumber to rectify." After a dramatic pause, Humphries said. "The plumber they used was Connor Ambrose. Apparently, Charlotte was at home on study leave at the time, and she developed a massive crush on him. There's nothing to back it up on the telephone records, but she told her friend that they regularly contacted each other after the work was complete."

"Leave it with us," Peter said. "We'll head over there now and see what she has to say."

"How are you two getting on?"

"We might have something," Fiona said. "Ruddle told us he was with Dale Wood, an old friend reminiscing about the good old days, the night Ambrose was killed. While waiting to confirm the alibi with Woods, a garage returned his car after completing bodywork on it. Remember the fatal, hit-and-run accident only a few miles up the road? It could be a complete red herring, but he seemed rattled by the prospect we knew about his car damage."

"What did he say happened?"

"The usual. Anonymous prang while it was parked up. As we're heading off to speak to Charlotte could you ask the garage for the damage report?" Ending the call after reading out the garage contact details, Fiona said, "Interesting that Charlotte took a shine to Ambrose Connor while his own daughter had a crush on his employer. Maybe there is a connection."

"I don't know much about schoolgirl fantasies," Peter admitted. "But alongside Ruddle's interest in young girls, things may be taking an interesting turn."

They were barely out of the car when the front door flew open, and Mrs. Searle, immaculately dressed in a tweed skirt and sweater stepped out. "Can I help you?"

Crossing the short distance to the house, Peter held up his warrant card and asked, "Is Charlotte here?"

Mrs Searle stepped off the doorstep, closing the front door behind her. "Why do you want to see her? I thought we had already explained the situation. As far as we're concerned the mattered is closed."

"I'm sorry to disturb you, only your daughter's name has come up in connection with the abduction of another girl," Fiona said. "Megan Ambrose?"

Mrs Searle firmly crossed her arms. "Never heard of her and Charlotte isn't here."

"Perhaps you could help us. I understand you recently employed a plumber to repair your boiler? Connor Ambrose?"

"Possibly."

"It's his daughter who was abducted."

"My daughter wasn't abducted." Feeling for the door catch behind her, Mrs Searle added, "I can't say as I took any notice of the man. I'm not sure I could even describe him to you." Opening the door behind her, she added, "I suggest you ask him about his daughter and leave mine alone."

"Unfortunately, we can't. He was recently killed in a vehicle fire."

Mrs Searle's hand shot to her mouth as her face paled. "The one that has been on the news, recently?" When Peter nodded, she lowered her hand and turned defensive. "That's terribly sad, but I still can't see how we can help you. He repaired our boiler and left."

"I believe your daughter was in the house when he was working on the boiler and may have spoken to him," Fiona said.

"She would have been in her room, studying for her exams. I can't imagine why she would have done anything more than politely make him a drink, but I'll ask her when she comes home."

Fiona stepped forwards before Mrs Searle could retreat into her house. "Please, if we could have a quick word about his visits."

Unenthusiastically, Mrs Searle opened the door wide and said, "You've ten minutes."

CHAPTER TWENTY-EIGHT

They left Mrs. Searle none the wiser. Charlotte had been sent to stay with family friends in Malta, and they were unable to contact her. Connor Ambrose had made several trips to the home to find a fault in their boiler and then to replace it. On at least two occasions Charlotte had been alone in the house with him, although her mother insisted that she couldn't imagine anything going on between her daughter and a tradesman. She wasn't that type of girl.

Fiona sighed, aware most parents were convinced their child wasn't that type of child, whatever that meant. The grey day had turned to a penetrating, cold darkness. She wasn't sure if they were onto something or the connection between the murders and the missing girls was wishful thinking. Teenage girls having crushes on older men was nothing new. If, however, there was a ring of middle-aged men, feeding these fantasies, it was a completely different ball game. One that might explain the murder of Ambrose and later India as a witness.

Fiona recalled the unused bedroom in Connor's house, with a sickening feeling. She had assumed it had been decorated for his daughter, Megan. What if it wasn't and he was part of the ring? It could be a case of double standards. It was acceptable for him to take advantage of teenage girls, but it was a different matter if men of his age were carrying on with his daughter. Could his reaction have led to a need for him to be eliminated from the group? If Ruddle was part of the same group, she wondered what transgression of the group rules had led to him being beaten up outside the airport.

Bone tired with the smell of rotten food from the well still clinging to her, Fiona closed her eyes and yawned. Peter looked across and said, "You look done in. Are you visiting your dad in hospital tonight?"

"Yeah. I'm on taxi duty again tonight."

"How about we put off visiting Albu until tomorrow? You said yourself, his call was worded more like a lunch date invitation."

"I don't know. What if he holds a vital piece of evidence?"

"I can't imagine it's something that can't wait a few hours."

"Oh, okay. Drop me at home. I'll call him from there and try to persuade him to say what was so important over the phone."

Fiona watched Peter pull out of the driveway and called Albu. Annoyingly the phone told her the number was temporarily unavailable and she should try later. A second attempt gave the same response without any option for leaving a message. What sort of businessman switches off his phone? She wandered to her car and sat on the bonnet while considering going inside for a hot shower and forgetting about Albu. Although tempted, a childhood of training in good manners made the option impossible. If she left now, there would be sufficient time to interview him and be on time to collect her mother. She could always grab something to eat in the hospital canteen. With a loud sigh, she opened the car door and threw her bag on the passenger seat.

She was surprised to find the housing development in darkness. She had expected the workmen to have finished for the day once darkness fell, but had anticipated the showroom would be open for viewings. She could see there was one light on at the rear of the building that doubled as Albu's office. Her sense of politeness jostled with an urge to drive off without stopping. For all she knew, he wasn't waiting solely for her to arrive. Working late could be his usual practice. To save on staff costs, maybe he personally showed prospective buyers around the show homes if they turned up unannounced. Her stomach gave a loud rumble to express its disapproval at her decision to park.

She grabbed the torch from the glove compartment. Outside

the car, the silent darkness was in sharp contrast to the brightly lit streets she had driven through moments before. She guessed those homeowners were relieved when the workmen and their noisy machinery finished for the day.

The access roads to the development were unsurfaced, making it a treacherous trek to the showroom. Even with the torch, the wet, uneven surface was slippery and awkward to negotiate. Keeping as much as possible to defined tracks, the light from Albu's office became obscured by buildings. Turning the corner alongside the first of the new houses, she nearly tripped over a bundle of electric cables and copper wires. As she emerged past the end of the building, she was relieved to be able to see the light again. It gave her something to focus on as she picked her way through the rubble.

Without warning, her torch was wrenched from her hand, and she was slammed up against a wall. The air was knocked from her lungs, and she was struggling to catch her breath. The light from her torch disappeared, plunging her into darkness as a rough hand covered her nose and mouth. Unable to suck in more air, she felt dizzy as she was dragged and pushed around the corner. Her wrists were grabbed, raised above her head and pinned against the wall. She gasped for air as the hand across her face slipped. The zip of her coat was yanked down in one swift movement, and a cold hand was shoved under her sweater.

Already light-headed and panicking, she reminded herself to breathe through her nose, as she realised, she was being attacked by at least two men. Filling her lungs with air, she jammed her knee into the crotch of one of them. He grunted and growled, "Hold her still, will you."

As she twisted and turned, she thought at least she knew one of her attackers was from Northern Ireland. Belfast, maybe. In her coat pocket, she always carried a rape alarm and pepper spray for all the good it would do her with her hands pinned against the wall. She struggled to free them as she rotated her body as far as the grip on her would allow and stamped down hard on one attacker's foot. Her hands were released, and she lashed out at the man in front of her, clawing at his face.

She was shoved back against the wall. The back of her head slammed into the wall. Pinpricks of light danced across her vision. She swung her fists as the attacker grabbled to restrain her arms. She gritted her teeth. This was not going to happen to her. She would fight them to her death, rather than let it happen. She kicked out as hard as she could and felt the satisfying crunch of the attacker's shin.

"Hold her, I said."

Fiona bucked and squirmed, convinced she was winning.

"For the love of God," her attacker muttered.

A hard kick knocked Fiona's legs to one side. She tried to fight gravity as she crumpled to the ground. A dull pain radiated from her hip as it hit the concrete. She kicked out wildly in all directions, while feeling in her pockets for her spray. Knowing how vulnerable she was on the ground, she swung her arm in an arc as she squirted pepper spray in the general direction of her attackers. She clearly hit her mark as she heard one of them stagger backwards.

"Hey!"

Fiona was flooded with the relief at the sound of running feet heading towards them. She shuffled backwards and scrambled to her feet. She could make out the shape of her saviour in the dark. He grabbed one of the men, pushed his arm against his shoulder and yanked his arm backwards with a violent jerk. The man screamed and dropped to his knees, cradling his arm dangling uselessly at his side. Instantly it reminded Fiona of the injury sustained by Ruddle. Pressed against the wall, willing her breathing to return to normal, so she could speak, she watched her rescuer haul the man to his feet and push him into his accomplice who was frantically rubbing his eyes.

"Get out of here! And don't come back."

Fiona desperately wanted to get her words out, but her voice refused to work. Feeling light-headed, she let herself slide down the wall. Watching her attackers disappear into the darkness, she dropped her head between her knees. Once her breathing slowed, she took deep breaths.

"Are you okay? Here, take this."

Fiona felt her torch being shoved into her hands. She rasped, "Why did you let them go?"

"Small men. Not important."

"What?" Fiona flicked on the torch and shone it directly into Albu's face. "Friends of yours?"

Albu reached his hand out. "I help you up."

Fiona considered pushing his hand away. Her adrenaline rush was dissipating, leaving her feeling weak with rubbery legs. She would look stupid if she rejected his help only to discover she couldn't get up unaided. She held out her hand and let him tug her to her feet. "Who were they? Site security?"

"I don't know. I help you to my office," Albu said, placing an arm around her waist.

Fiona stepped back from him. "I can manage, thanks." She felt unsteady on her feet, but there was no way she was accepting more help from him. Shining her torch ahead of her and walking a safe distance from him, she said, "If you had held onto them, they could have been arrested and dealt with."

"I will deal with them."

"You said you didn't know who they were."

"I will find out and deal with them."

"No! You give their names to the police and let us deal with them."

"They are nothing. Small men."

"You said that before. What do you mean by it? They aren't nothing. They are dangerous thugs, and the police will take action against them. If you hadn't arrived when you did..."

"But I did arrive," Albu insisted.

"What about the next time? When they attack another woman when you're not around?"

Albu opened the door to the showroom and flicked on the light. Frowning, he said, "I can punish them?" Ushering Fiona inside, he added, "Make sure it never happens again."

Not wanting another circular conversation, Fiona said, "How

did you know to come out when you did?"

"I see from my window. Hey, stop. There is blood on your head."

Fiona gingerly felt the back of her head. It was tender, and there was blood on her hand when she pulled it away."

Albu pulled out a chair. "Sit. I drive car to door and take to hospital."

"Hospital!" Fiona checked her watch. Damn, she was supposed to be collecting her mother in less than an hour. She spun around, knocking into him. "Sorry, I have to go."

"Sit. You no good to drive."

"I'm fine, and I need to drive to my mother's house."

Albu blocked her exit. "You no good to drive, and mother will be shocked to see you like this. You sit. I drive to hospital."

"You don't understand. I have to go," Fiona replied, trying to dodge past him.

Albu moved to block her path.

She gave him a determined stare. "Excuse me, please."

"I have a plan. You go to bathroom and clean up. I collect my car and follow you until you arrive at mother's house, safe.

Infuriated and reluctant to lead a suspect to a double murder, possibly more, to her parents' home, she started to object.

Albu interrupted her with a maddening smile. "Or I take you to hospital."

Fiona's shoulders slumped in defeat. He was the most exasperating man, but she was running out of time and lacked the energy to argue. "How about you follow me to the police station, and from there a colleague will drive me?"

Albu broke into a wide grin. "If this makes you safe. You sit. I go get car."

CHAPTER TWENTY-NINE

Fiona entered the station the next morning with a pounding headache. A nurse had patched up her head wound while she waited for the end of visiting time. At she had been given pain-killers that were stronger than over-the-counter ones.

Overnight her attack had played on her mind leaving her feeling first angry and then vulnerable. Had Albu lured her to the building site on purpose, to warn her off while at the same time deflect attention from himself by posing as her knight in shining armour? He had wanted to take her out to lunch in an isolated spot. Would that have suited his aims better? Had she been deluding herself by thinking there was a romantic spin to the invite? Her stupid vanity leaving her exposed.

She was the one who decided to meet him at the site in the dark, alone. Why shouldn't she be safe to walk alone in the dark? It wasn't that late. For six months of the year, it was dark by six o'clock.

Even more annoying, she hadn't asked why he had wanted to see her in the first place, and he hadn't volunteered the reason. She chastised herself for worrying about her own fears and inse-curities rather than concentrating on the case. Thinking back, she was convinced the injury Albu inflicted on her attacker was identical to that sustained by Ruddle outside the airport. Albu clearly had some idea who her attackers were and helped them to escape from the scene. Her mind fixated on the most prob-able explanation. He had employed the men in the first place.

When she entered the office, half of the team were already at work. Peter appeared behind her, making her jump.

"Sorry, I didn't mean to scare you," Peter said, stepping back. "I've just spoken to the hospital. Megan is stable, but unconscious. They are more optimistic about her making a full recovery, but couldn't give a time frame for when we can talk to her."

"That's something at least. Have the media picked up on the story, yet?"

Peter shook his head. "Her mother's earlier reluctance to pursue the matter has worked in our favour. There's an officer outside her room, just in case."

Fiona asked, "Anything more about Charlotte?"

"Nope. The connection between Charlotte and Connor Ambrose isn't looking as promising as first hoped."

Nodding towards the whiteboard, she said, "I was surprised not to see the possible connection between the girls up there."

"I was about to add something," Peter said, walking towards the board.

Fiona wandered to her desk and picked up the report on the hit-and-run accident. It concluded the unknown vehicle was a red SUV, but was no more specific. Disappointed, she put it to one side. She had hoped for something that would firmly point the finger at Dale Wood. "Has the garage sent us the repair report on Wood's car?"

Peter replied, over his shoulder, "Humphries requested it, but it hasn't turned up yet. I'll chase it later."

A quick search of her desk revealed that the estate agent hadn't rung through details of the owners of Lilac Cottage, as he had promised. Fiona rang the estate agents only to be left on hold, listening to tinny, classical music. While she waited, intrusive thoughts about her attack resurfaced. She should have been more alert and aware of her surroundings. If she had been, she would have reacted quicker and not let them get the upper hand. She had only herself to blame.

Peter pulled up a chair next to her, placing a coffee on her desk. "You look like you need it."

Fiona hung up the phone and took a grateful sip.

"I think we should widen our investigation," Peter announced. "Devote some time to discovering who else might have wanted to harm Connor Ambrose and his daughter."

"Whatever the motive, the killer must have known about Connor's campervan and where it was stored." Flicking back through statements, Fiona added, "Most of his friends were aware he had one, but only his family knew where he parked it when not in use." Skim-reading the statements reminded her how Megan's mother made it difficult for Megan to visit her father. "What about Megan's stepfather, Owen Wagstaff? He would know about the campervan."

Drumming her fingers on the desk, Fiona's mind started to work in a new direction." She grabbed a pen and wrote down some names. "Wagstaff is an architect, Wood, a lawyer, specialising in property law, Albu is a property developer and Ambrose, a plumber." Written down, the connection seemed obvious. "Should we be looking for a past building project they worked on together?"

Leaning his head to one side as he considered the list, Peter said, "Looking at it that way, the only odd man out is Ruddle."

"Ruddle has to be involved, doesn't he? He was the person India saw at the scene of the fire. The man on the television. Depending on the contents of the damage report on Wood's car, we may be able to prove he was in the area as well around the same time." Fiona rubbed her eyes, forcing herself to concentrate, but her mind continued to run through her attack.

Peter picked up his phone. "I'll contact the garage to ask what is causing the delay."

"Damn." Fiona thumped her hand, causing Peter to jump and put down his phone. "The television footage I watched with Abbie was stripped of advertising breaks. The cheaper advertising slots are filled with low-budget commercials produced by property developers. They often feature the business owners rather than actors. We need the full footage, inclusive of advertisements."

Checking the file for the contact Abbie had used to obtain the original footage, Fiona said, "Albu is the most charismatic and likely to enjoy being in front of a camera."

"You've really got a bee in your bonnet about him, haven't you?"

"Not particularly." Bristling at Peter's suggestion. She found the number she needed and half-turned away from him to make the call.

Peter studied her, before spinning the laptop around to face him and started a search on all the past Highfield Homes developments. Hearing the click of the receiver being replaced, he asked, "Did you get through?"

"Yes. They'll send it over."

Peter swivelled the laptop back to its initial position. "So far I haven't found anything to suggest Wagstaff or Wood had an involvement in any of the Highfield Homes developments."

"That doesn't mean there isn't a connection. The men could have joined forces on a completely different project. They could have been working together to thwart bids from competitors to Highfield Homes. Albu's alibi for the night Ambrose was killed was a planning meeting."

"Reading the minutes of all the local town planning minutes is feasible, but it would be a tedious exercise," Peter said. "How far back do you suggest we should go? It would be far easier to revisit the man. We're supposed to be seeing him anyway. Did you manage to speak to him yesterday?"

Fiona was saved from commenting by her phone ringing.

"Was that the estate agent?" Peter asked when the call ended.

"No. They've found traces of blood in the bedroom of Lilac Cottage. Initial thoughts are they were less than a week old. They will have something more conclusive in a couple of days. I'll ring the agent now."

This time, her call was answered after a few rings. "You said you would call through the details for the owners of Lilac Cottage." Reaching for a pad and checking her pen was working, Fiona said, "Can you give me the details of the owner and last year's booking, now?"

Ending the call, she showed the list to Peter. "These are the people who stayed at Lilac Cottage last year. I've also got the name and address of the owner."

Studying the list, Peter said, "Why don't I make a start on these while you interview the owner of the house? Before I leave, I'll ask Abbie and Rachel to go through all the recent planning meetings."

◆ ◆ ◆

An hour later, Fiona pulled up outside a large, Georgian town-house in a quiet street behind the main town centre of Ampney. The door was opened by a plump woman with her hair neatly tied back in a bun, in the process of removing an apron. When Fiona introduced herself, the woman smiled brightly and said, "I'll go and call him for you. I'm afraid I won't be able to stay as I'm meeting my daughter." She reappeared shortly later and led Fiona through a spacious hallway with arched doorways to other rooms. "Here we are," she announced and opened the door to a compact room lined with bookcases. "Geoffrey, your visitor is here. I'll see you tomorrow," she said, closing the door behind her.

Over the top of a sumptuous, red, two-seater sofa Fiona could see a shock of white hair. As she stepped into the room, he rose to greet her. With a surprisingly firm handshake, the elderly man introduced himself as Geoffrey Olive and invited her to take a seat. Fiona sunk into a matching sofa and started to explain why she was there.

Geoffrey looked over half-moon glasses and waggled his finger. "Refreshments before we start. As Betty has abandoned me, I will do the honours. What would you like?"

"There's no need," Fiona started to say, but sensing Geoffrey would be offended, she said, "A coffee would be lovely." After watching him shuffle out of the room in slippers and a baggy cardigan, Fiona reached forwards to read the title of the book he had been reading. A biography of Winston Churchill. She stood and walked behind the sofa to look at the books that lined the room. They were all non-fiction hardbacks covering a range of subjects. He had told her over the phone, he was a retired professor, but hadn't disclosed the field he was in. Other than the two sofas and coffee table the only other piece of furniture was a piano squashed into the far corner, next to a marble fireplace. The small window looked out onto a pretty garden surrounded by small trees and shrubs. She returned to her seat when she heard the shuffle of feet moving along the corridor.

After patiently waiting for Geoffrey to organise the mugs and snacks, Fiona started to explain why she was visiting. She forced a smile to cover her irritation when Geoffrey told her the estate agents had already contacted him to say his property had possibly been used for criminal purposes.

"So, you understand why we need to know who rented your cottage last week."

"I'm afraid I'm not going to be able to help you," Geoffrey replied sadly. "Whoever was in my cottage was there without my knowledge or permission."

"I understand you occasionally let the cottage privately. Would you be able to provide us with a list of those people?"

Geoffrey pulled a crumpled sheet of paper from his cardigan pocket and handed it over. "I have no detailed records as such. I don't let the cottage for profit. Occasionally, family members or close friends have holidayed there free of charge. These are all the people I can remember who have visited the cottage. You'll find them all as elderly and infirm as I am." With a shrug, he added, "I was told there was no forced entry suggesting the person had visited previously and made a copy of the key. I will now be arranging for all the locks to be changed."

Disappointed she had met another dead end, Fiona smiled and said, "Thank you for taking the time to see me today and provide the names."

"You're not leaving so soon, are you? I was hoping you could explain how a pretty, young woman such as yourself became a detective." With a playful look, he added, "Single as well. How could that be?"

Fiona deflected attention away from herself by saying, "You've a beautiful home. I especially like this room with all the books. What was your speciality?"

"Political history. A very dry subject for some, but I find it fascinating. And relevant. We must learn from the past to prepare for our future." Tapping the book next to him, he continued, "Take Churchill, for instance. A man full of contradictions. Revered by many for defeating Hitler, yet his views were remarkably similar. It could be argued the only difference was his concentration camps were on different continents out of sight of his countrymen."

"Really?"

"You should read up on your history. Things are rarely as straightforward as they seem when dealing with powerful men."

Fiona set her empty mug to one side and stood to leave. "Thank you again."

"I'm only sorry I couldn't be of more help. I hope you don't mind me saying I will follow your investigation with interest. Unexpected things rarely happen when you reach my age."

From her car Fiona telephoned Peter. "Any progress with Lilac Cottage visitors?"

"Nothing so far. Mostly couples from cities seeking a weekend in the countryside who can prove they were at work miles away this week."

"I've a list from the owner of private bookings. I'll check out the few that live in this area before driving back. Anything else come in today?"

"Nothing of any note."

Geoffrey stood behind a curtain watching Fiona drive away. He shuffled along the corridor to his study and unlocked the bottom drawer of his desk to retrieve a phone. The number he called was pre-programmed. "The police have been around. A good job Rob warned us of the antics of our newest member. Deal with him and the investigating officer, DI Fiona Williams, there's a good chap. Maybe they could disappear along with our damaged stock. I understand all our properties have fire insurance. Throw in any other evidence that may be hard to explain."

CHAPTER THIRTY

Other than getting drenched by a heavy downpour of rain, Fiona achieved nothing by checking the three elderly couples nearby who had spent time in Lilac Cottage during the past year. They were retired businessmen, mostly friends of Geoffrey from the local golf club. Once back at the station, she would check the ages of the remaining names on the lists and eliminate them over the telephone. There still might be one that raised alarm bells she reminded herself.

She detoured to her home to change into a dry set of clothes. Pulling into her driveway, she spotted what looked like a bouquet of flowers on her doorstep. Locking her car, she assumed they were probably delivered to the wrong address. There was no one in her life likely to send her flowers.

Pulling the card from the sopping wet arrangement, she nervously looked along the street before unlocking her door. What if Carl, her violent ex had returned? Inside, her eyes darted along the hallway and up the stairs, looking to see if anything had been disturbed. Listening for sounds of movement, she rushed to the kitchen to check the back door hadn't been forced open. A shake of the handle confirmed it was locked. She left the bouquet on the kitchen table and returned to the front door to attach the safety chain.

She racked her brain, trying to remember if she had closed the living room door when she had left that morning. It wasn't something she usually did. With her heart beating and mobile in her hand, ready to call for help, she slowly opened the door and stepped inside. It looked exactly as she had left it. She neatly folded the throw she liked to snuggle under at night and picked up the paperback she had started but abandoned reading the week before and returned it to the small corner bookshelf.

Her heart was still pounding in her chest as she made her way upstairs to check the bedrooms. Satisfied, no one was lurking under the beds, or behind the shower curtain, her breathing started to return to normal as she made her way back to the kitchen. She skirted nervously around the table to look out over the empty back garden. Eyeing the bouquet suspiciously, she made herself a mug of hot chocolate. She took a sip leaning against the counter, staring at the puddle of water that had formed on the table under the flowers. Taking another sip, she wondered if she was the only woman in the world who reacted to a flower delivery in such a paranoid way. It wasn't as if the flowers could hurt her. She took another sip reminding herself that the sender could.

Leaving her mug on the counter, she tentatively stepped toward the table and picked up the small envelope with her name written across the front. She teased it open and scrutinised the small card inside. White with pre-printed pink roses in the top right-hand corner, it contained a solitary letter, S. The only S that came to mind was Stefan Albu. He had flirted with her and asked her out for an expensive meal. She sat down heavily on a kitchen chair. If that explained the who, it did nothing to explain how on earth he knew her home address.

She shivered as an onslaught of rain was thrown against the kitchen window. Her heart leapt as the back door rattled from a powerful gust of wind. Her damp clothes added to the chill running down her spine. She gave the bouquet a last look before heading upstairs to change. The flowers would soon wither and brown if she didn't move them to a vase. She would leave them rotting in their cellophane wrapper in case they were evidence. Evidence of what she was still to determine. Climbing the stairs, she called Highfield Homes to be told Albu was away from the site and was not due to return until late afternoon.

Fiona dashed across the station car park at the same time as Humphries. Opening the door for her, he asked, "Any joy with the cottage owner?"

Fiona shook her head. "Not a lot. How did you know that's where I've been?"

"Peter said. A couple of labourers were badly assaulted last night. As one of them had worked for Highfield Homes in the past, Peter thought they were worth seeing."

"How did it go?"

"They're drifters doing odd jobs here and there. The one with possible connections to Highfield said he only worked a couple of days cash in hand to cover for a mate."

Fiona swallowed. Could these be the two men who attacked her? She should have mentioned something first thing this morning at the earliest. "Did they know who attacked them?"

"They said it was due to a misunderstanding over a girl and they don't want to press charges."

"Did they have strong Northern Irish accents?"

"Yes, they did. Hard to understand at times. Why? Do you know them?"

Fiona instinctively knew they were her attackers and Albu had kept his word. She should have called in her assault straight away. She couldn't even explain to herself why she hadn't. At first, she had been in shock and didn't want to make the call, in front of Albu. Then she was rushing to pick her mother up on time. It would have distressed her mother if she had made the call from the car. Earlier in the station, her mind had been elsewhere. This was probably her last chance to say anything. "No, I've just heard the accent when I've been out on site."

Humphries gave her a quizzical look, but let the matter drop as they walked along the corridor. Peter waved them over while he completed a telephone call. Beaming, he said, "Good news. Megan Ambrose is off the critical list."

"How soon can we see her?" Fiona asked.

"Not yet, was the only answer I could obtain as she remains

heavily sedated. On the plus side, we've managed to keep her survival out of the newspapers, and once she does come around, she can tell us everything," Peter replied.

"That's great news, but the trauma she's been through could cause memory loss. Plus, we don't know how much she did know about her father's death," Fiona said.

Are we satisfied the same person who assaulted Megan killed her father?" Humphries asked.

"I would say so. The two things have to be connected, don't they?" Fiona asked as she was overcome with a moment of doubt. Pushing the thoughts aside, she said, "The campervan fire was on an isolated stretch of road. Lilac Cottage where we found Megan is the only house in the area."

"How close is it?" Humphries asked.

"On foot, across the fields, the distance is about half a mile. There is no direct road link, so by car, it's more like three miles," Fiona replied.

"Could they both have been held at Lilac Cottage?" Humphries asked.

"We're waiting to hear more from forensics about that possibility," Peter said.

"Connor's work van was found where he stored his campervan. The driver's seat had been adjusted for a shorter driver. We've been working on the assumption his killer overpowered him elsewhere and then used his van to transport him to the campervan."

"The work van could have been driven to the farm later to distract our attention away from the cottage," Peter said.

"Maybe," Fiona said, pulling up google maps on her phone. While examining the screen, she said, "We think India was killed because she saw Ruddle at the scene of the fire. The hit-and run-accident was only a short distance away. The paint found at that scene is a possible match to a vehicle driven by Ruddle's friend, Dale Wood." Fiona turned her phone around to show Peter and Humphries. Pointing, she said, "If they were heading back to the cottage, they should have taken this single-track lane a few hundred yards before."

"They could have missed the turning?" Humphries suggested.

"Or they were heading back to return the work van," Peter said. "Possibly speeding and that's when they hit the moped. I don't believe for a minute Wood's car was damaged in a car park as he claims." Turning to Humphries, he asked, "How did it go with the assault?"

"Argument over a girlfriend. Neither of them wants to press charges." Humphries replied.

Fiona opened her mouth to say something, but remained silent.

"Ruddle is still in hospital as by chance they picked up he is diabetic. That's what the tests he mentioned related to. He is due to be discharged from hospital tomorrow," Peter said to Humphries. "It would be good to have some idea why Ruddle and Wood would want to kill Ambrose and his daughter by then."

As Humphries left, Dewhurst entered. "Any progress on the murders? I've a press conference later today."

Fiona looked at Peter, before saying, "We've a few ideas, but nothing concrete."

"I read through the file last night and had a thought that I want you two to check out," Dewhurst said. "Have you spoken to Megan's teachers?"

"I spoke to her form teacher," Peter said.

"How about her computer science teacher? What if she's a computer genius and the brains behind the Ruddle app?"

"There's nothing to suggest that could be the case," Peter said.

"But you haven't checked?"

"We'll do so now, Sir," Fiona said.

"Okay. Let me know how you get on and bring me something more concrete as soon as you can."

CHAPTER THIRTY-ONE

Fiona watched Dewhurst leave. His interest in the case seemed excessive. Or was it protecting Albu that was so important to him? Or could it simply be he missed being actively involved in investigations? Talking through ideas, seeking new ways of putting the pieces of the puzzle together in the hope it would lead to a breakthrough was her favourite part of the job. Even if those fragmented pieces were often the crumbled remains of destroyed lives. Would that explain his request? If he had read the report thoroughly, he would have seen her interview with Ruddle's partner, Robert Murray, so why the delaying tactic of asking them to contact the school?

Peter muttered beside her. "Condescending idiot."

"Sorry, what?"

"His attitude stinks, suggesting we overlooked something so basic. I already know Megan was far from a model student, and you've spoken to the technical brains behind the Riddle app." Shaking his head, Peter asked, "Are we agreed we've hit a dead end with the list of people who have recently stayed at Lilac Cottage?"

"There's still a few we haven't managed to contact."

"I would like to have one last talk to Lisa, the other girl who went missing. We can concentrate on tracking down the other visitors afterwards. Did you find out what Albu wanted?"

"Not yet." To change the subject, Fiona quickly said, "If Charlotte's mother is anything to go by, Lisa and her parents aren't going to be keen to speak to us."

"Lisa's mother is far easier to deal with."

Before we go, I want to talk with Megan's computer teacher." Fiona ignored the face Peter was making. "Dewhurst is likely to ask later if we checked. I would prefer to be able to give him an honest reply."

"Whatever," Peter said, moving towards the door. "Meet me downstairs once you've made the call."

As he left, Abbie walked in, followed by Rachel. Another unwelcome reminder she seemed to be rubbing everyone up the wrong way recently. To be fair, if someone had thrown her out of the car like she did, she wouldn't be so ready to accept an apology. She painted on her brightest smile, covering her recurring thoughts about applying for a transfer and starting over anew somewhere else, and said, "Hi. How are you getting on with the planning meetings?"

Rachel groaned. "Slowly. Is there anything else you would like us to do?" Something more interesting than planning meetings, please."

"There is something. Could you pull up a list of the holiday homes in the area? I'm thinking of cottages in isolated areas and whether any are currently rented out. And a check on recent past bookings."

"Sure. We'll make a start on it, now," Rachel replied, her mood brightening.

"What are we looking for?" Abbie asked.

"I'm not entirely sure," Fiona said, feeling flustered. Typical of Abbie to pick up on her half-formed thoughts. "Something out of the ordinary. Not young families or pensioners. Regular bookings by the same person or via a company, maybe."

CHAPTER THIRTY-TWO

In the car, Peter smirked when Fiona confirmed Megan was not a computer genius. "I could have told you that." Handing his phone to Fiona, he said, "Slight change of plan. Take a look at the last e-mail."

Fiona looked up from the screen, as Peter started the car. "The damage to Wood's car is consistent with a collision with a motorcyclist."

"Correct," Peter replied. "Which is why we're going to have another chat with him before meeting Lisa."

Inside Wood's office, when Peter showed him the accident report, his reaction was one of relief. Mopping his brow, he said, "In a way, I'm pleased you have found out. I've been a nervous wreck these last few days and I was thinking of handing myself in, anyway."

Peter exchanged a surprised glance with Fiona, before saying, "Would you like to explain what happened?"

Wood nodded. "Very much so. Keeping it to myself has been killing me. I've driven that road a hundred times at night and never seen another vehicle. The lad came from nowhere. I had no chance of avoiding him." Wood's Adam's apple bobbed up and down as he swallowed. "I want you to know, there's no way I would have left the scene if he had been alive. When I realised that he was dead, I panicked and drove home."

"What happened before the accident? Why were you on that stretch of road in the first place?"

"I was driving home after a few drinks in the Holford Arms. I wasn't drunk, but technically I may have been over the limit to drive."

"Do you remember passing a camper van a few miles before the collision?"

Wood's forehead crumpled in thought. Slowly he said, "Possibly. Parked on the side of the road. Was that the one that caught fire?"

"It would seem likely. Did you see anyone near the van?"

"No, but then I wasn't looking. It was just a van parked up."

Peter rubbed his hand across his chin. "Afterwards, instead of coming forwards you contacted your friend, John Ruddle, to give you an alibi. Is that right?"

"No," Wood replied, furiously shaking his head so his jowls wobbled. "I was ready to come forwards and admit what I had done. It was John who contacted me a few days later. When he said he saw what happened, I thought he was going to blackmail me. Instead, he offered to provide me with an alibi, if I would do the same for him. I wasn't comfortable with the situation from the start, but he persuaded me to go along with his plan. I haven't had a proper night's sleep since. The whole thing is giving me ulcers. I'm genuinely pleased it's all out in the open. What happens now?"

Peter leaned back in his chair considering Wood. "I'm confused by the timing. The campervan was parked at the side of the road when you passed?"

"I think so. The whole evening is a blur, to be honest."

"Were there any other vehicles in the area? Either near the campervan or travelling on the road?"

Woods scrunched his face in thought and closed his eyes. "There might have been. Behind the campervan, maybe." Opening his eyes, he added, "Sorry, I can't be sure. I wasn't taking much notice. I've driven that road so many times I almost do it on autopilot. Then, bang. Without warning the moped appeared from nowhere."

"What happened after the collision?"

"I stayed in the car for a while. In shock, I guess. I can't tell you how long for. A loud noise, like an explosion brought me back to my senses and I walked over to check the motorcyclist." Wood gulped and covered his face with his hands. "It was a young lad. He couldn't have been much more than a teenager."

Peter prompted him to continue.

"Yes. Of course, sorry," Wood said, removing his hands from his face. "Once I was sure there was nothing I could do, I returned to my car to call the police. I sat there a long while. I lost track of the time as my mind went blank. Or maybe I was waiting for someone to come along and take the decision out of my hands. I decided to make the call. I was going to tell the police everything. I heard a car engine as I waited for my call to be answered. Not wanting to be seen, I ended the call and I slipped down in the seat. The vehicle slowed right down and then sped away. I assume it was John and that was when saw me. We never were friends at school, you know."

"Did you see the vehicle?"

"Only from the back as it sped away. It was a van. It was too far away for me to tell you the colour."

"And then?" Peter prompted again.

"The boy was dead. I felt numb and disorientated. The next think I remember is driving up to my front door. As I had left the scene, it was too late to call the police to explain." Wood looked up, his face pale. "I knew it was wrong, but I tried to forget about it. And then John contacted me. What will happen, now?"

Peter looked at the floor and back up at Wood, before saying, "We need to be somewhere else. If you drive yourself to Birkbury Station and hand yourself in, we won't log this visit. If you don't, we will return to arrest you."

CHAPTER THIRTY-THREE

When Peter and Fiona arrived at the school gates, Lisa was waiting for them sitting on a wall, smoking a cigarette. She wore her school blazer with the collar up and earbuds dangling from the iPod inside the breast pocket behind the school emblem. The oversized tie knot hung low, and she wore more makeup than Fiona would wear for an evening out. Out of school uniform, she could easily pass for much older.

Lisa stubbed out her cigarette when they approached. She flicked a wary eye over Fiona before dismissing her and giving Peter a smile. "It's cold standing here. Are you going to take me somewhere nice and warm? There's a pub up the road."

"There's also a café on the high street. We'll go there," Peter said, opening the rear passenger door of the car.

Lisa jumped down from the wall and hefted her school bag over her shoulders. Slinging it across the car seat before climbing in, she said, "I can get served in all the pubs."

From the front seat, Peter looked at her through the rear-view mirror. "I don't doubt it, but the café is more appropriate. And put your seat belt on."

Fiona caught a twinkle in Peter's eye as he started the car. She settled back, happy to let him take the lead as he'd had prior contact with the girls. Lisa was a pretty girl with an athletic figure, and it wasn't hard to see why males would find her attractive.

"A hot chocolate is better than nothing, I guess. Any chance of a cake to go with it?"

Tucked away in a quiet corner of the cafe, they waited for her to devour a chocolate chip muffin.

"Now you're finished, are you ready to answer our questions?" Peter asked.

Lisa gave him a sullen look before wrapping her hands around her mug and raising it to her lips.

"What did you and Charlotte do the week you went missing?"

Replacing the mug on the table, Lisa gave him a defiant look and said, "I can't tell you anything more than last time. Or the time before that." With a bored expression, she picked up her bag from the floor and said, "I thought you were going to be asking something new. If you're not, I may as well get going."

"Sit down. There is something new." Once Lisa had re-settled herself, Peter asked, "How do you know Megan Ambrose?"

Keeping quiet and closely watching Lisa's reactions, Fiona caught a look of shock and fear that flitted across her expression, before she hid her face behind her mug. There was a slight tremor in her hand when she slowly lowered it to the table and busied herself lining it up square on the coaster. Looking down, she said, "Who?"

"Your friend, Megan Ambrose," Peter said.

"I've never heard of her. What do you want her for, anyway? Shoplifting or something more interesting?" She snatched up the box containing various sugars and sweeteners. "Don't give you much choice, do they?" she said, shaking a white sugar sachet.

"Stop messing about Lisa, this is serious. Megan disappeared too, only she wasn't as lucky as you and Charlotte. She's been hurt."

"Hurt? How hurt? And what has it got to do with me?"

"Badly hurt," Peter said. "Tell me how you and Charlotte really met and why you went into hiding in Plymouth."

Crunching the sugar sachet between her thumb and the tabletop, Lisa asked, "How badly hurt?"

"Badly. Why did you bolt to Plymouth? Was there anyone else

with you?"

Lisa rubbed her nose before grabbing a handful of the sugar sachets. "I think I'll take these for later."

"Can you answer the question."

"Why should I? You haven't answered mine." Lisa slumped back in her chair with a heavy sigh and said, "I met Charlotte in the train station. We hit it off immediately and decided to take a break in Plymouth. I've told you this already, so why do you keep asking?"

"Because I don't believe you," Peter said.

"It's the truth. Can I go home now?"

Fiona decided it was time to intervene. Leaning forward, she asked, "Are you scared of something?"

"I'm not scared of anything."

"If you were threatened, we can protect you. And your family," Fiona said, trying to make eye contact with Lisa.

Looking down at the tabletop, Lisa said, "I wasn't threatened. Why aren't you asking Charlotte these questions? Why do you keep bothering me?"

"We will be speaking to Charlotte when she returns and Megan if she makes it," Fiona replied.

"Returns from where? Where's Charlotte and what do you mean by if Megan makes it?"

"She suffered a serious assault and was left to die." Fiona left time for the statement to sink in before adding, "It was only by luck we found her. We still don't know if it was in time. Would you like me to pass on a message from you if she recovers?"

Lisa opened her mouth as if to say something, then shut it and looked away. "I told you. I don't know her."

Sensing Lisa was weakening, Fiona said, "If she does recover and says something different, you could be in trouble. If you have anything to say, now would be the time. Nobody needs to know you spoke to us. We can keep your identity a secret. Provide you with protection. We really need your help... Please ... Why did you run to Plymouth and who were you with? I think you would feel a lot better if you told us."

Lisa nervously shifted in her seat, looking around the room, her face racked with indecision and possibly fear. In a quiet voice, she said, "If I said something, could it be off the record? No statements or anything like that?"

Instinct told Fiona, this was the best and possibly their only chance to get some information from Lisa. Afterwards, she would clam up and say nothing. She thought about India Williamson with regret. If only she had pushed harder with her. "If you could give us something that we could check out, then we wouldn't have to say it was you who pointed us in the right direction."

"Like an anonymous tip-off?"

"Maybe. Or maybe a lucky break we worked out by ourselves."

"Are you sure we can't go to the pub?"

"Here is fine," Fiona said. "What can you tell us?"

Lisa looked furtively around and said, "And no one will know I spoke to you?"

"We won't release your name to anyone. Peter here is desperate to take the credit."

"And Megan? Is she somewhere safe?"

"Yes."

Once Lisa started, her words came tumbling out in a rush to be heard. "Okay. I met Charlotte and Megan at a photo shoot. We were taken to a big, old, posh house. Me and Charlotte stuck to headshots, but we think Megan agreed to something more. While we were waiting, we took a sneaky look around, and Charlotte said she saw a dead girl. Then she panicked when she realised that she had dropped her false ID. She called Megan's dad, and he said he would sort it. Charlotte was all shaken up and didn't want to go home, so Connor said we could stay a few days in his campervan. I think she thought he would be stopping with us. Only, he didn't. It got claustrophobic, and we decided to go to Plymouth. Next, we hear Connor has been fried alive in the van, and Megan is with Bob. He said if we said anything, he would hurt Megan. I guess he did anyway, but now you say she's safe."

"Whoa! Slow down," Fiona said, raising her hands. "Can we go through everything a bit at a time?"

Lisa nodded.

"Who organised the photo shoot, and how did you hear about it?"

"Bob King. He contacted me after listening to my songs online. He said he was a freelance promotor and had all the right contacts."

"Can you describe him?" Fiona asked, assuming the description would match Ruddle.

"Blond and bronzed. A bit of a Bondi Beach, surfer-boy thing going on. Amazing green eyes. On the short side. Old, about thirty or even forty, maybe, trying to look younger."

Fiona exchanged a look with Peter, who pulled a no-idea-who-that-could-be face, before asking, "Would you recognise him again?"

"I reckon so, although Charlotte said it wasn't his real hair. He could have been bald."

Fiona pulled up a picture of Ruddle and showed it to Lisa. "Could this be him wearing a wig?"

"Bob didn't wear glasses."

"Imagine him without the glasses and blond hair."

"It could be. I don't know, though. I'm not sure."

Peter said. "We can have someone play about with the image. Change the hair colour and remove the glasses, and you can look at it again."

Lisa grabbed the photograph and studied it. Handing it back to Fiona, she said, "No. That's not him."

Confused, Fiona said, "Would you be happy to work with someone to create an image of this man, Bob?"

"Sure. He's definitely not the man in your photograph."

"What can you tell us about the house? Did it have a name, and where was it?" Fiona asked, wondering who the blond, tanned man could be. Only the age was vaguely correct for any of their suspects.

"I don't know. Bob said it belonged to a famous star who

valued his privacy. We were blindfolded in the car. He did say something about the Amethyst. I'm not sure if he meant the house or something else."

"Roughly how long were you in the car?"

"I'm not good with time. More than half an hour, but less than an hour, I think."

"You said you had a look around the house. What was it like?" Fiona asked.

"Really old and posh. Like those Jane Austen programmes. Not as big as Downton Abbey, but that kind of place."

"When you went upstairs, how many bedrooms were there?"

Lisa started to count in her head. Eight, I think. But I can't say if they were bedrooms. The doors were all locked. We only saw inside one of them."

"And was that the only floor or were there more stairs?"

"All I saw was that great long corridor with locked doors. I didn't see any more stairs."

"Were you able to look out through any windows?" Fiona asked. "Was it in an isolated spot, or could you see other houses? A church spire, maybe?"

"It was in the middle of nowhere, as far as I could tell. There were some hills and woods in the distance."

"Do you remember if there was a private driveway to the house?"

"I think so."

Fiona turned to Peter. "Can you get the descriptions of Bob and the house to Abbie and Rachel? They are looking at holiday lets in the area. Tell her to widen the search to private houses if she doesn't find anything to match the description."

Turning back to Lisa, Fiona said, "You're doing really well. How did Charlotte describe seeing the dead girl?"

"She didn't really. She only saw an arm."

"Go back again. Where did she see this arm?"

"We were looking about upstairs when we heard voices. We hid behind one of those big, old clocks. Charlotte kept poking her head around the side. She said she saw two men carry a body, wrapped up in something from one of the rooms and take it down the stairs."

"Did she describe the men?"

Lisa shook her head.

"What happened next?"

"We decided not to say anything and went back and sat on the chairs to wait for Megan's shoot to finish. Bob drove us back to town. That's when Charlotte realised her ID was missing."

"Was Megan with you?"

"No, she was still in the car. We were dropped off first."

"Then what happened?"

"Charlotte called Connor, and he came to collect us. I'm not sure what Charlotte said to him, but he took us to his camper-van. That was on a stinking farm somewhere. Once we ate the food Connor left us, Charlotte suggested we wait in her parents' place in Plymouth, instead."

"Why didn't you say anything before?"

"Charlotte told me not to. When she heard about Connor, she tried to contact Megan. Only Bob answered her phone. He said if we breathed a word, he would kill Megan. But you said she's safe now, and you won't tell anyone I've said anything."

"We'll take you home and arrange for officers to keep a discrete watch. We will speak to your mother. It would be best if you stayed at home as much as possible over the next few days. We'll be contacting Charlotte's parents as well."

"You said you wouldn't tell," Lisa whined.

"It's for your own safety. The only people who will know anything about our conversation are your mother and Charlotte's family."

CHAPTER THIRTY-FOUR

They dropped Lisa home and explained the situation to her mother, which caused a blazing row between mother and daughter. Fiona whispered to Peter, "Time to make a quick exit?" Peter nodded, before interrupting the argument to say they were leaving. He confirmed they would be arranging some protection before withdrawing from the firing line.

Outside, Fiona said, "I expect we'll have a similar reaction at Charlotte's home."

"I'm going to update Dewhurst and ask him to authorise the protection. Could you ask Humphries to visit Charlotte's parents?"

"Wouldn't it be better if we went?"

"Possibly. But once we've requested protection for the girls, we're heading to the Amethyst."

"You know where it is? Why didn't you say?"

"I'm not sure it is the same place that Lisa mentioned. It's not even a house. There's a club in Birstall called Amethyst."

"Really? I've never heard of it?"

"Not surprising. It keeps itself under the radar. I was taken there once by an old friend with more money than sense. My eyes watered at the prices, so don't go ordering any cocktails."

"The description of this Bob character Lisa gave puts a spanner in the works. I thought we were getting somewhere when Wood put Ruddle at the scene at the right time," Fiona said.

"It was you that said there were two people involved. When

you speak to Humphries ask him to check the description against everyone we've spoken to so far," Peter replied.

Half an hour later they parked in a small, courtyard car park behind the main high street. Peter led the way through a covered walkway. They passed a series of artisan stalls before he turned up a narrow, cobbled side street, without pavements. Fiona hoped it was closed to traffic as if a car appeared, they would be forced to dive into a doorway. Peter slowed and checked the doorways as they walked along, coming to a stop outside a nondescript, white, wooden door.

"Are you sure? This looks like a private house," Fiona said, looking up at the narrow three-storey townhouse.

Peter pointed to a small brass plaque on the outside wall, before rattling the doorknob. "Locked."

Fiona stepped back and said, "There's a light on in an upstairs window."

Peter banged the brass knocker three times and stood back to wait.

The door creaked open, and an elderly man in a dinner suit looked out at them. "Can I help you? You look lost."

"No, I think we're at the right place. Can we come in?" Peter asked.

"Do you have a membership card?"

"Not exactly," Peter said, holding out his warrant card.

"I'm afraid this establishment is members only." With a polite smile, the doorman started to close the door.

Peter shot out a hand to stop the door from closing.

With an affronted look, the doorman said, "I'm dreadfully sorry Sir, but without membership or an appointment with a member you cannot enter. And you have neither."

A muffled voice came from within. "Is there a problem, Alfred?"

Fiona leaned in to listen, sure she had heard the voice somewhere before.

With a look of disdain, Alfred turned his head and said, "Two police officers are asking to enter."

"Do they have warrants?"

Peter said in a loud voice, "That could be arranged."

"Show them to the bar, Alfred, rather than doing a scene on the doorstep. I'll see if I can uncover someone to conversation with them."

The awkward use of language jogged Fiona's recollection of the voice. "Stefan! Stefan Albu?"

The door was pulled back, and Stefan appeared in the doorway. "Ah! The elusive and beautiful detective." Addressing Peter, he added, "With her considerable associate."

"We've been trying to reach you," Peter said, while Fiona looked away.

"And you have cleverly located me," Albu said jovially. "Alfred is correct. The rules do not allow me to bring in guests without a reservation. We may take a stroll if that would suit?"

"We're here to speak to the club owners," Peter said. "Is there somewhere inside we can wait while you find someone to speak to us."

Albu turned to Alfred, "I think today we could make an exception?"

Alfred shook his head and walked away without commenting.

"Shadow me, and I will try my best." As they walked through the door, Albu continued, "I am unable to say who I will find. At this time of the day, maybe no one. I was here for lunch and was about to leave when I hear commotion at the door."

They entered a room of leather armchairs clustered around small tables. Stefan walked to a small, corner bar, where a young man was polishing glasses. He placed a £50 note on the bar, saying, "Please provide my friends with refreshments."

Once settled in the corner of the room, Peter said, "Well, this is pleasant. You don't get this in my local boozer. There again, you don't get £50 notes either."

"So, what is this place? A private club for businessmen?" Fiona asked.

Counting the conditions on his fingers, Peter said, "I think it's open to anyone who knows it exists, has more money than sense and of course has the all-important contacts."

Leaning forward over the coffee cups, Fiona said, "Interesting Albu being here." Looking around, she added, "It's rather cliché, don't you think, if it turns out these are the people running a sleazy sex operation?"

"Sickening more like. Can I suggest you don't make a direct accusation in here? Cliché, like you say, but I have the impression their security may be discrete but very much present. I would like to leave here alive."

"Great. It's a bit late to be saying that now."

"It didn't seem so clandestine when I came before."

"So, what are we going to say?" Fiona asked quietly. "I don't fancy being buried in concrete."

"We could say the name cropped up in our questioning of Ruddle."

Fiona glanced around the room, taking in the understated elegance and seductive lighting. "This is the kind of place he might aspire to, but I'm not sure he has any of the requirements for entry."

"The rich and powerful need gophers to handle the dirty work. It is possible he's small fry. It could be, they regret letting him have a glimpse of their playground."

"You're saying the assault at the airport may have been a punishment for breaking their rules in some way?"

"Could be. All we know for sure is that he was in the vicinity of the vehicle fire and has a false alibi for the evening India was strangled. Either way, I think we'll be on safer ground if we say we're here as we're investigating him, personally. I won't even hint we think he might be a part of something bigger. That at least should mean we walk out of here unscathed. We'll need a lot more evidence before we start making any direct accusations against a place like this."

"That works for me." After taking a sip of coffee, Fiona said, "If we have stumbled in on an elite organisation, once we've briefed Dewhurst the case will be transferred. I would like to have something watertight on Ruddle before that happens. I don't want his responsibility for the deaths of Connor and India to be lost in the bigger picture. The same goes for Stefan Albu. What do you think he's doing here? He must be a part of it."

Peter checked his watch. "Right now, I'm more concerned about what is taking him so long. I have a bad feeling about this place. How about we leave now? We've already agreed we aren't in a position to question anyone. In fact, we could be jeopardising a larger operation, just by being here."

"Agreed," Fiona said. "We need to make our hasty retreat look casual, though. We don't want them thinking we're running away."

In the corridor, Fiona let out a gasp as Albu appeared from the shadows in front of them, blocking their exit.

"Leaving so soon? I thought you wanted to parley with some urgency."

"We've taken a call asking us to attend another scene. We'll come back another time," Peter said.

"With an appointment," Fiona added.

Albu continued to block their path, rubbing his chin as he looked them over. His cold, blue eyes returned to Fiona. "You no longer wish to talk to me, either?"

"We do, but we are in a hurry to get to this call," Fiona replied.

"Ah, I see. A more pressing concern. This is a great shame. Although there is no one here who could talk with you, I was given permission to give you a guided tour of the building. This offer may not be available another time. Such a pity you should miss the opportunity. It will not take long."

Peter stepped forward. "It's a kind offer, but please step aside. We are needed elsewhere."

Peter turned at the sound of Fiona's phone ringing.

"Perhaps you should answer that? Maybe, you are not needed, after all," Albu said, looking hopeful.

Eyeing him suspiciously, Fiona retrieved the phone from her pocket and slowly raised it to her ear. "When is he due to be discharged? ... We're on our way." Putting the phone away, she said, "Move out of our way""

Albu gave her a quizzical look and said, "Where is it you need to be?"

"Now! I won't ask again."

Albu bowed his head and stepped aside as Fiona and Peter brushed past him.

Outside, Peter said, "Who was that on the phone?"

"The hospital rang the station to say Ruddle is due to be discharged shortly, and he has a car waiting for him in the hospital car park."

"And we're speeding our way up there on nothing more than that?"

"It got us out of a difficult situation, and I don't have anything more pressing to do. Do you?"

"No, but do you know who called from the hospital? The timing of the call is bothering me. Albu was stalling us. Before you took that call, he gave no indication he was going to move out of the way."

"I'll call Humphries from the car when we have a clearer idea where Ruddle is heading."

CHAPTER THIRTY-FIVE

As predicted, a black Mercedes with tinted windows was waiting for Ruddle in the hospital car park. Fiona ran a check on the plates to discover they belonged to a recently stolen Fiat Panda. Satisfied Humphries was on standby to arrange for a back-up team once they arrived at their destination, they settled back for the long drive assuming they would be returning to their own area. At Swindon, they exchanged worried looks when the Mercedes pulled off the motorway several junctions earlier than they anticipated.

"Do you know this area?"

"Vaguely. Depending on where they go, we could end up on the edge of our area," Fiona replied. "You concentrate on driving, I'll update Humphries. If we keep an eye on the road signs, he can explain the situation to the local station."

"What did Humphries say?" Peter asked, as soon as Fiona ended the call.

"He'll see what he can do. Also, when he ran a check on the description Lisa gave, he discovered Bob King was involved in a similar case in Manchester a couple of years ago. Two girls went for a photo shoot session. One girl was dropped home safely the other hasn't been seen since. Manchester is sending a file over, but they hit a dead end. Bob King doesn't exist, and they found no one matching the description the surviving girl gave."

"Interesting. We need to work out who this Bob King really is."

"Humphries is checking whether Ruddle spent any time in Manchester," Fiona replied.

They followed the Mercedes along a dual carriageway a few

cars back, until the car pulled off onto a busy road which ran parallel to the motorway heading in the general direction of Snowshill. Peter took his time at the roundabouts they crossed, allowing new cars to overtake so they weren't directly behind. After several miles most of the cars branched off onto a dual carriageway, leaving only one car between them and the Mercedes. The road twisted through narrow country lanes until the car separating them turned into a private driveway. Peter dropped his speed. "Any closer, and there's no way we can pretend he doesn't know he's being followed. I don't know about you, but I've got a bad feeling about this. Do you think we're being set up?"

"I wish I knew. I think it could be Ruddle who is being set up as someone isn't happy that he has attracted our attention."

"The attack in the airport wasn't sufficient?"

"They were interrupted," Fiona replied, her mind instantly spinning to her encounter outside Highfield Homes.

"Although we can put Ruddle at the scene of the fire, it concerns me that despite extensive searches we've found nothing to link him to Connor let alone a reason to kill him."

"If he had an innocent reason for being at the scene why didn't he do anything to help? Or at least come forward after the event?" Fiona asked.

"Do you think it's possible he only witnessed what happened and has been threatened not to say anything?"

"It's a possibility," Fiona said. "Except how do you explain him asking Wood for an alibi for the death of India? She went out to meet someone after watching his segment on the shopping channel."

"I agree, that's harder to explain. Maybe India was killed by the same person who attacked Ruddle."

In a quiet voice, Fiona said, "I think it was Stefan Albu who attacked him."

"How have you come to that conclusion?"

"I should have said something before. I went out to speak to Albu by myself. I was attached walking through the building site."

"What! When was this? Were you hurt?"

"A few days back. The thing is, Albu knew I was on my way. He appeared halfway through the attack when I was getting the upper hand. He let the men escape, but not before giving one of them a similar injury to the one Ruddle sustained to his shoulder."

"Why the hell didn't you say anything before? I'm even more unhappy about this now. I'm convinced Albu was stalling us back at the club. Probably setting this little charade up."

"Possibly, but what option do we have other than to check out the tipoff?" Turning her attention to the road, Fiona said, "I guess he just wanted to take the scenic route. I know where we are now. If he carries on in the same direction, we'll come out near the back road to Brierly. Maybe the motorway driving was making him drowsy."

"Maybe," Peter replied, unconvinced.

Fiona picked up her phone, saying, "I'm ringing Humphries." When he answered, she gave an update on where they were. Before ending the call, she said, "Could you also check if Stefan Albu would have been in Manchester a couple of years ago?"

Up ahead the Mercedes indicated to turn right onto an unmarked road. Peter drove past as Fiona craned her neck to see the Mercedes disappear along a single-track lane. "It was a road, not a private driveway. Turn around. We need to follow them a little longer if we want to know where he is heading."

Peter took his time completing a three-point turn in the narrow lane. The fading light dimmed as they drove through a thick avenue of trees, the branches touching above their heads. After a short distance, the road split in two, with nothing to indicate which fork the Mercedes had taken. Peter stopped the car and stepped out. "I say we accept we've lost them. On the way back you can explain why you went out to visit Albu when we decided to leave it until the next day. I thought you were having problems pinning him down to a new time."

Fiona joined him outside the car, her eyes peering into the

gloom in the hope of seeing the taillights of the Mercedes. "I'll call the station and ask what properties are out here. I can't imagine there are many."

Before she could reach for her phone, they were surrounded by the thundering of quad bike engines. She turned to clamber inside the car and ran into a solid chest of muscle. Pulling back, she caught sight of Peter being wrestled to the ground. She was spun in a circle. A rough hand pulled her mobile from her pocket and bent her arm behind her back so far, she feared her shoulder was going to pop out of joint. She was expertly bound and gagged within seconds. The car boot was popped, and she was thrown inside. An equally trussed-up Peter was thrown on top of her and the boot slammed shut hurtling them into blackness.

The deep rumble of the car engine vibrated through the floor of the car. She rolled to one side as the vehicle lurched forward. Every bump in the road was magnified and disorientating. The weight of Peter wriggling on top of her, pinned her to the floor. She struggled to suck air into her lungs, past the gag across her mouth. Just as she thought she was going to be crushed, Peter's weight fell to the side of her. Caught between him and the side of the car, she was still unable to move, but at least she could breathe freely. Relief that she hadn't been travelling with Humphries and have his weight to deal with gave a brief respite from thinking about the situation they were in.

Peter continued to writhe next to her, bashing and squashing her. Unable to shout at him to stop, she resorted to kicking out at him. This wasn't the time for him to be having some sort of panic attack. She had to think. She had given out their location moments before they turned into the avenue of trees, but how long would it be before they sent out a search party. Long enough for them to be driven miles away, killed and dumped in shallow graves. They were on their own, desperately in need of an escape plan. If she could only free her bindings she could leap out and surprise them when they opened the boot.

If that was their intention. What if their intention was to torch the car with them inside? Recalling the black silhouette of Connor in the driver seat of his camper van, she started to join Peter, writhing on the floor of the car, trying to free herself. Panic and claustrophobia set in at the uselessness of her efforts.

"Fiona! Stop a minute."

It took a while for Fiona to realise, Peter had removed his gag.

"I've a penknife in my back pocket. If we lie back-to-back, do you think you can get it out?"

Through the gag, Fiona managed a muffled grunt.

"I'll take that as a yes," Peter said, shifting his body. "You need to turn over, so your back is to me."

In the darkness, Fiona was losing knowledge of which way was up or down. Forcing her confused mind to operate, she worked out which way she had to turn and started to flip herself over. A jolt from the car worked in her favour, rolling her over into a good position. Straining against the bindings she felt the bulge in Peter's back pocket.

"That's it. Can you pull it out?"

The bindings cut into Fiona's wrists as she managed to slip the fingers of one hand inside the pocket. Ignoring the pain from the restraints she closed her thumb and two fingers around the smooth metal and pulled out the pen knife. "How do I get it open?"

"Pass it to me. My fingers are probably stronger, and I know how the catch works."

They rocked against each other as the car came to a halt.

"Quick hide it," Peter said, moments before the boot lid popped open above them.

CHAPTER THIRTY-SIX

They were half-carried, half-dragged toward a substantial farm-house. Fiona scanned the area for landmarks, but all she could see were brown, ploughed fields in all directions before they were bundled inside. They continued along a narrow corridor between walls adorned with old paintings and into a large room decorated in a similar way to the Amethyst Club.

Ruddle was already strapped to a wooden chair. Motionless, his head hung down. The beating he had taken to the side of his face was evident. They were roughly shoved across the room to two more waiting chairs. Peter pushed back into one of the men forcing him to take his weight while kicking out with his bound feet. His feet connected to one of the thug's chest and caught unawares he went spinning back before falling over backwards.

Fiona watched feeling helpless. She hoped the kick was intended as a distraction so she would be bound to a chair without them checking her pockets and Peter wouldn't try anything else. She flinched when the fallen man pulled himself to his feet and launched himself at Peter. She closed her eyes when the onslaught began. Held upright by the others, Peter had no way to protect himself as the man's fists pummelled his face.

Satisfied with the damage he had inflicted, the thug shook out his fist and growled, "Tie them both to the chairs and let's get out of here."

Fiona's concern for Peter, slumped forwards in the adjacent chair, was tempered by the fact she had been bound to the chair without being frisked. Her hands remained tightly tied behind her back in a position from which she was sure she could retrieve the knife from her back pocket. Peter's jaw and cheek-bones were probably broken, but she could see the rise and fall of his chest, and she had the means to get the three of them out alive.

The thug who Peter had kicked appeared to be in charge. Fiona kept her eyes focussed on the floor as she felt his eyes pass over her. This wasn't the time for a show of defiance. It was a time to sit quietly and wait for them to leave so she could get to work initiating their escape. The damage to Peter's poor face wouldn't be in vain. She looked up at the sound of the door opening. Three men left, leaving the one who seemed to be in charge standing in the entrance. Itching to check she could reach the knife she averted her eyes to the floor willing him to leave. The last thing she wanted to do was attract attention to herself and him to realise she hadn't been searched.

She could hear doors being opened and the flooring creaking out in the corridor and wondered what the other men were doing. It sounded like they were moving methodically from one end of the house to another. As their steps crept closer, her nostrils flared at the smell of petrol. Looking up, the thug at the door smiled broadly, at the recognition in her eyes. He laughed, as she started to struggle against the bindings.

The three men returned to the doorway. After a brief exchange, the leader took hold of one of the petrol cans. Laughing, he caught Fiona's eye. "It seems you didn't pull the lucky straw after all." Nodding towards Peter and Ruddle, he added, "Shame they're going to miss the show." He crossed the room and sloshed petrol over the window curtains and the soft chairs in the room. After a pause to assess his handiwork, he shook the can to check its contents and returned to the entrance door. He poured the last dregs of petrol around the door before throwing the empty can across the room. "Enjoy!"

Once the footsteps and laughter retreated along the corridor, Fiona gave herself a moment to calm herself. Panicking and dropping the knife would be a death sentence. She took one final, deep breath and started twisting her wrists so her fingers could reach into her back pocket. By the time she heard engines starting up, she had secured a firm hold on the knife. She contorted herself to withdraw it from her pocket. She forced the sting of the bindings digging into her wrist from her mind, telling herself it was a darn sight less painful than being burnt alive.

She could hear the crackle of fire by the time she finally located the catch to open one of the blades. She caught the first whiff of smoke as she manipulated the knife into a position that would cut the bindings from her wrists. Sweat trickled down her side, itching as it went. She dreaded the knife slipping from her sweaty palms. The angle at which she dragged the knife backwards and forwards made it impossible to put any real weight behind it. She had to hope the slight movement forwards, and backwards would be enough to cut through the plastic ties. The thugs setting the fire in a way to cause the most fear as it edged slowly closer gave her additional time, but not that much. She had to free herself and the other two before the flames reached the curtains, blocking their only means of escape.

Her heart leapt as she felt her grip on the knife slip. She caught it just in time. She had to focus on the job in hand. Not get ahead of herself thinking up escape plans. The knife was at a more awkward angle as she resumed sliding it up and down the bindings. A slight give in them told her she was nearly through and had a few millimetres more to manoeuvre her efforts. Feeling them give again, she clasped the knife and jerked her hands apart in the hope of breaking through the last of the plastic. As her hands sprang apart, a tall figure dressed in black appeared in the doorway. Tears pricked behind her eyes as the knife slipped from her hand and clattered to the floor.

Anticipating the end, she closed her eyes and thought of her parents. Of a beach holiday in Cornwall when she was little. Hearing footsteps coming close she hoped he would kill her outright. Not let her watch Peter and herself burn to death. She quickly dispelled thoughts of the agony of being burnt alive and tried to recreate the sunny day on the beach in Cornwall.

With her eyes tightly closed, she felt hot breath on her face. Fear coursed through her as she held herself rigidly still. Maybe he would leave her alone, and she still had a chance. Hidden behind her back, her hands were no longer bound. She wasn't out of options if only he would leave. If he didn't spot the knife, she could rock the chair until it fell. Drag herself across the floor and start again with the knife to free herself from the chair.

The pressure around her waist and chest lifted. She could breathe much easier. She felt hands fumbling around her ankles. Instinctively she kicked out. Bindings cut into her ankles, making her kick impotent. She heard something snap and her legs were free. Confused, she raised her head and opened her eyes.

The stranger in front of her was dressed head to toe in black. He wore a balaclava, so only his startling blue eyes were showing. As the gag was gently removed from her face, she opened her mouth to speak. He placed a finger to his lips, silencing her. Bending forwards, he picked up Peter's penknife and handed it to her. She looked down in surprise, dumbfounded. When she looked back up, he nodded his head towards Peter and Ruddle still slumped unconscious in their chairs.

Slowly, it dawned on her. He was here to save them. But who was he? The stench of smoke was growing more potent, but the fire remained outside the room. They had plenty of time to escape through the window. The stranger worked at Ruddle's restraints while she started on Peter's.

She was cutting the restraints from Peter's ankles when the stranger hoisted Ruddle over his shoulder. Balancing him there, he released the window catch and pushed him out of the room. Cutting through the last binding holding Peter's ankles, Fiona stood and turned to face the masked stranger. "Who are you?"

The stranger stood back, saying nothing. He motioned for Fiona to move so he could pick up Peter. She stepped back, but as he put his arms under Peter's armpits, she shot forwards and pulled the balaclava over his head. For a moment, they stared at one another in shock.

Albu straightened, leaving Peter's head to loll backwards.

"Please, do not say I was here. Promise." When Fiona, remained silent, too busy taking his presence in to speak, he continued, "If they know I help you, I am dead. Please, promise. Whatever happens."

Fiona took a step back. She didn't know what to think. If he was here, he had to be a part of it all. She would need to give his name. His assistance would stand for something, but he couldn't escape justice. Not if he was involved in murder and abduction.

"Fiona! It is important. They will kill me. I promise I will come to you later and explain. Whatever you think you see do not always believe. Please. Promise."

Fiona crossed her fingers behind her back and slowly nodded. "I promise."

Albu beamed a smile, pulled the balaclava down over his face and returned his attention to lifting Peter from the chair. He carried him across the room and propped him up against the wall next to the window. His voice was muffled by the wool of his face covering. "You climb through. I will hand him safely down to you. From there you call ambulance and fire engine."

Fiona climbed through the window and dropped the short distance to the ground next to Ruddle's crumbled body. Looking back at Albu heaving Peter's body to the window frame, she asked, "Where are we? I need to know to call the emergency services."

A moment of panic crossed Stefan's eyes. "I not know the house name. The last road sign I saw said Whitley."

"Okay, that's something," Fiona replied, raising her arms to receive Peter. When Stefan released his hold of him, she staggered backwards under his weight, narrowly avoiding falling as she lowered him to the ground.

Albu's head appeared through the window, his eyes full of concern. They really were the most beautiful, expressive eyes. Breaking out of the trance, Fiona could see the way the fire had taken hold of the bottom floor. "Come on!"

"You can pull them to safety?" Albu asked.

"With your help, yes."

"Promise me again, you will not say my name."

"I promise. Come on out!" Fiona shouted.

Albu threw a mobile phone to Fiona. "You call for help. First, I need to check there is no one on the upper floors."

"What? I'll come with you." As soon the words out of her mouth, the window was slammed shut and Stefan vanished inside. Fiona felt around the window, searching for a way to prise open the window from outside. Accepting it was impossible, Fiona turned with her back against the building and called the emergency services. She was surprised when she glanced back at the building how quickly the fire was taking hold on the ground floor. She grabbed hold of Peter's jacket and started to drag him away from the burning building.

She was breathing heavily and drenched in sweat by the time she hauled Ruddle alongside Peter to the sound of approaching sirens in the distance. She was horrified to see flames were now licking at the window they had escaped through. She shouted, "Stefan," and started to run back towards the building.

After a loud crash to the side of her, she heard his voice, "Over here." She turned and raced back along the front of the building. Albu staggered through the smoke billowing from the front door, each arm wrapped around a girl. The girls were thrust into her arms. She looked over their heads as they clung to her, coughing and spluttering. Stefan mouthed the words, "You promise me," and faded back into the smoke before she could react.

Moments later loud sirens pierced the air, and she was surrounded by firemen. A loud crash from somewhere in the building sent sparks shooting high into the air like fireworks. Fiona grabbed the arm of the fireman pulling her away. "There's still someone in there."

Glancing back at the burning building, the fireman continued to pull her away. "Sit down over here, and I'll arrange for two of my men to go in."

"Hurry, please," Fiona said, before moving away to kneel next to Peter. She watched two men pulling on breathing apparatus before running towards the building, just as another section of the roof collapsed. The building was fully ablaze and beyond help. She wiped a tear from her eye, realising there was no way Albu could have survived inside the inferno. Paramedics placed a blanket around her shoulders, while others crouched over Peter. Torn between accompanying Peter to the hospital and keeping vigil for Albu's body to be carried out, new tears welled up. The decision was made for her as she was forcibly led towards a waiting ambulance. She glanced back at the roaring flames as the ambulance doors slammed shut.

CHAPTER THIRTY-SEVEN

After her minor injuries were patched up, Fiona headed toward the Accident and Emergency reception desk to discover where Peter was being treated.

She was intercepted by Humphries. "How are you doing?"

"A little wobbly, but I wasn't injured. Where's Peter?"

"He's in surgery. He will make a full recovery, but you won't be able to see him tonight."

"And Ruddle?"

"There's an officer outside his room, and we will be able to speak to him tomorrow."

"And the two women?"

"What two women?"

"There were two young women. A ... the stranger returned inside the first time to bring them out. Where did they go?"

"It's the first I've heard of them."

"Damn. They must have sneaked away while I was checking Peter."

"We could put out an appeal for them to contact us?" Humphries suggested. "Can you describe them?"

Casting her mind back, she said, "Bottle blondes in their late teens or early twenties, skinny. They were dressed in miniskirts and T-shirts."

"Not exactly dressed for a hike in the countryside, then. Someone might have seen them."

Fiona shook her head. "They're long gone. I doubt we'll ever see them again."

"There is some good news. We can speak to Megan Ambrose for ten minutes. I was headed that way. Do you want to come along?"

"You bet." When Humphries led her deeper into the hospital, Fiona asked, "Did the fire service find a body in the house?"

"I don't think so, but maybe it's too early to say. Any idea why he went back inside?"

"I guess he thought there might be more girls upstairs. The building started to collapse moments after he ran inside." Sighing, she said, "It's unlikely he survived."

"And you have no idea who this masked saviour was?"

Fiona hesitated for a heartbeat, before shaking her head. "He was dressed in black and wearing a balaclava." Changing the subject, she nodded towards the file Humphries carried. "What have you got there?"

"Photographs of our main suspects." Handing it over, he said, "Do you want to take it?"

A nurse greeted them outside the door to Megan's room. "Ten minutes. Not a second longer and if you upset her, you'll have me to answer to."

The officer sitting outside the door to Megan's room looked up and exchanged a glance with Fiona and Humphries. The look he gave indicated he had already been firmly put in his place by the senior nurse.

Looking pale and drawn, Megan was propped up by pillows. Her mother was sitting in an easy chair next to the bed, reading a fashion magazine.

Aware they would be limited to ten minutes, Fiona moved directly to the bedside. A bruise covering one side of her face, changing from purple to yellow accentuated the paleness of Megan's skin. "Hello, Megan. I'm a police detective. I'm the one who found you. You have been incredibly brave and resourceful, and in time we will need the full details of your ordeal. But for now, all our efforts are on capturing the man who abducted you."

"He killed my Dad. It's all my fault."

"Why do you say that?"

"Because it was. I had a second phone, and I telephoned Dad. He overheard me and took the phone. Then later ..."

Fiona stepped back as Megan's mother awkwardly comforted her. Megan pushed her mother away. "It's fine, I'm fine. Everything is bloody fine." Looking up at Fiona and Humphries, she said, "One of the nurses said he is in here. Is that, right?"

"Possibly," Fiona said, pulling out a picture of John Ruddle. "Is this the man who attacked you?"

Megan gave it a dismissive glance before leaning back on her pillows. "I have no idea who that is. I've never seen him before."

Megan's mother pushed herself forwards. "So, my daughter is still in danger. Not only do you not have him in custody, you don't even know who he is."

Fiona held up a hand to silence her while addressing Megan. "Can you tell us about him and what he looked like?"

"He said his name was Bob, the King. He was blond with startling green eyes."

"Your friend Lisa thought maybe he wore a wig?"

"No way. It was his own hair, although his tan was too orange to be natural. But his eyes. His eyes were something else." Megan shuddered. "I see them when I close my eyes. So cold and unfeeling." As tears filled her own eyes, she said, "Go away. I can't help you." Pointing to the photograph, she added, "That isn't him. He's still out there."

"Before we go," Humphries said. "Roughly how old was he?"

"Thirty or forty, maybe."

"Tall, thin, fat?"

"Average height, maybe a little weedy."

The nurse from earlier bustled inside, heading directly toward Megan. Turning to glare at Fiona and Humphries, she said, "Your ten minutes are up. She needs her rest. Come back tomorrow."

Walking across the hospital car park, Fiona said, "I know I probably should return to the station to write up my report, but I need some time to think things through. Neither girl recognises Ruddle. Maybe Peter was wrong, and this dodgy photographer has nothing to do with the murder of her father."

"Except you heard her. She blames herself for her father's death. And since when has Peter ever been totally wrong about anything?"

"True. We talked earlier about the vehicle fire set-up needing two people. Did the doctors say when we can speak to Ruddle?"

"I told you. Tomorrow. Can you describe the mysterious saviour who appeared out of nowhere to rescue you all?"

"We would have escaped the fire without his help. Thanks to Peter I had the knife."

Opening the car door, Humphries said, "Could the stranger, who helped you slightly, be described as of average height or weedy?"

"Hardly," Fiona replied. "He was able to hoist Peter and Ruddle over his shoulder with ease."

"What else can you say about him?"

Fiona fought with her conscience. Why was she lying to a colleague for a criminal she had met briefly? A criminal with gorgeous, blue eyes and a grin that turned her stomach inside out. Which was beyond ridiculous in the circumstances. "He wore a balaclava and didn't speak. I was too busy trying to free Peter to take down his measurements."

"And you've no idea who he was or what he was doing there?"

Sliding into the passenger seat, Fiona said, "As he died in the fire, we'll be able to identify him when his body is found. We may never know why he was there or why he chose to risk his life saving us."

"Until they find a body, we can't be sure he died," Humphries said, starting the car. "Straight home?"

"Can you go via the station so I can pick up my car?"

"Or I can take you home and give you a lift into the station tomorrow morning?"

"Thanks, but I would prefer to collect my car."

Once home, although she was exhausted, Fiona headed upstairs to run a bath. For the second time in a week, she reeked of smoke. She hoped a hot, long soak would help her think through the last twenty-four hours.

Refreshed and fed, if not more enlightened Fiona curled up on her sofa and surfed through the television channels. Accepting she wasn't going to find anything to take her mind of Albu and the look on his face when he disappeared the final time, she grabbed a notepad and pen. Concentrating on solving the case might just stop her eyes from welling up every time she thought about him.

Writing out bullet points of what they knew for sure by hand might dislodge something from her brain that would lead to a breakthrough. Feeling disloyal to Peter she marked three separate headings. The vehicle fire, Megan's abduction and the house fire. One thing was immediately apparent. Albu was connected to all the victims, except one, Ruddle. Fiona flicked back through her pad to the notes she had made about a possible planning or building regulations connection. Again, the odd man out was Ruddle.

Fiona hugged her knees to her chest and stared at her lists in frustration. Now they knew Ruddle wasn't the photographer who had dumped Megan in the well they had nothing to connect him to Connor. Could he have been an innocent bystander too scared to come forward as Peter suggested? The hospital would be her first port of call in the morning, and she wouldn't leave without some answers.

Her mind returned to Albu. He was charismatic, mesmerising, physically strong and had no qualms about dislocating shoulders. If he was alive, he would have more questions to answer than Ruddle. Like, what was he doing at the house, why did he help them escape, and how did he know there were two girls upstairs?

Her head started to throb, and her eyelids droop as the day's events began to catch up with her. After a last look through her notes, she checked the downstairs locks and turned off the lights. Drawing the curtains, she spotted a police car parked a short distance away. She turned away with mixed feelings. Annoyance she hadn't been told jostled with a sense of reassurance. Deciding to play it safe, she returned to the kitchen. She slipped a pepper spray into her dressing gown pocket and grabbed the heavy-duty torch from the counter, before heading upstairs to bed.

She let out a shriek as she opened her bedroom door, before swinging the torch and slamming it down on Albu's head.

CHAPTER THIRTY-EIGHT

Fiona sipped coffee at the kitchen table watching Albu nurse a whisky while holding a packet of frozen peas wrapped in a dishcloth to the side of his head. His forehead and hands were red raw from burns and starting to blister. Where the ice was melting, it began to drip down the side of his face. He went to pull his hand away.

"Keep it there," Fiona ordered, "and explain what you were doing at the house."

"I followed you there." Albu glanced over at the sink and smiled. "My flowers have arrived. Why not paraded into a pot?"

"Really?" Fiona asked, with a raised eyebrow. "You followed us through Dymmoc?"

"Naughty, Fiona," Albu said, wagging his finger. "You want to trick me. You go from Amethysts to Hillingdon hospital. We pause short time. Then, you follow a black car until you stop in a knife in the road."

"Okay. Okay. You know the route we took. Why didn't we see you?"

"I'm better at hiding than you."

"Why did you follow us?"

"So many asks. To answer all will be a long night, no? You will be a busy wasp tomorrow. Maybe, you should not drink so much coffee. It will keep you alive."

Determined to not become distracted, Fiona asked, "Why follow us all that way? What were you hoping to gain?"

Albu stood up from the table. "I find something better for you to drink. Maybe, we could share some wine. I think my story will be much better with wine. I will feel much relaxed. Let down my guard and tell you all. Good idea?"

"Sit down," Fiona ordered. "I don't want you wandering about." When Albu retook his seat, giving another of his disarming smiles, she stood and said, "I'll find a bottle and a couple of glasses." Returning, she said, "So come on. Your story."

"How is your work friend?"

Opening the wine bottle and filling their two glasses, Fiona said, "He will be fine. Stop wasting time, or we will do this at the station. A night in the cells might loosen your tongue just as much as the wine."

Albu rolled the wine around his glass and took a sip. Putting it to one side, he said, "Will you still love me if burns leave scars?"

Fiona leaned forward across the table. "This is your last chance."

"Three years ago, my sister travel to England to make a new home. All was arranged by an English gentleman. He is very charming. My family believe Alina will be safe, and carefully looked after. We have not heard anything from her since she left. I come here to find and take Alina home."

"And if you can't find her?"

"I will find Alina."

"Why do you believe she is in this area?"

"The English gentleman give address to be from near here."

"Have you found him?"

"I am near. The name given to us was untrue. The name he give was a man from Streed. I visited his home. It was not the same man. His person was stolen without his knowing."

"So, why keep looking here?" Fiona asked.

"I judge some bad people of the Amethysts are knowing."

"Do you have names?"

"I work hard to be trusted by these men and not be viewed." Albu broke into a broad smile and pulled a sheet of paper from his inside, jacket pocket. "I have here the club's people list. This is what I was doing when you came in. Your telephone call worried me."

"Why?"

"I hear Alfred making a phone call. He tells phone you and friend are in club and asks what to do. I scared for the safety of the love of my life, so I follow you."

Shaking her head to show disapproval, but unable to suppress a smile, Fiona reached for the sheet of paper. "May I?" Quickly scanning it, she recognised several names, Owen Wagstaff, Megan's stepfather, Geoffrey Olive, the owner of Lilac Cottage along with John Ruddle and his partner, Robert Murray. The name that made her eyebrows shoot up was Ian Dewhurst. "What else can you tell me about the club?"

"Very small. Mostly is old men talking about the good old days when women and foreigners knew their place. Many are stupid bigots, but I think there is also a group who are dangerous and unpleasant men."

"At the house, you begged me not to say you were there. You were the hero of the hour. Most people would want that publicised. You seemed genuinely afraid. That's the only reason I haven't given your name. It could be, that after the shock wears off, my memory returns, and I suddenly recognise your voice."

"Then you will sign my death warrant. Searching for truth of my sister, I pretend to be like them. To use and hurt for money. They are bad men who would not take kindly to knowing what I do."

"If what you say is true, the police would give you protection."

Albu laughed. "Your trust in your police is good, but I prefer my chances. I feel safer alone."

"The girls you brought out of the house have disappeared. Do you know where?"

Refreshing their glasses, Albu laughed. "They feel the same as I do. They are free now to do their own way. Good luck to them."

"Unless their dependence on drugs drags them back into the mire. Same situation, different place. None of this really explains your interest in our investigation. You drove a long way on nothing more than snatches of an overheard conversation."

"For you, I would drive to the end of the World."

"Why did you come here tonight?"

"To know you were okay."

"And that I hadn't mentioned you?"

"That is truth, also," Albu admitted.

"What can you tell me about this group of men you claim to have become close to?"

"They are bad men, although they ... how you say ... keep their noses clean. They have the money to do bad things, but they stay hiding."

"And you pass details of what you know to Birstall Station regularly?"

"I have talks with Mr. Strickland. We know each other."

"And how does John Ruddle fit in with all this?" Fiona asked.

"I do some digging after you show photograph. I don't know how this man fits."

Fiona sighed. "That makes two of us."

"I like to think of us." When Fiona glared at Albu, he added, "I think he is occupied by one of the members. Maybe a personal thing?"

"And Connor and Megan Ambrose?"

"That is a mystery. I find no connection. Do these things help and now you have no need to give my name?"

"We'll see. How about the name, Ian Dewhurst?"

"The bells don't ring for this name."

Fiona drained the last of her wine. Exhaustion was overriding her earlier adrenaline spurt. She needed to think through the relevance of what Albu had told her with a clear head. "What do you plan on doing now?"

"It is very late. I'm broken, but I go so I arrive at work tomorrow as though no events have happened." Closing his eyes, he added, "So tired, I could sleep here."

"You're in no fit state to drive. You can sleep here," Fiona stood and carried the empty glasses and bottle to the sink. "I'll show you to the spare room, but I expect you to be gone by tomorrow.

Preferably without anyone seeing you. Do we have an understanding?"

"Absolutely."

Fiona hesitated at the kitchen door. "What did you do before you came to England?"

"I am dentist. You have great teeth, Fiona."

Fiona frowned to hide her amusement, and her teeth.

CHAPTER THIRTY-NINE

Her phone's ring tone jolted Fiona from a pleasant dream. One where she and Albu spent balmy evenings walking along a deserted beach. Shaking such foolish fantasies from her head, she felt along her bedside cabinet for her phone.

Without preamble, Peter said, "What happened yesterday? I remember being taken to a house, but that's about it. No one is telling me anything other than there was a fire."

Fiona closed her eyes and looked at the ceiling. "It will be easier if I come in to see you. When are visiting times?"

"No idea. Drive over as soon as you can. You can take me home when you arrive. They're all talking nonsense in here."

Fiona swung herself out of bed and put on her dressing gown, wondering if Albu was still in the house. Her heart started to beat erratically at the thought. "You can't be discharged this early in the morning. They won't let you leave," Fiona said, checking her reflection in the mirror before heading downstairs.

"I've spoken to the doctor. I can leave once I have a prescription for antibiotics and pain killers."

"You were in surgery when I left yesterday. Are you sure you should be leaving?"

"They put some wires in. I'm fine. What's happening about Ruddle?"

In the kitchen, Fiona flicked on the kettle to make coffee. "I'll explain when I arrive, but he wasn't the photographer. Like Lisa,

Megan doesn't recognise him."

"Megan? You've spoken to her?"

"Briefly. I can be there within an hour." Fiona was distracted by Albu walking in, dressed in the clothes he wore yesterday with ruffled hair. He gave her a broad smile that caught her unawares, sending her heart rate soaring. She wrapped her dressing gown tighter around herself and forced her attention back to the call.

"And Albu? Have you brought him in?" Peter asked.

Moving from the counter, Fiona sunk onto a kitchen chair. Her eyes followed Albu across the room while she wondered what on earth to say to Peter. "Not yet. I will give you a full update in an hour," she said, ending the call.

Albu had already found two mugs, coffee and milk, so she let him carry on. She looked away as fragments of her earlier dream danced around inside her brain. She stood and moved to a window to check whether the police car was still outside. Turning, she found a steaming mug of coffee on the kitchen table and Albu in the process of cooking breakfast. She closed down the voices in her head, telling her she could get used to this. Taking a seat at the table, she said, "Once I've drunk this, I will be getting ready for work. I won't have time for breakfast. There's a police car outside. I assume it will leave as soon as I do. Once it does, you need to get going. Please don't let anyone see you."

"Of course, I will always protect a lady's honour."

"I was thinking more about my career," Fiona replied.

Peter was sitting on the edge of his hospital bed, wearing the same clothes as the day before, clutching a paper bag filled with boxes of tablets. His face was bruised and swollen, almost beyond recognition.

"Good grief! Have you seen your face? You can't return to work looking like that."

"That good, eh?"

"You'll scare people half to death." As an afterthought, Fiona asked, "Does it hurt?"

"The drugs help," Peter said, holding up his bag of medication. "You can tell me what has been happening in the car. Are you okay to drive me home? I need to change my clothes before heading into the station."

"I can, but as I'm here, I was going to see if Ruddle is up to a visit. I'm not sure if you should come in looking like that."

"Nonsense. Be good for him to see what we went through to rescue him."

"I'm not sure the staff on the ward will see it the same way."

As Peter slowly stood, he swayed.

Grabbing his elbow to steady him, Fiona asked, "Are you sure about this?"

"Yes."

"And you don't have to wait for a doctor?"

In response, Peter held up his bag. "I've got all I need in here." Following Fiona into the corridor, he said, "And Megan has confirmed Ruddle had nothing to do with her ordeal?"

"That's what she said. I didn't have the impression she was lying."

"So, what was he doing that led to him ending up unconscious in that house?"

"I'm hoping he's going to tell us," Fiona replied.

Ruddle's face was in a similar state to Peter's. Beneath the swelling and bruising, his expression was one of defeat when they entered, and Fiona hoped they were going to get somewhere at last. He slowly reached for a beaker at the side of his bed and sucked on the straw, before saying in a quiet, husky voice, "I hope this time you're here to talk about my assault."

Fiona pulled the hardbacked chair closer to the bed and sat. "I hope this time you're going to be more helpful."

Ruddle replaced the beaker on the side table, leaned back on his pillows and closed his eyes.

"Mr Ruddle, if you want us to help you, you need to tell us what is going on. Two assaults in a week is a rather strange coincidence."

Ruddle opened one eye and closed it again. "You're telling me."

Fiona glanced up at Peter, who remained standing, leaning against the wall. He shrugged and indicated she should carry on.

"Do you know who the men that attacked you were?" Fiona asked.

With closed eyes, Ruddle replied, "Nope."

"We know you left the hospital in a black Mercedes that was parked in the car park for you, with the keys left under the wheel arch. Who left the car there for you, and why did you drive to that house?"

"I had a call from someone wanting to talk about my app. They claimed to be from a private school consortium. They wanted me to work on the school curriculum, producing books that would bring subjects, such as history and geography, to life." Ruddle opened his eyes and snorted. "I thought it sounded too good to be true."

"What was the name of this interested party?"

"They called themselves Grittleton Academia."

Peter pulled out his phone to search for the group on the internet. "There is a group going by that name. We'll check it out, later."

Turning back to Ruddle, Fiona asked, "And that's your story, and you're sticking to it?"

"Yup. Unfortunately, my phone has been destroyed, so I can't prove the call was made."

"The records won't be," Fiona replied, although she doubted a check would lead to more than an untraceable mobile and the fusty old men of Grittleton Academia had probably never heard of the Ruddle app. "Why do you think this group went to all that trouble and expense to lure you out to your death? You must have some inkling what this is about."

"Sorry, nope."

"Who is Bob King?"

"I have no idea."

"What can you tell me about Connor Ambrose?"

"You asked me this before. I don't know who this man is."

"You were seen on the road to Hinnegar at the time his vehicle magically burst into flames. What were you doing there?"

"They must be mistaken. I have no recollection of being on that road, let alone witnessing a fire."

"India Williamson? She contacted you after seeing you there. You strangled her and left her body near Lordswood."

"I absolutely did not. I have already told you where I was the nights of these dreadful events."

"Try again. Your alibis for those nights have been withdrawn," Fiona said. "Wood has admitted to the hit-and-run accident and explained how you contacted him asking for alibis in return for your silence."

"I've changed my mind. I'm not prepared to speak to you without a solicitor present."

Peter pushed himself away from the wall and said, "You have clearly upset someone in a big way. Had we not intervened you would not be alive today. I believe you know who those people are, but if you're not prepared to name them, then there is nothing we can do. I will relieve the police standing guard outside of their duties. I wish you the best of luck."

Ruddle opened his eyes and visibly paled, but said nothing.

Peter shook his head and announced, "We're out of here."

Fiona gathered her things and returned the chair to its position. Leaning over Ruddle, she said, "If you don't help us, we can't help you. I hope you know what you're doing."

After a momentary flicker of concern crossed his face, Ruddle closed his eyes and replied, "I know nothing."

In the corridor, Fiona said, "Why is he lying?"

"Unfortunately, he is more scared of whoever is behind this than us."

"Are you really going to stand down his guard?"

"Of course not," Peter replied. "Where next?"

"To see Megan. I want to show her some new photographs."

They were met at the ward entrance by the same nurse who had intervened the day before. "I can't allow you to see Megan this morning."

"I only need a couple of minutes to show her some pictures," Fiona pleaded.

"I'm very sorry. She is resting after undergoing treatment, so you will have to come back later. If you telephone ahead, you could save yourself from another unnecessary journey."

Realising she wasn't going to get past the nurse, Fiona stormed off. Peter stumbled when he turned to leave.

"Are you feeling okay?" the nurse asked.

Peter reached for the wall to steady himself as he experienced a sudden surge of heat, followed by an intense shooting pain in his jaw.

The nurse grabbed a wheelchair from behind the reception desk. Peter half fell before she pushed him into the chair. The nurse grabbed his wrist and read the medical armband he still wore and said, "Wait there. I will arrange for someone to come down to collect you."

Peter mumbled, "I discharged myself." His words sounded slurred and disjointed to his own ears. The nurse didn't respond, so he was unsure whether his words made any sense. A short while later, Fiona returned, but by then the pain from his jaw had radiated through his body, and all he heard was a vague whooshing sound as people moved around him.

CHAPTER FORTY

It was almost lunchtime by the time Fiona arrived at the station. Humphries met her as requested. "Where have you been? Dewhurst is going spare. You were supposed to be in here first thing to provide a full update on what happened yesterday." Checking his watch, he added, "He's has a press conference in forty-five minutes."

"I know, I know. I'm going to do that now," Fiona said.

"Good luck!"

"Did you complete the background checks I requested?"

"Wagstaff looks clean. Olive had an eventful younger life, flitting on the fringes of organised crime before settling down to a productive career as a renowned historical professor, resident at Harrow School. Over the last few years, his travel history is interesting."

"And Murray, the brains behind the Ruddle app?"

"I've not been able to find much about him," Humphries admitted. "Wealthy parents who socialised on the edge of Royal circles. Most notably, Prince Andrew."

"Not something to crow about these days."

"He attended Harrow at the same time as Olive. Harrow was followed by Cambridge studying computer technology. There is a closed record relating to an event during his early-teens. I haven't been able to gain access to it, and there is nothing to give any indication of what it related to."

"Are his parents alive?"

"Both dead. A double suicide about six years ago. Loads of rumours in the local press covering everything from satanic rites to financial problems, but nothing substantiated."

"Siblings? While I'm with Dewhurst can you keep digging and contact the hospital and ask when we can see Megan Ambrose."

"Sure. How's Peter?" Humphries asked.

"An infection has set in. Once they get it under control, he will be fine, but he's going to be out of action for a few days."

Fiona left Dewhurst's office, disappointed but not surprised. The case was being handed to Strickland from Birstall station, and he was waiting for a full final report from her. She understood the situation. As a small station they didn't have the expertise to handle such a potentially explosive case. It was why she had jumped at the secondment to the Met. Thoughts resurfaced about making a permanent transfer request as soon as her father recovered. What was keeping her in Birkbury? Here was comfortable, but she craved something more. She wasn't getting any younger, and if she didn't make a move soon, it would be too late.

Humphries accosted her as soon as she entered the incident room. "You're going to want to see what I've found out about Murray."

Fiona sighed and walked past him to the coffee machine. As the machine mechanism clunked away in response to her selection, she said over her shoulder, "Put it in the report. Dewhurst is passing the case to Birstall."

"Which part of it?"

"The part that suggests there's some sort of perverted-gentleman's-club angle with connections to organised crime and large-scale people trafficking."

"Maybe there is in the background, and our investigation has ruffled some feathers, but what I've uncovered suggests something different. Come and take a look. I haven't been able to get into the closed record, but I discovered Murray had an older sister. She died in mysterious circumstances when she was alone in the family home with him. There are no details anywhere that explain how she died, other than an unfortunate accident at home," Humphries said, tapping away at his keyboard.

Fiona sipped her coffee as she took a seat next to Humphries. "I'm assuming there's more?"

"Oh yes," Humphries said, glancing up from the keyboard. "Shortly after his sister's death, Murray was whisked away to a private clinic in Switzerland."

"Who will refuse to release any details."

Undeterred by Fiona's negativity, Humphries continued, "The parents' suicide raised some questions as well. Completely out of character according to friends. They were financially secure and planning for early retirement." Satisfied he had reached the screen he was looking for he turned the screen around to face Fiona. "Look familiar?"

Fiona's brain whirled as Humphries showed her a series of photographs of an attractive teenager engaging in various sporting activities and social events. While Charlotte, Lisa and Megan shared more than a passing resemblance physically, Murray's sister and Megan could have been identical twins. Looking up at Humphries, Fiona said, "Peter fixated on how similar Charlotte and Lisa looked when they first disappeared, but this is uncanny."

"The anniversary of the sister's death was a couple of weeks ago. Wait until you see this," Humphries said, his fingers skipping over the keyboard at speed. "Well?"

Fiona stared at the picture Humphries had brought up. "Is that Megan or Murray's sister?"

"Neither. It's the girl who went missing in Manchester following a photo shoot." Looking up, Humphries said, "Do you want to hazard a guess where the Murray family lived?"

Fiona's thoughts were at warp speed as pieces of the puzzle slotted into place. "Tinted contact lens and a fake tan," she muttered half to herself. "Did you contact the hospital about visiting Megan?"

"Not possible until this evening."

"A positive identification would be helpful as I want to take some backup with us when we bring him in, but it can't be helped."

"Do you think we need full, armed backup? Your initial report didn't flag up any concerns."

"Don't remind me. I was completely taken in by his reclusive nature and fear of germs. If he was a paid-up member of the Amethyst Club, he must have been leaving his house at some point. The most likely explanation for Ruddle being seen by India at the scene of the vehicle fire is that he was helping Murray. Ruddle has known him for several years. If he was petrified enough to help him dispose of a body and refuse to give his name after two attempts on his life, there must be a good reason. Can you arrange it while I go back to see Dewhurst to explain whatever group we've stumbled upon is secondary to the murders of Connor and India?"

◆ ◆ ◆

Fiona and Humphries pulled up outside Robert Murray's home along with two, marked police cars. After a quick discussion, it was decided two officers would accompany them to the door while one would cover the rear of the property and another remain in his car out front.

The wind dropped as they waited outside the silent front door. The sun made an appearance, turning the wet grass to a shimmering field of emeralds. "Try again," Fiona said.

"Could he be in the grounds somewhere?" Humphries asked, looking around at the extensive range of outbuilding and sprawling garden sloping down to the river.

Following Humphries' gaze, Fiona said, "I was told a gardener is responsible for all this by people in the nearby village. Although, I'm guessing it was Murray in disguise they saw entering and leaving the house."

Turning to the uniformed officer, Humphries said, "Grab the battering ram."

Fiona mumbled, "Something isn't right, here."

The officer stepped forwards to examine the door. "This is fully reinforced. I suggest we start with a window, although they're toughened safety glass."

"I don't care how you do it. Get us in there." Humphries said.

"No!" Memories of Nick Tattner's death surged to the forefront of Fiona's mind. "The guy is a computer geek with all sorts of tricks and gadgets. If he's in there hiding, he's got nowhere to go. Get an explosives team out here, before you touch anything."

"Will do," the officer said, stepping quickly away from the door. "I'll get on to it now."

After he walked away, Humphries said, "What now? It could take hours before we can get inside."

"I know, I know," Fiona said, walking small circles as her frustration built. "We need more officers out here." Walking back to the car, she added, "I want this place surrounded in case he makes a bolt for it."

"I hope you've called this correctly."

"Thanks for the vote of confidence," Fiona replied, already hearing the reprimands about wasting police resources unnecessarily. "It's better to be safe than sorry."

Once Fiona had completed her requests for more officers and explained her justifications to the station and herself several times, she wandered over to Humphries. She was irritated by the way he had stepped away, leaving her to make the calls, passing his time leaning on a post and rail fence looking up at the building. As she approached, he dropped his cigarette and stamped on it to put it out. Fiona looked down at the collection of cigarette butts by his feet. "I thought you had given up?"

Humphries shrugged. "I did." Looking up at the house, he said, "There haven't been any signs of movement. I don't think he's in there. They've checked around the back, and there's a car missing. While you were busy, I put out an APB on it."

"Brilliant. Thanks."

"Do we wait?"

"Only until someone arrives to take over," Fiona said. "Then

I want to get back to interview Megan, regardless of whatever that nurse has to say about it."

They were returning to more familiar territory when Fiona's phone rang.

"Have you seen this morning's gazette?"

Fiona mouthed, "Peter," to Humphries while scrolling through to find the gazette's on-line edition.

"Megan's mother has gone to them criticising us for going after the wrong man and not having a clue who really abducted her daughter," Peter said.

Fiona paled as she scanned the article. "They've given out the hospital's details."

"I know. Is there still an officer outside her room?"

"Just the one. We're about ten to fifteen minutes away. We'll get there as soon as we can."

"I'll wait for you outside her room."

"No! Wait," Fiona said to the empty line as Peter had already disconnected the call.

CHAPTER FORTY-ONE

Peter received confirmation from Abbie that officers were on their way as he gingerly tried to stand. He knew he was too weak to do much more than warn the officer stationed outside Megan's room to be on full alert. Just his presence, alongside the officer, might cause a short delay while the potential attacker re-evaluated the situation.

His jaw throbbed, and his legs felt rubbery as he took his few wobbly steps towards the door. He listened and waited while somebody on squeaky rubber soles walked along the corridor. He edged open the door and peered along the passageway. It was empty, but he knew he had to move as fast as he could. He took a deep breath, and pulled himself upright. Staring straight ahead, concentrating on walking in a straight line, he made his way along the corridor. He squinted his eyes to keep the world in focus.

He counted three nurses huddled over a computer screen at the central desk. His intended route took him to the side of the central station, but it was unlikely he could slip by without them noticing unless they were distracted by something. His head was throbbing, and his neck ached under the strain of holding his head still as he waited. Finally, a group of cleaners, pushing a trolley entered the ward, laughing and chatting away to themselves. It gave him the distraction he needed. When one of the nurses rebuked the cleaners, Peter steeled himself and pushed off from the wall and walked out of the ward. Once he was in the main hallways, as long as he kept his pace up and didn't do something stupid like faint, he was unlikely to be apprehended.

When he arrived on Megan's ward, the central station was empty. At the far end of the ward, a doctor flanked presumably by trainees was doing her rounds. He had considered warning the staff to be on their guard, but as there was no one available he made his way towards Megan's room, praying she hadn't been moved since he had last been there with Fiona. Turning the final corner, he saw the officer slumped forwards in a chair, snoring loudly with an empty cup and saucer pushed neatly under his seat.

Muttering to himself, Peter tried to shake the man awake. The man lolled to one side before sliding from his chair. In his condition, there was nothing Peter could do to cushion the fall. He looked around, hoping the sound of the chair crashing to the floor would bring people running.

Peter stepped over the man sprawled on the floor, still snoring and grunting loudly. If he wasn't found, he would at least provide a trip hazard to anyone attempting to flee from the room. He threw open the door shouting, "Oi!" as loudly as he could at the male nurse leaning over Megan's bed.

The nurse turned with a syringe held aloft in his right hand. His shocked, startling green eyes met Peter's briefly before he regained his composure. "Go back to your room. I'm treating this patient."

Peter felt the room spin and the smiling nurse split into three. He fumbled behind for the door handle to steady himself. His tongue was thick and uncooperative. He managed to croak, "Stop," before a flash of movement sent his already fuddled brain spinning.

Megan used the split-second hesitation to snatch at the syringe. She dislodged it from the nurse's hand, but was unable to hold on to it, and it tumbled to the floor, the glass smashing on contact. She clawed wildly at the nurse's face, which was now inches from her own.

Peter remained upright only because he had propped himself against the wall. He watched in horror as the nurse easily batted Megan's hands away before fixing his own hands around her neck. Megan continued to squirm and buck in the bed as the nurse continued strangling her. As the girl's kicks slowed, Peter knew he had to act fast.

He slowly bent to pick up the plastic wastepaper basket, nearly toppling forwards as he was assaulted by a dizzy spell. He didn't have the strength to attack the nurse, much less to restrain him. He reminded himself help was on the way. All he had to do was delay things. Holding that one thought, he pushed away from the wall and propelled himself across the room holding the basket over his head. He clamped the upturned bin over the nurse's head and held on with every ounce of energy he had left, praying the cavalry was only seconds behind. As the nurse thrashed about Peter hung on the bin using his weight to keep it firmly over his head.

A sudden punch to his stomach sent him reeling backwards, releasing his hold on the bin. He crumpled to the floor, his vision fading. The nurse had returned to squeezing his hands around Megan's neck. Sweat poured down Peter's face blurring his already distorted vision as he crawled across the room, focussing on the nurse's legs. Knowing he wouldn't be able to pull himself up to a standing position, he rolled onto his back. From there, he kicked out with both feet hitting the nurse with all the force he could manage behind the knees. It had the desired result. The nurse's legs buckled. The air was forced out of Peter's lungs as the nurse fell backwards on top of him. Unable to catch his breath, his vision dimmed to nothing as the door crashed open and the thudding of heavy feet vibrated through the floor.

CHAPTER FORTY-TWO

Fiona sat on Peter's bed, waiting for the doctor to arrive to officially discharge him. A condition of his discharge was he moved in with someone while he recovered. Offering little resistance, Fiona agreed to temporarily move into Peter's cottage. She would have preferred Peter to stay with her, but it avoided the risk of him seeing Albu turn up on her doorstep. Or in her bedroom. The relationship wasn't sustainable and maybe this would be the best way to bring it to a close. Contrary to Peter's earlier assessment she knew Stefan was a minor thief and occasional fraudster and she was far from convinced it was all part of his elaborate cover. His supposed role as her protector set alarm bells rings. And still she melted at his lopsided grin.

Peter jogged her train of thought. "What's happening about Dewhurst?"

"Would you be surprised to know nothing. He claims the club membership was suggested by a friend when he moved to the area, and he only visited the place once. He accepted he made a slight error of judgement and has cancelled his membership." Fiona shuddered as she remembered his comment to her about how we all make occasional mistakes about people. The way he said it, suggested he knew about her and Albu.

"So, has everything been handed over to Birstall, already?"

"Pretty much. Strickland is taking over everything related to the Amethyst group. I'm shocked, Geoffrey Olive, the old man who owned Lilac Cottage is involved. He seemed such a lovely old man and completely harmless."

"And the murder charges against Murray?"

"Staying with us. It was an uphill battle, but I received the final confirmation yesterday morning. Although there is a clear over-lap, the murders and the abduction of Megan are being treated separately."

"Another feather to your cap."

"Yes, although ..."

"You would like to be involved in the Amethyst group investi-gation."

"Possibly."

"You could apply for a transfer," Peter pointed out. "You could do well within a major crimes squad."

"I'm tempted, but ..."

"But?"

"There's Dad for one thing."

"You wouldn't be much further away."

"I know. I'm not discounting the idea. I would like to see Dad settled back home before making any major decisions." She punched Peter lightly in the arm. "Plus. I would miss you too much. I'm going to be a right Florence Nightingale the next few weeks between you and Dad."

"I would miss you, but it's your career. Your future."

"I'll give it some more thought once our case against Murray is fully watertight."

"There's no chance of him getting off, surely?"

"Hopefully not. The three girls have positively identified him, so I'm confident of a conviction for the abduction and at-tempted murder of Megan. I'm meeting with officers from Man-chester tomorrow. They are hoping he'll admit to killing the young girl from there. Megan will also give evidence that he told her he had killed her father."

"So, why the concern?"

"I have this nagging worry that with all the money behind him, he will wriggle out of the murder charges."

"I thought once Murray was in custody and Wood withdrew his alibi, that Ruddle gave you chapter and verse about how Murray forced him to help set fire to the camper van and it was Murray who met up with India?"

"He did, but Murray's solicitors are working hard to discredit him and say due to greed, it was him who killed Connor and India."

"Is that likely?"

"No, but it's muddying the waters. If it takes off, the Ruddle app is going to make him a rich man. There really is interest from schools in America."

"One thing that has always bugged me. Was it ever discovered who called the emergency services? They arrived far too quickly after I reported the fire."

"According to Ruddle, Murray rang them moments before he set fire to the petrol can he had put among the gas canisters on a pay-as-you-go mobile. He then threw it to Ruddle, laughed and told him he had better get a move on and drive the van back to the farm. Too panicked to object, Ruddle started to run towards the van that was parked a short distance up the road. That was when he saw Barney's car pull into the layby and India get out."

"How did Murray leave?"

"On foot, as far as Ruddle knows. Probably back to the cottage. I still can't get over how we missed it all by minutes."

"How do you mean?"

"If we had left the hospital ten minutes earlier, we may have seen them at the scene. The same goes for Barney and India. If they had left the restaurant ten minutes earlier, or if Barney had told India not to worry about the figures, they would both be alive."

"Don't dwell on it. It will mess with your mind," Peter advised. "Where's the phone now? That could prove Ruddle's account."

"Unfortunately, after using it himself to report the hit-and-run Ruddle stomped on it and threw it in the river. Still in panic mode, he hadn't seen Wood as an alibi, but a scapegoat."

"Do you know why the Amethyst group were planning to kill Ruddle? Maybe he was more involved than you think."

Fiona shook her head. "He only visited the club twice, both times with Murray. After Charlotte's ID card was found upstairs, Murray created rumours that Ruddle had discovered the house's location and taken the girls out there. As our investigation brought us closer to the group, Murray worked hard to deflect all blame away from himself and onto Ruddle."

"We know from the girls, that's not true," Peter said. "It also shows he was lying to you when he claimed to be a recluse and had never met Ruddle."

"I'm waiting for his solicitors to bring in psychiatrists to claim the reclusive Robert had no knowledge of the actions of the philandering Bob. They are probably keeping that in reserve, depending on the conclusions of the new investigation into the death of his parents and sister."

"Whether it's a psychiatric hospital or a prison, he's going to be locked up for life."

"He knew exactly what he was doing. My concern is that the solicitors are throwing elements of doubt into the ring, so they can negotiate a deal." Fiona's voice turned angry. "If Strickland and Dewhurst think they are going to come to a shady agreement in return for Murray giving evidence in the Amethyst case, they'll have me to answer to. It will be over my dead body." She stopped when she saw the look on Peter's face. "What?"

"I know you think you want to progress through the ranks, but you're way too good for that."

"What do you mean by that?"

"The type of concessions and compromises you'll be forced to make won't give you the satisfaction of a job well done. Like you get when you put the right people behind bars."

"You're such a cynic."

"No, a realist."

"Thanks for the vote of confidence. Maybe I'm strong enough to change the system from within."

"Maybe you are." Peter added, "The doctor should be here any minute. I should just have time for a quick change, and we'll make The Horseshoe before last orders. We can put the World to rights over a pint."

Thank you for reading my book. I hope you enjoyed reading it as much as I enjoyed writing it. During these strange times, please stay safe. Reading and writing has proved a great distraction for me. While we are all under some level of restriction, books really can take you places when you have to stay where you are.

Other titles

DCI Peter Hatherall Mysteries
The Skeletons of Birkbury
mybook.to/Birkbury
Bells on her Toes
mybook.to/Bells
Point of no Return
mybook.to/Point
Who Killed Vivien Morse?
mybook.to/VivienMorse
Twisted Truth
mybook.to/TruthTwisted
The Paper Boy
mybook.to/Paperboy

The Trouble Series
Trouble at Clenchers Mill - mybook.to/ClencherMill
Trouble at Fatting House - mybook.to/FattingHouse

Standalone novels

Fool Me Once - **mybook.to/FoolMe**
Debts & Druids - **mybook.to/DebtsDruids**

Printed in Great Britain
by Amazon